"I thought I ha
good defenses,
beat all."

"I don't know what you're talking about."

"The difference between us is that I'm willing to admit what I want, and willing to hope I might find it. You aren't even willing to hope," Rafe said.

"That's not true!"

"Sure it is. I drive you crazy, don't I, with the way I get close and then pull back? And I don't blame you for feeling that way. But you don't get close, then pull away, you shut the doors and pull up the drawbridge."

"That's not true," Angela insisted again.

"It sure as hell is. And it's getting more and more obvious, so I must be getting too close. Just keep one thing in mind, Angela. I may pull away when I get scared, but I keep coming back."

Dear Reader,

Welcome to another month of fabulous reading from Silhouette Intimate Moments, the line that brings you excitement along with your romance every month. As I'm sure you've already noticed, the month begins with a return to CONARD COUNTY, in *Involuntary Daddy,* by bestselling author Rachel Lee. As always, her hero and heroine will live in your heart long after you've turned the last page, along with an irresistible baby boy nicknamed Peanut. You'll wish you could take him home yourself.

Award winner Marie Ferrarella completes her CHILDFINDERS, INC. trilogy with *Hero in the Nick of Time,* about a fake marriage that's destined to become real, and not one, but *two,* safely recovered children. Marilyn Pappano offers the second installment of her HEARTBREAK CANYON miniseries, *The Horseman's Bride.* This Oklahoma native certainly has a way with a Western man! After too long away, Doreen Owens Malek returns with our MEN IN BLUE title, *An Officer and a Gentle Woman,* about a cop falling in love with his prime suspect. Kylie Brant brings us the third of THE SULLIVAN BROTHERS in *Falling Hard and Fast,* a steamy read that will have your heart racing. Finally, welcome RaeAnne Thayne, whose debut book for the line, *The Wrangler and the Runaway Mom,* is also a WAY OUT WEST title. You'll be happy to know that her second book is already scheduled.

Enjoy them all—and then come back again next month, when once again Silhouette Intimate Moments brings you six of the best and most exciting romances around.

Yours,

Leslie J. Wainger

Leslie J. Wainger
Executive Senior Editor

Please address questions and book requests to:
Silhouette Reader Service
U.S.: 3010 Walden Ave., P.O. Box 1325, Buffalo, NY 14269
Canadian: P.O. Box 609, Fort Erie, Ont. L2A 5X3

RACHEL LEE

INVOLUNTARY DADDY

Published by Silhouette Books

America's Publisher of Contemporary Romance

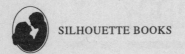 SILHOUETTE BOOKS

ISBN 0-373-07955-9

INVOLUNTARY DADDY

Books by Rachel Lee

RACHEL LEE

wrote her first play in the third grade for a school assembly, and by the age of twelve she was hooked on writing. She's lived all over the United States, on both the East and West coasts, and now resides in Florida.

Having held jobs as a security officer, real-estate agent and optician, she uses these, as well as her natural flair for creativity, to write stories that are undeniably romantic. "After all, life is the biggest romantic adventure of all—and if you're open and aware, the most marvelous things are just waiting to be discovered."

To Deletta Walton,
for suggesting that Nate might have a brother.
Of just such things, entire books are born.

Acknowledgments

My sincere thanks to Vicki Lemonds, Walta Slagle and
Pat Bonano for their timely and helpful responses to
my questions about juvenile onset diabetes.
Within the dramatic requirements of the book,
I tried to stay true to all you taught me.

Prologue

Rafe Ortiz slouched his way into the Drug Enforcement Agency offices looking as though he was ready for a trip on somebody's yacht. He wore a white cotton shirt, razor-creased khaki slacks and deck shoes. His inky-black hair was caught in a little ponytail at the back, and a large diamond winked in his left earlobe.

It was eight o'clock in the morning, and he hadn't slept in nearly forty-eight hours. The only thing he could think about right now was his bed—if he could remember where he really lived. The past six months undercover had made his real life seem distant, as if it belonged to someone else. As usual, he had the feeling that he didn't know who he was, that he had never known.

It was a safe way to live, playing one role or another, always acting a part. At least until he got tired. Then everything started to get jumbled, like the pieces of a puzzle he couldn't quite put together.

He needed sleep. The adrenaline rush had quit hours ago when he had arrested LeVon Henry and his crowd, and he'd been running on empty ever since. After another hour or so here at the office tying up loose ends, he was going to split and rediscover where he'd left his own bed six months ago.

"Rafe?" The far too pretty receptionist with the brilliant white teeth smiled at him. He saw her so rarely that he could never remember her name, but he always remembered her teeth. He had the feeling she was hoping he would ask her out sometime, but he never would. There was no room in his life for anything except work.

"Yeah?"

"Seton Hospital called. Some friend of yours is in critical condition and asking for you."

Rafe stilled. His mind rifled quickly through the agents he worked with and could come up with no one who should be sick or injured. Hell, he'd talked to them all in the last couple of hours as they'd wrapped up the bust. "Who?"

"Raquel Molina."

In the instant before he slammed the door on any possible feelings, he felt his heart skip a beat. His face suddenly felt wooden. "She's not a friend of mine."

"All I know is she's asking for you. Who is she?"

"The sister of Eduardo Molina."

Carefully penciled eyebrows lifted. "The guy you busted last spring? Hey, he was a real big fish, wasn't he?"

Rafe didn't answer.

"Maybe she's got some info for you, wants to get it off her chest before she dies."

Rafe looked down at her, his eyes burning oddly. "Yeah. Maybe." Turning on his heel, he headed for the door.

"Hey," she called after him. "Whaddya want me to tell Keits?" Keits was the agent in charge.

"I'll be back in a coupla hours."

"I'm sorry, Mr. Ortiz," the young woman in blue scrubs said to him. She looked as exhausted as he felt. "Ms. Molina died about an hour ago."

He didn't know what to say. He stood looking at the doctor

as if she must have something more to say, something that would clarify matters.

"It was a gunshot wound," she said finally. "The police can tell you more about what happened. We did everything we could."

He continued staring at her, thinking that this was how Alice must have felt as she slipped down the rabbit hole.

"I hardly knew her," he said finally.

Something in the doctor's face tightened. "Really? Well, there is this little problem you need to take care of."

"Problem?"

"She wanted you to take the child away from Miami, away from her family."

"Child?" Raquel didn't have a child. At least, not one she'd told him about. "What child?"

The doctor's expression grew distinctly disapproving.

"We delivered an eight-pound baby boy by cesarean just before she died. Mr. Ortiz, you're a father."

Chapter 1

Rafe Ortiz sat facing Kate Keits across her desk. As bosses went, Keits wasn't as bad as some he'd had. Right now, though, she was irritating the hell out of him. She was a slender brunette who always looked as if everything in her life was in order. Looking at her reminded him of how out of control his life had gotten in the past couple of months.

"You're sure it's your kid, Rafe?" she asked. "It'd be just like those damn Molinas to try to find a way to work on one of us. Especially you. You nearly brought down the whole family."

"It's my kid."

"You can't be sure."

"I *can* be sure, Kate. Don't take me for a dope. I got a DNA test. The results came in last week. My kid. My problem."

"It's a problem, all right. You have to find somebody to take that baby off your hands, or I'm going to have to reassign you."

He knew that. He knew as sure as he was sitting here that

he couldn't go undercover when he had a kid on his hands. But he also didn't know anybody who could take the baby for months on end. At least, not anybody he'd trust.

"You never should have gotten involved with a subject."

He knew that, too. "It just kind of…happened." Lousy excuse. There was no excuse.

"What about adoption?" Kate suggested.

"I thought about it." At least a dozen times, he'd even headed out for an adoption agency to set the wheels in motion. Every time he turned right around and headed back home—such as it was, his hole-in-the-wall apartment that he'd spent only a few months in since he'd rented it two years ago. Now it was worse than ever, smelling of baby poop and baby spit-up, and cluttered with a crib and stacks of disposable diapers. Hell. That was what his life was these days.

"So?" Kate pressed.

"So I can't do it. I'm all the family the kid has, unless you count the Molinas, and they don't count for much." He had the uncomfortable sensation that Kate Keits was trying to hide a smile. What the hell would she be smiling about? There was nothing funny in any of this.

"So what are you going to do?" she asked. "I need you on the street. If you can't go on the street, then I need to get someone who can. Make up your mind, Rafe."

He nodded. He'd been thinking about this little problem of his and had just about decided what he was going to do. "I've got family out in Wyoming," he said finally. "Give me a month off. I'll take the kid up there and see if they want to look after him."

"Sounds good to me. I'll put in the papers. You can be out of here Friday."

It sounded good, all right, he thought as he walked out of her office. What he'd neglected to tell her was that this "family" consisted of a brother he'd never met, a brother who didn't even know he existed. The guy was a cop, he'd heard, but he still might be some kind of bum he wouldn't trust anybody's kid to, let alone his own.

But there didn't seem to be any other option. He knew what foster care could do to a kid; he'd been there himself. He would die before he'd turn the kid over to the Molina clan. They'd probably have him running drugs by the time he was four.

That left him, and any family he could rustle up. Cripes, he hoped this brother of his was a deacon in his church. Anything that would help him avoid the twinges of guilt he was beginning to feel every time he thought about giving that kid up.

On the way home from work that night, he picked the kid up from daycare, then stopped to get more formula and a road atlas. He needed to figure out where Conard County, Wyoming, was, and how long it would take for him and the peanut to get there. And man, was he getting sick of these middle-of-the-night feedings. He was beginning to wonder if this kid was ever going to sleep all night.

The kid had a name, he reminded himself. Raquel had named him Rafael. Just like him, except that where the name fit *him,* it didn't fit eleven pounds of squalling baby. Too much name for such a little bundle, so he usually just thought of him as the kid or the peanut.

The peanut managed to sleep all the way through the pharmacy and the bookstore, despite all the cooing ladies giving Rafe looks that left him feeling like a steak dinner in front of a starving person. However, halfway home, Rafe Jr. woke up and squalled until Rafe Sr. wanted to stuff cotton in his ears.

You didn't have to be a daddy long to know what that noise meant. Every time the kid woke up he wanted something going in one end or had something coming out the other.

"Hold your horses, Peanut," he called over the squalling. "Just two more blocks."

Two more blocks and he could change another messy diaper and shut the kid up with a bottle. Why in hell did anybody ever want a baby, anyway?

Rafe was getting good at juggling things, so he managed to get into his apartment with baby, formula, diaper bag and atlas all in one trip. By this time, the peanut was seriously angry with the world.

Rafe dropped everything else and grabbed the baby, heading for the improvised changing table on the bathroom counter. One thing you could say for the kid, he thought as he washed, dried and diapered the little bottom: his problems were easy to fix. As soon as he was clean, Junior's sobs subsided into little hiccups.

"Okay, little man. Time for food."

Rafe had tasted the formula and thought it was pretty awful stuff, but the kid seemed to like it, guzzling down a few ounces, then burping contentedly. One more change, then the baby went right to sleep in the crib.

All in all, he thought, it was easy. He had a feeling it got harder as they got older.

For now he had a little peace and quiet. It was time to heat up a frozen pizza, pour himself a glass of milk and kick back with *Dr. Spock's Baby and Child Care*.

He was halfway through the pizza when he nodded off in his easy chair while reading about colic. His dreams were filled with images of mountains of diapers and a sea of sticky formula. When he awoke a couple of hours later to the sound of the baby's cries, he had the frustrated feeling that he hadn't managed to escape for even a few hours.

He forgot about that, though, after he cleaned the peanut up and fed him. The kid didn't seem ready to go back to sleep, so he held him for a while, cooing at him and watching the kid's eyes track the diamond in his earlobe.

After a bit he put the peanut down on the floor on a blanket and watched him flail his arms and legs as if he didn't even know they were attached to his body. He looked content and bright-eyed, though, happy enough just to be awake and alive.

Maybe there was a lesson in that.

A knock on the door sent Rafe's adrenaline into high gear. Nobody knocked on his door, and certainly not at this time of night.

If he'd been undercover, he would have assumed it was one

of his contacts. But he wasn't undercover, and that knock sig-
nified danger. Someone he'd sent up the river? Someone with
an old score to settle?

He went for the gun that was on the table where he'd left
it. He pulled it out of its holster, released the safety and went
to the door, standing to one side.

Then, in a moment of awful clarity, he looked back at the
baby on the floor. For the first time in his career he was risking
something besides his own life, and he didn't like the feeling.

Instead of opening the door, he called, "Who's there?"

"Manny Molina."

Hell! Rafe stood for a minute, unmoving. Manuel was the
only Molina he'd never been able to tie into the drug operation. Manny seemed to be exactly what he claimed: a restauranteur. "You alone?"

"Hell, yeah, I'm alone. I just wanna talk."

Rafe opened the door a crack and peered out. Manny was
alone. "How'd you find me?"

"How do *you* find somebody?" Manny shook his head. "I
had you followed."

The hairs on the back of Rafe's neck stood up. "Why?"

"The kid. I want to talk about the kid. That's all, I swear.
And if you think I'm going to tell anybody else how to find
you, you're wrong, Ortiz. That's my nephew in there."

"I feel a whole lot better."

Manny shrugged. "I got no ax to grind with you. My
brother got what he deserved. What kind of guy imports
drugs? I got kids of my own, and I don't wanna see none of
that stuff on the streets where my kids could get it. Raquel
didn't like it, either."

Rafe remembered that clearly, but he hadn't let it get in his
way. As he saw it, he was like an angel of justice, and angels
couldn't afford to let feelings keep them from their missions.
No way. Raquel had gotten him close to Eduardo, and that
was all that mattered.

"Hey," said Manny, "can we talk inside, or you wanna
come out here?"

"Just what do you want, Manny?"

"To see the kid. My flesh and blood. My dead sister's only child. What's so wrong with that?"

Still reluctant, his pistol firmly in his hand, he opened the door and let Manny inside. The man was dressed in a dark suit and tie, every inch the successful businessman.

Suit notwithstanding, he crossed the room in a flash and knelt on the floor beside the baby.

"He looks like you," Manny said after a moment. "I read somewhere that kids look like their dads for the first year."

The peanut gurgled and waved his arms and legs.

Rafe stuck his head out the door, checking the balcony and the courtyard below. Seeing no one else, he closed and locked the door.

Turning, he looked at Manny and the baby, and had to bite back an instinctive protest when Manny picked the kid up. Rafe leaned his back against the door, barring Manny's exit.

"He's a cutie, all right," Manny said, cradling the baby expertly in his left arm and chucking the little chin gently. He rose, bouncing the baby gently, and began to pace the small room. Rafe began to feel like a jerk, hanging on to a gun he would never fire at the man as long as he held the kid.

"What do you want, Manny?"

"To see the kid." Manny turned to face him, patting the little bottom. "Like I said. I got my own. Eduardo ain't never gonna have any, since you're sending him up for life, and my younger brother Tomas don't like the ladies, you know? So this is Raquel's only child, probably my only nephew. I wanna see the kid sometimes. And my mother wants to see the kid sometimes. It's her grandchild."

"Raquel wanted me to keep the kid away from the family."

Manny snorted. "She didn't mean me and Mama."

"She didn't exclude the two of you, either."

"Well, she ain't here to argue now, but I am. It's all we got left of Raquel. You don't wanna bring the kid to us, we'll come to the kid. Here. In a park. You name it. But we wanna see the baby. Besides, how you gonna work undercover with this kid? Maybe you should consider letting Mama take care of the baby while you work.''

Rafe, who had realized the instant he set his eyes on Manny on his doorstep that his days of working Miami undercover had ended, didn't bother to tell him that. What he wanted was for Manny to get out of here *now*. "Okay," he said. "I'll think about it.''

Manny nodded. "Good. Don't think too long. Mama's having crying spells over seein' the kid. What's his name, anyway?''

"Raquel named him Rafael.''

"After you, eh?'' Manny nodded and looked down at the baby in his arms. "She was real broken up after you had Eduardo arrested.''

Rafe didn't want to hear it. "I never lied to her.''

Manny suddenly cracked a laugh. "Yeah, who believes a guy who tells the sister of a big-time drug dealer that he's a D.E.A. agent? She even told Eduardo you said that. Man, you had it psyched right. Eduardo thought it was the funniest thing he ever heard.''

"He should have paid attention.''

Manny cocked a brow at him. "No sense of humor, eh?'' He nodded and carefully put the baby down on the blanket. The peanut was looking a little drowsy now.

"You got some *cojones,* man. Well, I ain't askin' you to do any big thing, but this baby should know his family, you know. His uncle, his grandmother, his cousins. And we ain't gonna hurt the kid.''

"I'll think about it.''

"I'll check back tomorrow night, okay?''

"Okay.''

Manny said good-night. Rafe stood in the doorway watching until the man had left the courtyard below, then he closed and locked the door, throwing the second security dead bolt. That was when he realized for the first time that he'd broken a cold sweat.

But everything was okay. The peanut was falling asleep safely, and Manny was gone.

He reached for the phone and dragged Kate Keits away from the late-night news.

"What the hell is going on, Rafe?" she asked irritably.

"Manny Molina was just here."

She was silent for a beat. "How the hell did he find you?"

"He had me followed."

She swore, a four-syllable word he'd never heard pass her lips before. "What did he want?"

"The kid. He says he and his mother just want visitation."

"You believe that?"

"Truthfully? No."

"Me neither. In fact, I consider it an implied threat."

"I've got to leave right away, Kate."

"Damn straight. Start packing. I'll take care of everything on this end." She paused. "You're off the streets for good, Rafe. You've got an Achilles' heel now. If the Molinas would use their own flesh and blood to threaten you, somebody else might be even more willing."

One of the advantages of being an undercover agent was that he rarely got a chance to spend any of his paycheck. That meant he didn't need to take much with him, because there was nothing he couldn't afford to replace on the road.

So he packed the kid's diaper bag with a few changes of clothing, some diapers, formula and bottles, enough to get through most of a day. Everything else he left behind, figuring he could get it another time. He didn't have much that mattered, anyway. The important thing was not to tip anybody off that he was leaving town.

They left at five in the morning, when even Miami's streets quieted down enough to make it easy to tell if he had a tail. He drove aimlessly for a while, and when he was sure he didn't have a shadow, he surprised himself. Instead of heading for the turnpike, he found himself driving toward the cemetery.

He'd never come here before. When he pulled to a stop, he

felt like a jerk. But he knew where Raquel's grave was, because for some reason he'd had a friend check it out over a month ago. He told himself he didn't care, but it seemed like the thing to do, to know where the kid's mother was buried. Someday the peanut would want to know.

And for some reason, he got out of the car with the baby and worked his way among the headstones until he stood in front of Raquel's.

Her family had picked a tombstone with a lamb lying on top of it. A lamb was the last thing he would have associated with the fiery, passionate Raquel, but maybe she'd seemed that way to her brothers and mother. The grave had been sodded, and it looked as if it had been there for years rather than for just a couple months.

He stood there holding the baby, feeling awkward and stupid, but feeling that there was something he absolutely needed to do.

Finally he spoke. "See?" he said. "It's the kid. He's okay, Rocky." The pet name he'd given Raquel felt odd on his tongue, his lips forming the syllables woodenly. God, was he really standing here talking to a stone and a patch of grass?

He looked away, then felt his gaze inexorably drawn down to the bundle in his arms. Rafe Jr.'s eyes were wide-open, staring at him as if the kid could understand every word.

"I'm getting him out of here, Rocky," Rafe heard himself say. "Manny wants him. I don't know about that guy. He's clean, I guess, but I just don't trust him. So Peanut and me are hitting the road, okay? When the kid gets older, I'll bring him back to see you."

Then, feeling all roiled up inside in ways he couldn't understand, with his eyes burning as if he'd gotten something in them, he headed back for the car.

"I'm sorry, little man," he said to the baby in his arms. "I'm sorry your mom got killed. I know I'm second best, but that's all there is."

And it was going to have to be enough. He took the turnpike north, then got on Alligator Alley. It was a straight shot west, and he didn't see another car behind him for miles. Five days to Wyoming, he figured. Five days.

It was going to be a whole different world.

Angela Jaynes pulled up to the curb, beneath the shade of a huge old tree, and switched off the ignition. Conard City hadn't changed much in the five years since she'd last come here to visit Emma, and Emma's house hadn't changed, either. It was still the same white clapboard two-story with black shutters.

The sun was sinking low in the west, and the October breeze was blowing dead leaves across the yards and sidewalks. Winter was on the way. How apropos, Angela thought. She would have felt offended if the day had been sunny, bright and warm.

She sat a few moments surveying the scene, a small, thin woman with blond hair and blue eyes that held a wistfulness nothing ever seemed to erase.

Getting out of the car, she stretched muscles stiff from the long drive from Iowa and surveyed the rest of the street. Rows of big old houses, neatly kept yards and grandfatherly trees. She wondered if Conard City ever changed, but was glad it didn't. It made her feel at home, even though she had never lived here.

The breeze gusted again, reminding her it was getting chilly out here. She decided to leave her suitcases until she was sure Emma was home. With such a long drive, she hadn't been able to tell Emma exactly when she would arrive, and she was here far earlier than she had anticipated.

She crossed the sidewalk and walked up to the wide porch with its swing and wicker chairs. The chairs were new, she realized, natural-colored rather than white, and inviting. Emma had been able to give up taking boarders since her marriage, and apparently things were even better than that now. Five years ago Emma had been barely making it on her shoestring librarian's salary.

Be home, Emma, she thought as she raised her hand to knock. She really needed to measure her blood sugar. It had been a little too long since her last meal, and she was begin-ning to feel the familiar sense of weakness in her muscles, the warning that low blood sugar was right around the corner. In her purse she had a roll of candy for emergencies, but she hated to do that. Invariably it started the seesaw going again.

She didn't have to wait long. The door swung open and Emma's warm, wonderful smile greeted her. An instant later she was enveloped in a bear hug, the first hug she'd had since her last visit.

"Angela," Emma said. "It's so good to see you!"

Angela hugged her back, truly feeling as if she'd come home. "You've gained weight!" she said on a laugh that was laced with tears of happiness. "It looks good on you."

"Eight whole pounds. Gage says it's because I'm happy. I think he's right." Emma stepped back, looking at her. "You look wonderful!" Then she shook her head, her beautiful red hair trailing over her shoulders. "Wonderful, but not well. Are you okay? You need something to eat?"

"Actually…"

Angela didn't have to say another word. Emma ushered her quickly toward the kitchen, and Angela caught a glimpse of herself in the hall mirror as they passed. Too pale, her eyes too big in a face that was too thin. Her blond hair was messed up, and her makeup had been gone for hours.

"Sit," Emma said, putting her in a chair at the round oak table that dominated the kitchen. Mouth-watering smells were issuing from the oven.

"I'm making a pot roast," Emma said, "since I didn't know when you'd get here. But it won't be ready for hours yet. What do you need? Crackers? Milk?"

"Both, please. And I need to get my test kit from the car."

"I'll get it. You just sit here and eat."

Emma put a plateful of crackers in front of her, and a tall glass of milk. Alone again while Emma went out to the car, Angela nibbled, waiting for her strength to return.

The main problem with being diabetic, she thought for the umpteenth time, was the way she was enslaved by her schedule. She had to eat at certain times, check her blood sugar level at certain times, inject her insulin at certain times—and nothing could be allowed to interfere with that. Lately, too much had been interfering.

Emma returned a few minutes later with the overnight case that held Angela's equipment. "Need me to put the insulin in the fridge?"

"Thanks." At least she didn't have to be uncomfortable doing this around Emma, she thought as she opened the glucose testing kit and pricked her finger. They'd been roommates in college, and Emma had gotten almost as proficient as Angela in dealing with the disease.

But Emma's acceptance didn't make it any easier to accept the necessity, Angela thought as she took the reading. She still hated her own inadequacy, hated being dependent on shots for her life.

The reading was low, as she had expected. Not too low, but low. With a sigh, she put the kit away and nibbled another cracker, hoping to eat just enough but not too much.

Emma sat across the table from her. "Are you okay?"

Angela nodded. "I'm fine. I just needed to eat something. Really."

"When you called you said...you were having trouble."

"Stress was getting the upper hand in my life, that's all. I was getting lax."

"Well, just let me know what your schedule has to be. I'm a little rusty."

"Sure. But for now let's talk about something—anything—that doesn't involve diabetes."

Emma laughed. "Fine with me. So, did you decide to quit your job or just take a vacation?"

"I quit." Angela tried to shrug as if it didn't matter, but didn't quite succeed. "I don't mind repossessing cars and that kind of thing, but I never, ever, want to foreclose on someone's farm again. God!" She shook her head and looked away. "I'd rather do anything else in the world."

"I can imagine."

Angela looked at her. "Are you sure it's okay with your husband to have me visit for a whole month? Won't he get sick of having someone else around all the time?"

"He doesn't mind at all," Emma said firmly. "You can ask him yourself when he gets home from work, but I promise, he's been looking forward to meeting you."

Angela smiled and reached for another cracker. "I'm looking forward to meeting him. He must be really something to get you over your fear of men after...." She trailed off, not wanting to mention the incident in college when Emma had been brutally assaulted and left for dead.

"He's special, all right," Emma said, her face softening. "We need to find someone like him for you."

Angela shook her head. "No way." It was bad enough that she had to live with her own illness. She couldn't ask that of anyone else. The one time she had been foolish enough to think someone could love her in spite of her diabetes, she'd lost both her baby and her lover. No man wanted a woman who couldn't have a healthy child, a woman who would periodically need to be rushed to the hospital as she too often had, and whose entire life consisted of an inalterable schedule of eating and self-treatment. A woman who could die on him at any minute. She'd made peace with that a long time ago and just wished her friends would, as well.

Just then the back door opened and Gage Dalton stepped into the kitchen. He looked exactly like the wedding photo Emma had sent Angela, except that he had gained a little weight, too, and looked less hard. He was wearing a light jacket, jeans and a white shirt. Angela remembered that Emma had once said he wore only black. That seemed to have changed.

He looked at her, and a warm smile split his face. "I recognize you," he said, his tone as warm as his smile. "Hi, Angela. It's about time you came to visit." He took the hand she offered and squeezed it gently.

"It's awfully kind of you to have me for a whole month," she said. "That's a long time to have a houseguest."

"We're looking forward to it." His dark eyes twinkled. "Hey, this town is so small it starts to feel inbred. A fresh face is always welcome."

He turned to Emma. "Speaking of which, do we have room for another houseguest?"

"Sure. Who?"

"I ran into a guy I used to know in the D.E.A. Well, I didn't know him very well. We met a few times. Anyway, he's in town to see Nate about something, and he's staying at the Lazy Rest. That would be okay, except he has his son with him, and he's less than three months old."

"That's no place for an infant," Emma said.

"That's what I thought."

"So ask him to come stay with us. We've got plenty of room." She turned to Angela. "Unless you think that would keep you from resting? Babies can be noisy."

"No, no," Angela said swiftly. "I love children. I wouldn't mind at all." Actually, she rather liked the idea of not being the only houseguest. It would keep everyone from fussing over her unnecessarily. She might *be* an invalid, but she hated to be treated like one.

"Good," Gage said. "Then I'll give him a call."

"First, honey, could you get Angela's bags from her car? She probably wants to rest after that long drive."

Ten minutes later Angela was ensconced in a room on the second floor with a view of the street. It was the room Emma had always given her when she visited, and it felt familiar and comfortable. Emma had made a few changes, brightening the room, and the mattress felt new. Still, it felt like coming home.

She was so glad to be back with Emma, back in Conard County. The thought buoyed her, driving back her fatigue long enough to take a shower and change.

Then she stretched out on the bed and fell asleep to the sounds of booted feet on the stairs and a baby fussing. Gage's friend had arrived.

Rafe was surprised by the phone call from Gage, and he hesitated before accepting the offer. But then he looked around the motel room, looked at Peanut sleeping in his portable bed, at the formula mess on the dresser and the disposable diapers already filling the wastebasket, and decided to accept.

He had been surprised to meet someone he knew here and instinctively felt uncomfortable about it. He'd stopped at the sheriff's office to introduce himself to Nate, but he still hadn't told the man they were brothers. Finding that he actually *knew* someone in this godforsaken place complicated things.

He wasn't sure exactly how, but for many years now he'd been playing things close to the vest, gathering information while giving none, learning to see information as power. He wasn't undercover now, and he told himself it was ridiculous to feel uneasy because he'd run into someone who knew he was with the D.E.A. For Pete's sake, what did it matter? It wasn't as if he was trying to deceive anyone. It wasn't as if Gage knowing him could put him at risk.

But he was uncomfortable anyway. He didn't like people knowing things about him, even minor things.

Entirely too paranoid, that was what he was. But paranoia had kept him alive, and it wasn't easy to relinquish.

And that conversation with Nathan Tate earlier—that had been ridiculous. "Hi, I'm staying in town for a few days and thought I ought to let you know I'm a D.E.A. agent, and I'm armed." As he stood there with the peanut in his arms.

Man, the sheriff must be wondering if he was off his rocker.

Tate had stared at him for a minute, then asked, "Are you expecting any trouble?"

Reasonable question. Tate had seemed okay. He'd looked younger than Rafe had expected of a man in his fifties, and there was nothing about him to put anyone in mind of the sheriff in one of those Grade-B movies. Just a competent, weathered, capable-looking man in an office buried in paperwork. Well, at least he knew his brother probably wasn't a sleaze. Although you could never really be sure. He'd met more than one crooked cop in his day.

But if Rafe had been looking for some kind of instant recognition, he hadn't found it. His brother didn't look like their mother. But then, neither did he. Looking at the one photograph he had of his old man, Rafe knew he resembled the rodeo clown who had fathered him. Nate probably took after his own father. Not one lick of their mother in either of them.

Both he and Nate had become cops. When he thought about it, that was downright interesting. Both of them had been sired by men who'd ditched their obligations. Maybe the way they'd been brought up had given them a desire for law and order?

But there was no way to know without talking to Nate, and he wasn't ready to do that. First he had to scope out the man's reputation around here.

No, first he had to pack up, check out and take the peanut over to Gage Dalton's house. He could probably learn a lot about Nate Tate from Dalton. That and getting the peanut out of this tiny room were all the motivation he needed.

He found the Dalton house without any difficulty and parked his beater behind a blue Toyota. He was hardly out of the car before Gage Dalton was coming down the darkening walk with a smile of welcome. Behind him, in the pool of warm lamplight that spilled out of the open doorway, stood a red-headed Valkyrie. A real knockout.

"What can I help with?" Gage asked.

Rafe popped the trunk, revealing a stack of cheap luggage he'd purchased on the road and the travel bed. "Anything you want to grab. I need to get the peanut. Thanks, Gage."

"No problem."

Rafe lifted the sleeping baby, car seat and all, and the diaper bag, and carried them toward the house. The woman stepped back to let him in. "Hi," she said. "I'm Emma Dalton."

"Rafe Ortiz. And this is Rafael Jr. 'Peanut' for short."

Emma peeked into the car seat and tugged the receiving blanket back just a little so she could see the tiny face. Women always did that. Rafe couldn't understand the fascination. His own kid, yeah, sure, he was interested in checking out the peanut, but somebody else's kid? Women were crazy that way.

"How adorable," Emma said.

"He's a good kid," Rafe said. "Thanks for asking us to stay with you."

Emma dazzled him with a smile. "We couldn't let the two of you stay in a motel. That's impossible with an infant. Your room's up the stairs, around the hall corner and at the back of the house. You can get settled in. Dinner will be in about an hour, but come down whenever you feel like it."

"Thanks." He headed for the stairs with Gage right behind him, carrying the luggage.

"We've got another friend staying with us," Gage said as he followed Rafe up the stairs. "She arrived just a little while ago, too. Nice lady."

Gads, another woman. Probably a *decent* woman. For some reason he was only comfortable with women if they were hookers, dealers or cops. Then he knew how to treat them. Too many dazzling, decent smiles and he was apt to get heartburn.

Well, what the hell, he told himself as he set the peanut and his carrier in the middle of the bed and turned to help unload Gage.

"Any of this you want me to take back downstairs?" Gage asked. "Formula and bottles, maybe? It'd be easier for you to deal with all that in the kitchen."

"Yeah, sure. That'd be great."

But before he could find the stuff and give it to Gage, the baby decided to wake up and demand immediate attention. Rafe looked at Gage and saw his own rueful look returned.

"I think I'd better take care of him first," Rafe said over the baby's squalls.

"Sure. If you need any help, let me know. I had kids of my own at one time." Something in Gage's face shadowed. "I'm good at feeding and diapering and pacing the floor in the middle of the night. Just holler."

"Thanks." Rafe turned to the kid as the door closed behind Gage. As soon as he picked the baby up, the cries quieted.

"Imagine that, Peanut," he said to his son. "Some other guy got suckered into this crap, too."

And looking down into those dark blue baby eyes, still damp around the edges, Rafe thought how easy it was to be suckered.

Peanut was still on Miami time, so he was ready to play after his diapering and feeding and didn't seem at all inclined to go back to sleep. Rafe took a few minutes to unpack essentials and organize things so that when he got hit with the inevitable two and four o'clock feedings he wouldn't be stumbling around half-awake trying to find them. He set the portable bed up in the corner, out of the way, but not too far from his own bed, and spread things out on the dresser to make a changing table.

"It looks like home sweet home, Peanut," he said as he surveyed his handiwork. Peanut cooed in response, waving his arms and legs from where he lay in the middle of the floor on a blanket.

"Guess we ought to go down, huh? Maybe I can learn a little more about your uncle Nate."

And didn't that sound weird? He was having trouble thinking of himself as a father, and thinking of a stranger as the kid's uncle—well, it was some kind of reality shift.

But what was new? Since the night Raquel had died, everything in his life had been mixed up. He'd better just get used to it.

With the baby in one arm, the diaper bag over his shoulder and a soiled diaper in his other hand, he went downstairs. Gage and Emma were seated at the table in the kitchen, chatting quietly. Rafe felt as though he were intruding, but they both looked at him with warm smiles and invited him to join them.

"I need to get rid of this first," he said, holding up the diaper.

"Out here." Gage took it from him and showed him the trash can in the little enclosed porch just off the kitchen.

He sat at the table with them, and there was a moment's awkward silence, broken by the baby's cooing.

"He's wide-awake, isn't he?" Emma said.

"It's his playtime. He's not sleeping as much as he did at first, though." End of that conversational avenue. He tried to think of another one.

"So," said Gage finally, "are you on vacation?"

"I guess you could say that." That was how it was marked back at the office. So far it hadn't really felt like one. He knew what they really wanted to know, though, and figured he might as well take the bull by the horns. "The kid's mom died when he was born."

"I'm sorry," they said at the same time.

Rafe shrugged. He didn't want to get into that. "Anyway, me and Peanut are hiding out for a while, right, kid?"

Peanut apparently agreed, gurgling and waving an arm.

"Well, this is a great place to hide out," Emma said. "Goodness knows, I hid out here myself for a long time."

"Me, too," Gage agreed.

"Me, too," said a lovely female voice from behind him. Rafe craned his neck to see a small, slender blonde standing in the doorway, looking as if she'd just woken up.

Rafe started to rise to his feet, an instinct he hadn't felt in a long time, but Gage put his hand on his shoulder, telling him to remain seated. Gage rose, though.

"Angela, this is Rafe Ortiz and his son. Rafe, Angela Jaynes."

The blonde came toward him and offered her hand. He shook it, feeling delicate bones beneath warm skin. Her smile was soft, a little uncertain, and he reckoned she wasn't used to men with ponytails and diamond earrings.

She turned her attention to the baby then, and for once he was glad of the instinctive response in women. Something about her blue eyes…something wistful… He shook his head, trying to shake off the pull he felt.

"What a little sweetheart," Angela said. She reached out, and Peanut grabbed her finger, hanging on for dear life. Then Angela laughed, a light, lovely sound that brought an answering smile to all the faces around her.

"What a grip!" she said.

"He is pretty strong," Rafe agreed, not even bothering to fight the fatherly pride he was suddenly feeling.

"I suppose he'll give me back my finger sooner or later." Angela took the seat beside Rafe, letting the baby continue to cling to her finger. "What's his name?"

"Rafael Jr. But I call him Peanut."

She nodded. "That's cute. I like it." Then she looked around the table, her smile lingering on her lips. "So we're all hiding out here, huh? Escapees from the larger, crueler world?"

Everyone laughed. Everyone except Rafe. He hadn't really thought of himself that way, but it kind of fit.

Angela turned to Rafe. "Gage said you were with the D.E.A.?"

He nodded, caution filling him. He didn't much like it when people started asking questions.

"What exactly do you do?" she asked.

It was an innocent question; even Rafe knew that. But it put him on edge, anyway. "I go after drug traffickers," he said finally.

"Undercover?" Her eyes widened a little, signifying her interest.

"Sometimes," he replied noncommittally.

"That must be...scary."

Scary? He didn't think of it as scary. Most of the time it was sheer fun or dirty, hard work. He got an adrenaline rush from it, but he didn't remember ever being scared until Manny had found him at home and wanted to see the baby. "What do you do?" he asked her, wanting to change the subject.

"I was a bank loan officer." She grimaced, and her wistful eyes grew sad. He wondered what had happened but didn't ask. "I made my living being nasty to nice people."

He nodded slowly. "You do what you have to." He'd been doing that his entire life.

"I guess. But I'm not going to do it anymore." She brightened, a visible effort, and turned to Emma. "What can I do to help with dinner?"

"How about setting the dining room table? I thought we'd be more comfortable out there."

Rafe watched the women rise and gather up the dishes and utensils. Then he and Gage were alone in the kitchen.

Gage spoke in a low voice. "Is somebody after you?"

Rafe shrugged. "Maybe." It was true.

The other man nodded. "You hide out here as long as you need to, Rafe."

"Thanks. I should get this mess cleaned up within a couple of weeks, though." If that long. Once he knew whether Tate would take the kid, and whether he wanted to leave the kid here, there would be no reason to stay. Funny how what had originally looked like a good way to handle an inconvenience had become the linchpin on which the rest of his life depended. He looked down at the baby in his arms and met that unnerving, steady stare.

Blank slate? Not likely, he found himself thinking. There was something going on in this baby's head.

He looked at Gage. "Your kids grow up?" He was surprised by the way the other man's face seemed to freeze.

"What do you mean?"

"You said you used to have kids. They grow up? Or did you get divorced?"

Gage's answer was clipped. "Car bomb."

Rafe could have nailed his tongue to the wall then, as he remembered. "That was you," he said haplessly. "God, I'm sorry...."

He'd heard about it. Hell, everyone in the agency had heard about the guy whose family had been blown up right before Christmas.... Damn, he should have thought of that. It explained the scar on Gage's cheek, the rasp of his voice. They said he hadn't stopped screaming for days....

"I'm sorry," Rafe said again. "I didn't know it was you."

Gage made a gesture, as if to wipe it all away.

Rafe looked down at the bundle in his arms, feeling something he hadn't felt in a long time: fear.

"Anyway," Gage said after a moment, "you can count on me. For as long as you need."

Rafe believed it. For the first time in a very long time, he felt a stirring of real trust. The feeling made him uneasy, as uneasy as the baby's steady stare. The world was going cock-eyed on him.

"Just don't say anything to Emma or Angela about it," Gage said. "Angela's here for a rest, and Emma—well, Emma has some bad things of her own in her past. I don't want them worrying."

Rafe nodded. "That's fine by me. I don't like telling everyone my business, anyway."

Gage cracked an unexpected laugh. "You've been spending too much time on the streets, Rafe."

Maybe he had, he thought, looking down at his son again. Maybe he had.

Chapter 2

Seeing as how Peanut didn't care that he'd moved to the Mountain time zone, the 2:00 a.m. feeding happened around midnight. Which was fine with Rafe, because he hadn't fallen asleep yet.

Unfortunately, though, when he opened the can of premixed formula he'd left on the bedside table, he discovered it was spoiled.

The baby was crying his little head off, red in the face, angry about the hunger pangs in his stomach. Nothing pitiable about this kid, Rafe thought. Hell, no. He was a scrapper.

He picked the infant up and headed downstairs, hoping the peanut didn't wake the entire world with his caterwauling. Then it occurred to him that he'd bought all the formula he had at the same store in Kansas City. What if it was all spoiled? He doubted this flyspeck of a town had any place he could buy formula in the middle of the night.

The kitchen light was on, he saw as he approached. The glow seeped around the edges of the closed door. Well, there was at least one person in the house that Peanut wouldn't be waking.

He found Angela Jaynes sitting at the table in her cotton terry-cloth bathrobe, nibbling on some crackers and drinking a glass of milk.

"Sorry," he said, pausing just inside the door. "Didn't mean to bother you."

"You're not bothering me." She gave him a wan smile. "Sounds like you have a problem."

Peanut let out another ear-splitting wail.

"Yeah, he's hungry. The can of formula I had upstairs was spoiled. There's more in the fridge."

Angela rose from the table. "Let me get it for you. Want me to pour it in the bottle?"

"Sure, but rinse it first. Thanks."

He'd forgotten to bring the can opener down, so Angela had to hunt for one. With nothing else to do, Rafe patted Peanut's bottom, bouncing him gently as he paced back and forth.

"How can I tell if it's spoiled?" Angela asked when she found the can opener.

"The last one was lumpy."

"Okay. How much do I pour?"

"Four ounces, a little more. He'll eat what he wants."

"Really? You don't have to measure exactly?"

Rafe, who was used to women he didn't even know telling him how to hold the baby and how to feed him, was surprised to have a woman asking him as if *he* were the expert. "Yeah. I only have to pay attention in case he starts eating less than usual."

"That must be nice."

"What do you mean?"

She didn't answer. "What now?"

"Warm it in a little hot water, will you? I don't know if it would hurt him to get it right out of the fridge, but he's not used to it. Why risk it?"

She nodded and ran the bottle under the tap for a few

minutes, then shook some on her wrist, just like a pro. "It's okay now." She handed it to him.

He popped the nipple into the baby's open mouth. It took a couple of seconds for Peanut to realize that food was at hand, but as soon as he did, silence, blissful silence, reigned.

Rafe blew a breath of relief. "Man, he's got a pair of lungs."

Angela laughed and returned to her seat. She nibbled a cracker and sipped milk, watching Rafe walk the floor as he fed the baby. For a few minutes there was no sound except the child's contented sucking and the father's slow, steady footfalls.

Then he remembered that Angela hadn't answered his question. He paused and looked at her. "What did you mean, it must be nice that I don't have to measure exactly what he eats?"

She hunched a little and looked down at her plate. When she looked up, her smile didn't quite reach her eyes. "I'm diabetic. I have to watch everything I eat."

"Really? That must be a pain."

"I've been doing it since I was eight. You'd think I'd be used to it by now."

"No…no…" he said slowly. "I can see how it would be difficult. Especially when everybody around you eats whatever they want whenever they want."

"Well," she said, squaring her shoulders, "most of the time I just do it without thinking too much about it. I'm pretty good at eyeballing food and guessing portions."

He nodded. "Yeah, I can imagine. I'm pretty good at eyeballing a kilo of cocaine."

That surprised a laugh out of her, and her blue eyes met his. They were still wistful eyes, he noted, but not as shadowed as they had been a few minutes ago.

"Well," she said, "I've been getting careless lately, so I'm here to get back on track."

"Yeah. This seems like a good place to do it. Nice folks."

"I've known Emma since college. This is the first time I've met Gage, though."

"I don't really know him," Rafe offered. "We met a couple of times, but we never worked together."

"That's what he said." She hesitated. "Would you...would you mind very much if I held the baby?"

Women, he thought. They just couldn't resist. But while he usually said no, for reasons he couldn't quite explain to himself, he didn't feel his usual resistance. Somehow it seemed okay for Angela to hold Peanut for a little while. And it sure would ease his aching arm.

He walked over and handed his son to her. She was a little tentative at first, and Peanut felt it. He let go of the nipple and made an irritated sound.

"Relax," Rafe said to her. "You're not going to drop him."

She settled the baby more firmly against her breast, tucked the bottle nipple back in, and Peanut went back to his midnight snack. "He's so incredibly light," she said. "Such a bitty thing."

"Until you've carried him for half an hour." Rafe shook out his arm as Angela laughed quietly. He took the opportunity to pour himself a glass of milk, then sat with them at the table.

"So how do you like being a father?" Angela asked.

Questions again. Rafe hated them. He chose to answer with humor. "I'll let you know when he's grown up."

She laughed again, a pleasant sound. "I'm from Iowa," she said. "Where are you from?"

"Miami."

"Wow. This has to be a change for you."

"Yeah, it is." A pleasant change, he found himself thinking. For the first time since Manny had shown up on his doorstep, he didn't feel a compelling urge to look over his shoulder. He hadn't exactly relaxed—he suspected that after the way he'd been living these past ten years, he would probably need months to completely relax. Nor was he sure it would be wise to let himself relax that much.

Peanut had lost interest in his bottle and was busy pushing the nipple back out.

"I think he's done," Rafe remarked.

"It looks that way." Angela put the bottle on the table, and Rafe took the baby, putting him on his shoulder and patting his back gently. The child clutched Rafe's shirt and bobbed his head as he looked around.

Angela laughed quietly. "He doesn't look sleepy at all."

"I'm not surprised. This one's a regular little night owl."

"He probably takes after you."

"How did you guess?" Their eyes met again, and again Rafe felt that inexplicable tug. He didn't like the feeling. When he had time to be aware of women, he was usually aware of a sexual pull. This was...different. Angela Jaynes wasn't the type of female he usually felt attracted to. For whatever reason, he tended to be drawn to Latinas like Raquel Molina, dark-haired and fiery. Not once in his life had he been interested in a blonde.

So he wasn't feeling sexually attracted to this woman, but he was feeling...drawn to her. At an emotional level. At some place where he'd never in his life felt pulled toward another human being.

Not good. He dragged his gaze away and returned his attention to bringing up a gas bubble. The peanut promptly obliged with a belch that would have done an adult proud. The sound brought another one of those pretty laughs out of Angela.

"Well, you'll have to excuse me," she said after a moment. "I need to go take my insulin."

He turned and looked at her. "You take shots?"

"Four times a day."

"That's miserable."

"You do what you have to." She went to the refrigerator and pulled out a Styrofoam box. Opening it, she took out a small vial, then put the box back in the fridge. "Good night," she said.

He watched her go, surprised to realize that he would have liked her to stay.

"Now isn't that ridiculous?" he said to the baby. "We don't even know her."

Peanut apparently agreed. He answered with another little burp, then closed his eyes and gave every indication of falling asleep.

Upstairs, Rafe changed the kid's diaper and put him to bed. Then he was alone again, with no company but his own. For a couple of hours he didn't have to play daddy, but he didn't have to play D.E.A. agent, avenging angel of the U.S. government, either.

It felt weird. At home he would have been kicking over what he had to do the next day. Whether he was undercover or between assignments, there was always something he needed to be planning or working on.

Now he was alone, with nothing to do, and the yawning chasm of his own self loomed uncomfortably before him. The feeling disturbed him. Without a role to play, he didn't quite know what to do with himself. He wasn't introspective by nature, and didn't want to sit around pondering the mysteries of life and the universe. Nor did he want to think about the shadowy self somewhere inside him.

Finally he grabbed a book off the shelf near the bed and opened it up to discover some thriller about a D.E.A. agent. It wasn't long before he was laughing quietly at the absurdities of the novelist's view of life undercover. Which was fine.

Anything was better than shaking hands with himself.

Angela woke in the morning feeling more rested than she had in months. She made quick work of testing her blood sugar and injecting herself in the thigh with fast-acting insulin.

Her thighs were a mess, she thought, looking at them. Needle tracks and little depressions from years of poking herself. Oh, well, nobody had to see it except her. She pulled on a sweatshirt and a pair of biker shorts that concealed the damage fairly well, slipped her feet into jogging shoes and headed downstairs.

Emma was in the kitchen making bacon and eggs and ready with a glass of orange juice. "Can you wait a few minutes to eat? It's almost done."

"Sure." The orange juice would tide her over.

"White or wheat toast?"

"Wheat, please."

"Did you sleep well?"

"Better than I have in a long time. Thanks, Emma."

Emma smiled at her. "I'm glad to have you here. You know that. It's been too long, Angela."

Emma put a plate of scrambled eggs and bacon in front of her, and a moment later added a couple of pieces of toast. "Is there anything else you need?"

Angela did a quick mental survey of the grams of carbo-hydrate on her plate. "This should be perfect."

"You know you can help yourself if you need anything, right?"

Angela smiled at her. "I know. Thanks."

Emma joined her with a cup of coffee. "I've got to leave for the library in about twenty minutes. You don't mind, do you? Being alone today, when you just got here?"

"I don't mind at all. I don't expect you to upend your whole life for me, Emma. Giving me a bolt hole is quite enough."

Emma waved a dismissing hand. "It's no trouble at all. We certainly have enough room. You just make yourself at home and let me know if you need anything."

"I will."

They sat in companionable silence for a few minutes while Angela ate.

"How sick have you been?" Emma asked presently.

Angela sighed. "My blood sugar has been all over the place. I wound up in the hospital twice in the past couple of months. I was lucky I passed out in public places. God knows what would have happened if I'd been alone."

"I hate to think. Was it just stress?"

"Stress and not paying attention to myself. I was so upset sometimes that I wouldn't eat enough. Or I'd forget my insulin. Hard to believe, isn't it? You'd think that since I've been doing this since I was eight it would be automatic. Or I'd be in the middle of a meeting with some couple, trying to work out how they could possibly save their home, and lunchtime would come and go before I realized it...." She shook her head. "My doctor says I was blaming myself for other people's problems, but it's hard not to, when you're sitting across the table from some decent couple who, through no fault of their own, have had a couple of bad years."

Emma nodded. "It would be hard."

"Especially since these people got to be my friends. It's not like the problems happened suddenly and they were total strangers. The trouble comes on for a long time. I did everything I could to keep them going. Darn it, Emma, I even got to know things like exactly how much they were spending on milk and clothes for their kids, trying to find some way to help them cut costs so they could make it."

"It sounds like you did everything you could."

"Everything I was allowed to do." She shook her head. "It wasn't enough. Anyway, it's obvious I'm not cut out for that kind of work. I couldn't even forget it when I went home at the end of the day. I was lying awake running numbers, looking for ways to work things out the same as I would have been if *I* were the one in trouble."

"And so you decided to quit."

"Now I've got to think about what else I can do with a background in banking." Angela grimaced. "My main fear is that I'm locked in."

Although that wasn't quite true, Angela thought after Emma left for the library. She was afraid of a lot more than that she might have to take another job in banking. That life was pointless, for example. Because it sure seemed like it.

She stepped outside and began her morning jog, heading up Front Street toward the downtown area. The air was crisp and dry, and small dark clouds scudded across a sky that was painfully blue. One of Emma's neighbors, an elderly man, was out raking leaves in his front yard and he waved as Angela jogged by.

Boy, was she out of shape, she thought after about a half mile. It had been too long since she'd jogged regularly. She'd forgotten how good it felt, even with her lungs burning and her legs aching.

But whether it felt good or not, there was still the pointlessness of her existence, and it shadowed her every step.

A life had to have meaning, she thought. It wasn't just enough to get through the day. There had to be a purpose. But somewhere along the way she'd become absorbed in just making it through the day and had lost track of the point of it all.

Just because she couldn't have a family and children, that didn't mean she couldn't have a purpose. The problem was, she couldn't find one. Without children to work for or a husband to take care of, it all seemed pretty pointless, a matter of getting up every morning and working so she could pay for her insulin, food and shelter, so she could get up the next morning and do it all over again.

So, she was depressed. Probably not depressed enough to need a doctor, but depressed enough that she needed to get her head screwed on straight before it got any worse.

When she reached the far side of town, she stopped jogging and turned around to walk back. She wasn't sure how this was going to affect her blood sugar, and she probably shouldn't have done it, she thought as her legs began to seem wobbly. When her blood sugar had started to roller coaster a few months ago, her doctor had changed her regimen, upping her number of shots each day to four to get better control.

When she reached the town square in the shadow of the courthouse, she sat on a park bench for a little while, watching the passersby and wondering if they were ever plagued by feelings of pointlessness, or if they felt fulfilled and content with their lives.

Probably not, she decided. She had certainly seen enough people in her office whose lives were messed up and who didn't seem to be able to hang on, no matter how hard they tried. By comparison, she supposed she was damn lucky.

A woman with twins in a side-by-side stroller walked by. The children looked happy and healthy, but the mom looked fatigued. Angela felt a twinge of envy but scolded herself for it. Some days that mother probably wondered if she was going to have enough energy to make it until bedtime.

Just then Gage Dalton came out of the sheriff's office on the corner and saw her. He waved, and she waved back, then watched him as he limped across the street. Funny, she hadn't noticed last night that he limped.

He joined her on the bench. "How's it going?" he asked.

"Great. I just took a run. It's a beautiful morning for it."

He shifted, as if sitting made him uncomfortable. "It most certainly is. I was getting cabin fever looking out my office window."

"So you decided to make a jailbreak?"

He laughed. "Actually, I was just playing messenger boy. We had a call from Miami today. Somebody needs to talk to Rafe. I tried to call him, but he's not answering the phone, probably because it's not his."

"A job that follows you on vacation, huh?"

His face sobered. "It's a job that never stops following you. Want a lift home? Or do you want to walk back?"

She accepted the ride, figuring she'd better check her blood sugar again to make sure she hadn't thrown it out of whack by running.

"So you know Rafe from the D.E.A.?" she asked to make conversation as they were driving down the street.

"Not really. I ran into him a couple of times. I heard he had a good reputation for working undercover. That he was a bit of a wild card."

"What does that mean?"

Gage shrugged. "Sort of…independent in his methods. Apparently whatever he's doing is working."

"It's a dangerous job, isn't it?"

"Oh, yeah. High on-the-job death rate. It's not for the faint of heart. It requires…hell, I don't know. Adrenaline addiction? You have to like living on the edge, taking risks. And you have to stay on that edge or you'll get yourself killed. It's not a great way to make a living.''

"But you did it, didn't you?'' Angela remembered Emma saying something about it long ago.

"Yeah. When I was young and wild. And it cost me. That's the thing. The piper has to be paid eventually. And there're a lot of ways he can get his pound of flesh. Rafe's evidently been at this a lot longer than most people.''

"Does it…do something to you?''

Gage nodded. "It sure does. It can get hard to remember you're one of the good guys when you spend most of your time acting like one of the bad guys.''

"I take it you mean you don't come home at the end of the day.''

"Too dangerous. No, you might live months or years trying to get close to the guys you're after, and all that time you have to be sure not to leave any trail that'll lead back to who you really are. I was married and had kids. The two things don't go together, so finally I had to get out of that end of it. Didn't keep somebody with a grudge from coming after me, though.''

He pulled into the driveway, parked and turned off the ignition. Then he looked straight at her. "D.E.A. agents might be the stuff of romantic legends, Angela, but we're lousy mates, at least when we're working the streets. And even when we're not, we can be away for days or weeks at a time when a case is coming to a head.''

She felt faint color stain her cheeks. "I was just curious.''

He smiled. "I know. But I figured I'd give the warning anyway.''

Feeling uncomfortable, Angela wanted to get to her room without running into Rafe, afraid he might suspect her interest in him the same way Gage had, but there was no way to manage it. Rafe was sitting on the front porch with the baby, the two of them evidently enjoying the beautiful morning.

"Hi,'' Rafe said as they came up the steps. Angela smiled

and tried to edge past Gage to get into the house, but couldn't do it without being both obvious and rude.

"You need to call Kate Keits," Gage told Rafe.

Rafe's smile faded. "Did she say why?"

"Afraid not."

Rafe rose and handed the baby to Gage. "Do you mind? Can I use your phone?"

"Help yourself." As soon as Rafe disappeared inside, Gage looked at Angela. "Can you take the baby? I need to get back. I've got an appointment in ten minutes with an attorney who wants to depose me for a case."

Angela nodded, figuring she could wait another few minutes to measure her blood sugar. She *felt* all right. But, for safety's sake, she sat in the wicker chair and made sure that even if she started to fog out the baby couldn't fall. Then she waited, hoping Rafe's phone call wouldn't take too long. Right now the baby was sleeping, but she wouldn't know the right thing to do if he woke and started screaming.

She found herself absorbed in looking down at the small, sleeping face. There was something so peaceful there. Something soothing just to behold. She also felt an unmistakable ache in her heart for something that could never be.

Rafe dialed Kate Keits's number with a reasonable degree of trepidation. He knew his boss, and knew if she was calling him here there was serious trouble afoot. Maybe some legal maneuvering in one of his cases. Maybe they needed him back for depositions. Or maybe she was getting ready to reassign him because he was useless to her. Or all of the above.

It turned out to be none of the above. Once he was transferred past the gate guardian with the blinding teeth, Kate came on the phone immediately.

"Rafe," she said in her usual brisk tone, "are you absolutely *sure* that kid is yours?"

The question took him by surprise. "Yeah. Didn't I tell you so?"

"You said you had a DNA test."

"That's right. What the hell's going on, Kate?"

"Are you listed as the father on the birth certificate?"

"Hell, yes. Kate, what's going on?"

She sighed. "Buckle your seatbelt, Ortiz. Four days ago Manuel Molina was here looking for you. He said you were supposed to meet with him about arranging visitation with the baby."

"I said that to get him out of my hair."

"I figured. Anyway, he wanted to know where you'd gone, and I refused to tell him. Said I didn't know, that you'd taken vacation."

"Thanks, Kate. I appreciate it." It didn't surprise him that Manny Molina wasn't going to go away easily, but it did surprise him that Manny would go to the extreme of contacting the D.E.A. Molinas, as a rule, had a violent, allergic reaction to law enforcement. Manny must have broken out in hives when he made that call.

"Wait, it doesn't end there. Today I got a letter from an attorney representing the Molinas. One of those smarmy iron-fist-in-a-velvet-glove letters, suggesting that this matter can be settled amicably—or not so amicably—and demanding to know your whereabouts."

Rafe swore quietly.

"Anyway, I'm going to stonewall it. You're on vacation, and I don't know your whereabouts. But you'd better watch your back, *compadre*."

"Yeah." He had that feeling again, that one he'd gotten when Manny picked the kid up that night. Only this time it was stronger. More like an urge to kill. He jumped as if stung. He didn't allow himself to feel things like that. Hell, he didn't allow himself to feel much. Feelings clouded his brain. They were dangerous. "What does Manny think he can accomplish by this? I'm the kid's dad."

"I don't know, Rafe." Kate's sigh was audible over the phone. "I'd feel a whole lot better if I was sure it really *is* the kid he wants."

"That's a fact."

"As to what he can do? Bankrupt you with legal bills in a custody fight. Keep you so tied up in court that you can't do your job. Try to prove you an unfit parent…and by the way, Rafe, your life-style the past few years isn't going to be much of a positive recommendation. Hanging out with dope dealers, prostitutes, murderers… That could be used to paint an ugly picture in court."

"I can paint an even uglier one of the Molinas, Kate."

"Sure. But that takes time and money. Listen, it strikes me that it's time for you to go undercover again."

"What?" Rafe wondered if Kate had been sniffing something from the evidence locker.

"Seriously. You know how you play a street buzzard with everything you have? Maybe you need to play the ultimate good dad for a while."

"I'm doing that already," Rafe said dryly. "What other kind of dad does two feedings in the middle of the night? I'm up to my ears in baby poop. It doesn't get much better than that."

Kate laughed. "You might be right. Excuse me, but I'm enjoying the notion of you buried in baby poop."

"Thanks a lot."

Her voice grew serious. "You know what I mean, Rafe. Play it to the hilt, watch your back, and stay the hell out of Miami until we find out what the Molinas are up to. In fact, stay right where you are. I'm putting a man on it. It makes me nervous when somebody gets too interested in one of my agents."

"Yeah, it's making my scalp crawl, too."

After he hung up, he stood staring blindly out the window. From where he stood in the living room, he could see Angela and the baby on the front porch. The view was so peaceful and perfect that he nearly wanted to barf. That wasn't his life out there. *His* life involved living with the lowlifes of society until he could get the goods on them. His life was the existence of an avenging angel, bringing the lawbreakers to justice, not wiping a kid's bottom.

But for now, he couldn't let anyone know that. While he might actually consider leaving the kid with his half-brother, he couldn't stomach the thought of letting the Molinas get the peanut in their clutches.

Which meant he would probably have to keep the kid close for a while.

It wasn't the way he had planned it, but some things were more important than his plans. Like his kid.

Running hadn't been her brightest idea ever, Angela found herself thinking. She should have remembered to reduce her insulin this morning, but it had been so long since she'd had the heart to follow her exercise regimen that she'd forgotten that necessary adjustment. The low-blood-sugar wooziness was all too familiar to her, and she gave in, popping a hard candy into her mouth.

She didn't understand how it worked, but she *did* know that exercising reduced her need for insulin. Now she had too much coursing through her system and was in danger of insulin shock.

She chewed the candy to help it dissolve faster, and popped another one into her mouth. God, how she hated this! This constant preoccupation with her illness was a bore. Even after twenty-seven years, she still resented the control it had over her.

The attitude was childish, she told herself. Diabetes was a fact of her life, one she simply needed to deal with the way other people dealt with weight problems, but sometimes she resented it so fiercely she wanted to cry. Sometimes she drowned in self-pity, wondering why she couldn't be like everybody else in the world, with a body that took care of things automatically.

Now she was sitting here holding a baby, and rarely had she been as aware of her disability as she was now. Even if she'd been able to have her own child, she wouldn't have been much of a mother, she thought now. She couldn't even risk getting up, because her blood sugar was falling and she might drop the baby. Pretty damn pathetic.

The door opened, and Rafe stepped out onto the porch. She looked up at him, smiling brightly. "I think you'd better take the baby."

He obliged at once, scooping the child from her arms with practiced ease. "What's wrong?" he asked. "You look pale."

"A little low blood sugar. I got carried away with my running this morning."

His face creased with concern. "Do you need anything?"

"I popped a couple of pieces of candy. I'll be okay in a minute."

"You're sure?"

He looked so genuinely worried that she felt a laugh rise inside her, but she swallowed it. She didn't know him well enough to risk offending him. "I'm sure."

He planted himself in the other chair with the air of a man who didn't intend to budge. "I'll just sit with you for a couple of minutes."

She was torn between feeling touched and irritated. "I really don't need a caretaker," she said. "I've been living with this for twenty-seven years. I know what to do."

"I don't doubt it."

"You don't need to sit with me."

"Maybe not."

She narrowed her eyes. "Are you always this difficult?"

"Yep. Are you?"

She was taken aback. "What do you mean?"

"Do you always tell people who are concerned about you to get lost?"

She could feel a hot blush rising in her cheeks, a feeling she wasn't used to since she'd left girlhood behind. "Yes," she said finally. "I guess I do."

"Yeah, me, too."

His answer astonished her, driving out her irritation. Finally a helpless laugh escaped her.

He shrugged, tilting his head to one side. "I just call the shots the way I see them."

"Funny, I would have thought a D.E.A. agent was more…circumspect."

"Most of them probably are. Me, I have a major flaw. I tell the truth."

"Even to drug dealers?" She was sure she had him with that.

"Even to drug dealers. You'd be amazed how many of them laugh themselves sick when a guy who looks like something that was just scraped out of a back alley comes up to 'em and says he's with the D.E.A." He shook his head. "Can't understand it, but they never believe me."

Angela found herself laughing again. "Oh, I can understand it," she said. "Believe me, I can understand it."

He looked down at himself. "I don't think I look that disreputable."

That sent Angela off into another gale of laughter.

One corner of his mouth lifted. "Honest, I walked up to a street pusher once—in fact, it was my first undercover assignment. I was supposed to make a score so we could start reeling him in. Usual procedure when you're working a local dealer. The guy looks at me and says, 'Who the hell are you?'"

He shook his head. "I got so rattled… I mean, I didn't expect that kind of question. I expected him to fob me off because he didn't know me, so I'd probably have to come back a few more times before he trusted me enough to deal me some crack. Or maybe that he wouldn't say anything at all, would just sell the stuff to me. But I didn't expect the question. Anyway, I was so startled, I said, 'I'm Rafe Ortiz, D.E.A.' The guy laughed himself sick and sold me a gram of crack. That's when I decided that honesty was the best policy."

"But not every time, surely?"

He shook his head. "Not every time. But often enough." His gaze grew distant, and he looked away from her, evidently lost in some corridor of memory. After a moment he returned his gaze to her. "You meet all kinds in this business. I've pulled up to a corner dealer in my car with government plates, flashed my badge and asked him what he had to sell me. The jerk actually gave me my choice. I figure he thought I wanted something for my personal use and was offering him protection when I flashed my badge. Or maybe he just didn't think at all. Not very many of these types are really bright."

"But it can't always be that easy."

"No. Depends on what you're after. Some of the big boys— well, it can take months or years to get close enough to major dealers and importers. They're a lot more cautious. Just figuring out who they are is a job all by itself, and then you have to get the goods on them. Not easy. But street pushers— they're a dime a dozen. Easy to crack. Hell, they practically hand you the evidence on a silver platter."

"What do you mean?"

"Suspicious traffic catches somebody's attention. Too many cars pulling up to an out-of-the-way place, or to a house, that kind of thing. It doesn't take long to make a few buys from these guys. But it always amazes me how many of them actually keep books. Just like businessmen. I've found detailed ledgers in more of these guys' houses than I can believe."

Angela nodded and popped another candy into her mouth. "I wouldn't even have thought of that."

"It surprised me the first time I saw it," he agreed. Suddenly he stiffened. "Um...you'll have to excuse us. We're wet."

Just then the baby let out a cranky cry. Rafe stood, and Angela could see that his slacks were damp.

"Diaper bypass," he said with a shrug. "You going to be okay?"

"I'm fine now. Really. Thanks for worrying about me."

He nodded, then looked down at her from eyes that were suddenly empty. "Just don't make too much out of it."

Angela stared after him as he disappeared into the house and wondered if it would be better to clobber him or give him the cold shoulder. "Don't make too much of it" indeed!

Of course, she admitted a few minutes later when her annoyance had died away, he *did* radiate high-wattage animal magnetism. There was something about Rafe Ortiz that drew even a disinterested woman's mind—such as her own—to places it didn't ordinarily go.

Unfortunately, she was afraid her straying thoughts had been written on her face. Why else would he have said anything to her about it?

He must just be used to women throwing themselves at him. That was all it could be; he couldn't possibly be a mind reader.

But now that she was alone, she indulged in a few moments of remembering how he'd looked sitting beside her. He had very broad shoulders, and when the fabric of his slacks stretched across his thighs, it was easy to tell that he had strong legs.

The direction of her thoughts surprised her, because she didn't notice these things about men anymore, and hadn't for years. Pheromones, she decided. He must exude some very powerful ones. What else could it be?

And he was arrogant, she decided. All the more reason to keep a polite distance.

But keeping a polite distance vanished a few minutes later when he returned to the porch with a glass of orange juice. "Here," he said, handing it to her. "It's better for you than that candy."

Then he disappeared back inside, leaving her to wonder what was going on in his mind.

Chapter 3

"Well, this sure isn't getting us anywhere, Peanut," Rafe said.

The baby was squirming on the floor, happy now with a fresh diaper, trying to creep toward a squeaky toy that was a few inches away.

"I can't hole up here indefinitely," Rafe said. Maybe it was time to go talk to the sheriff and lay it all out. Better than skulking around, anyway, and he'd never been much good at skulking. He also wasn't any good at hanging around and doing nothing.

What had he been thinking, anyway? Coming out here to check out his half-brother made sense, but he should just have told his story. If he started poking around and asking questions, people were just going to run to Tate, anyway, and tell him what was going on. Then he would be explaining to Tate why a D.E.A. agent was asking questions about him. Not a good way to begin a familial relationship.

"I must have left my brain in my other pants, Peanut."

Peanut cooed.

"Yeah, I agree." He packed the baby into the car seat, slung the diaper bag over his shoulder and carried the whole kit and caboodle downstairs.

Angela was still sitting on the porch, half a glass of orange juice in her hand. He paused, looking down at her. "Are you okay? Really?"

She looked up, but there was no smile for him. "I'm fine."

He hesitated. "You don't look fine," he said.

"Too bad."

"Oh." It dawned on him that she was annoyed with him. "Did I do something wrong?"

"Just quit hovering, okay?"

"Okay." He stepped away, just one step. "Anything else?"

"Yes. Explain to me where you got the notion that every woman within ten feet has to be attracted to you."

"Did I say that? I never said that."

"You *implied* it."

He shook his head. "I didn't imply anything. Why? Are you attracted to me?"

"No, I'm not!"

"Then there's no problem, is there?" He flashed a smile, the one Rocky used to call his thousand-watter. "I'm glad we have that all straightened out."

"We don't have anything straightened out. And you are a maddening conversationalist."

"Actually, this isn't a conversation. It's more like a cross-examination." He watched as another blush stained her cheeks and tried not to notice how pretty it made her. "Look, I'm sorry if I said something that made you think I think you're attracted to me. Because it never entered my head. I'm not your type."

"What?" She looked stunned and disbelieving. "You don't even know me. How can you say any such thing?"

It was pathetic, Rafe thought, but he was actually enjoying this ridiculous farce of a conversation. "Maybe because you're not my type," he said finally, then descended the steps, whistling as he went.

"Just answer me one thing," she called after him. "Do you ever talk in a straight line?"

"What's the point?" he asked over his shoulder. "Nobody ever believes me, anyway."

He buckled the baby into the car, then climbed in behind the wheel. He cast a glance toward the woman on the porch and saw that she was still sitting there, looking utterly uncertain. Maybe he shouldn't have made that crack about her not being his type. Maybe that had made her feel bad.

Nah, he decided as he pulled away from the curb and headed down the street. She was a blonde. In his experience, blondes thought they had the world by the tail.

But maybe that wasn't a fair assessment. He turned it around in his mind for a minute, then dismissed the concern. When all was said and done, it didn't matter one way or the other, because they would shortly go their own ways and never meet again.

And why, he wondered suddenly, had he started to care what total strangers thought of him? Concerns like that could only get in the way of his job—if he still had a job when all this was over.

Oddly, that prospect didn't make him feel as gloomy as he had expected. It was the baby thing, he decided. The arrival of Rafe Jr. in his life had overshadowed everything else. He needed to do something about that.

He parked in front of the sheriff's office and sat for a few minutes, contemplating what he was about to do. For years now he'd pretty much had to fly by the seat of his pants, making snap decisions in dangerous situations, but this was different. This time he had the luxury of reflection, and he had the choice of not acting at all. It would be easy to walk away right now and never tell Tate that they were half-brothers. He could just turn his back on the whole idea and make other plans for himself and his son.

Or he could walk in there and shake up Tate's life and his own with a revelation that might not be at all welcome. Too, now that he was getting closer to the prospect, he found that the idea of dumping Peanut on a relative didn't sound half so good as it had sounded back in Miami. If nothing else, the kid deserved better of him. Then, there was that responsibility thing. He'd always been a responsible person, and ditching his kid with a near stranger didn't strike him as at all responsible.

"Hell," he said.

He gave some serious thought to turning around right then and letting the proverbial sleeping dog lie, but it struck him that if something happened to him, Peanut was going to be in serious need of some family besides the Molinas.

That was enough to make him get out of the car, retrieve the baby and diaper bag, and head into the sheriff's office. Apparently he hadn't been thinking too clearly over the past few months, not since he'd found out about the baby. Where in the world had he gotten this harebrained notion to look up a brother he'd never met and dump his kid on him?

Nate Tate was standing in the front office talking to the dispatcher. He was a tall, sunburned man with a strong face that had been creased by the clements. His voice was gravelly as he spoke to the dispatcher, an old prune of a woman who was filling the air with her cigarette smoke.

Rafe wanted to tell her to put the damn thing out, that it wasn't good for the kid, but he decided that wouldn't be the best way to start.

Tate finished speaking to the dispatcher, then turned to him. "Well, well, well," he said with a friendly smile. "Our D.E.A. agent and companion. What can we do for you?"

"I was wondering if I could have a private word with you, Sheriff?"

"Come on back to my office. I'd pass on the coffee, though, if I were you. Velma makes it thick enough to spread with a knife."

"I make *real* coffee, boss," the dispatcher called after them. "It puts hair on your chest."

"Like I don't already have enough," Nate said. He ushered Rafe into his office and waved him into a chair, then closed the door. Nate walked around behind his desk and sat.

"So," Nate said, leaning back in his chair and folding his hands across his flat belly, "did you lose your weapon, or did you run across some big-time drug dealer on Main Street?"

There was antagonism there, Rafe realized. The sheriff resented his presence. Well, of course. He probably figured Rafe was here on assignment, and he didn't like being cut out of the loop.

He sat back, patting the baby's bottom gently, and looked at the sheriff. "I don't usually bring my son with me when I'm on assignment, Sheriff."

"Why not? A baby would make great cover."

"Would you believe I'm just stopping over on vacation?"

Tate leaned forward, resting his elbows on the desk. "No. This isn't the kind of place people come for vacation. The only tourists we get come off the state highway to get groceries or directions. There's no rodeo in town at the present, we don't have a Wild West show, or even dinosaur bones to show off. Just a small town with a lot of hardworking people. And the last time I checked—which was this morning sometime—we don't even have a drug problem. Unless you count alcohol. Oh, I see some marijuana from time to time, and I suppose some of our folks have even tried cocaine, but nothing that ought to interest a big-time fed like yourself."

"I'm not here on government business, Sheriff."

"Then maybe you ought to explain yourself a little bit better. Being sheriff, I get a little paranoid about strangers who don't add up."

"Well, I'm staying with Gage Dalton. He's one of your investigators, isn't he?"

"Gage is my only full-time investigator. He says he met you a couple of times but doesn't know you."

So Tate had been checking him out, too. Rafe felt a smile start to stretch his mouth. "Seems we have a lot in common, Sheriff. I came here to check *you* out."

Tate didn't like the sound of that. His face hardened, and the lazy drawl disappeared from his gravelly voice. "Maybe you want to tell me why the D.E.A. would be interested in me.''

"The D.E.A. isn't. I am."

Nate nodded slowly. "Okay. So...are you congenitally incapable of just laying it out for me, or do I have to sit here and ask a million questions?"

Rafe realized something about himself suddenly. He *was* incapable of just laying it out. Too many years on the streets had made him prone to answering with monosyllables and misdirection. But realizing it didn't mean he could change it.

"Did you ever know a Marva Jackson?" he asked.

Nate stilled. Something in his gaze grew distant and cold. "Yeah. A long time ago. She in trouble?"

Rafe shook his head. "She's dead. She's been dead for over twenty years."

"Then why are you asking about her now?"

Rafe hesitated, suddenly reluctant to blurt it out, though he didn't know why. But it wasn't like him to hesitate, and sooner or later he was going to have to say it, anyway. "She was my mother."

Nate might have been carved from stone. For the longest time he didn't move or even breathe. Peanut stirred in Rafe's arms and managed to get his fist into his mouth. Content, the baby sucked on it once or twice, then settled back into slumber.

Finally Nate spoke. "She was *my* mother."

"I know."

"Well, hell, son, why didn't you just say so right off?"

Rafe felt unaccustomedly embarrassed. "I don't know," he said after a moment. "I had some notion about checking you out first, finding out what kind of person you were before I spoke to you."

Nate nodded. "I guess I can see that. Unwanted relatives can be a pain in the butt. My wife has a couple I'd as soon ditch in Death Valley."

"I wouldn't know," Rafe said. "I've never had any." He felt almost ashamed to admit it, as if it were his fault somehow.

He looked down at his sleeping son. "Well, that's not true any longer, I guess. I have Peanut now."

"No wife?"

"We weren't married. She was killed the night the baby was born."

"I'm sorry."

Rafe looked out the window. "I didn't really know her."

Nate leaned back in his chair, and it creaked a protest. "I reckon you must have been born right after Marva disappeared."

"Disappeared?"

"That's the way it looked. I went off to the army when I turned eighteen. Came home from my first year in Vietnam and she was gone, lock, stock, and barrel. No forwarding address. I tried a couple of times to find out where she went, but no luck. Or maybe I didn't try very hard. I didn't exactly miss her. She was a terrible alcoholic, and abusive as all get-out. These days we take kids away from parents like her. Did she clean up when she left here?"

"For a while, I guess."

"So where did she go? What happened?"

Rafe sighed and unconsciously held the baby tighter. "She ran off with a rodeo clown. My dad, Paul Ortiz. They wound up down in Killeen, Texas. My dad ran off a little while after I was born. She went back to drinking, and by the time I was ten they took me away from her. She died a year later."

"I'm sorry."

Rafe lifted his head and looked across the desk at Nate. "Why? It sounds to me like your childhood wasn't any easier. Maybe it was worse."

"If I'd known I had a half-brother, I'd have moved heaven and hell to get you away from her. I'd have raised you myself."

Rafe didn't know how to react to that. He felt something inside him shift and had the feeling that he was never again going to be the same person. He didn't know if he liked that or not. "You didn't know," was all he said.

"Maybe I should have looked harder."

"I didn't come here to make you feel guilty. I just wanted to find out about you. I've had the advantage all these years. She used to talk about you."

"Did she? Well, she couldn't have had much good to say. She always thought I was a pain in the butt."

"Actually, she didn't say anything bad about you at all. Just that she had a son up here. When I was in foster care, I thought about trying to get in touch with you, but I didn't know how. Then I got older, and it seemed crazy to even think about it. Then I got…the baby here."

"And family seems important?"

"You could say that." He sure as hell wasn't going to admit what his original plan had been.

Nate nodded. "Well, you've got family now, son. I've got a wife, six daughters, one son, a bunch of sons-in-law, and a few grandbabies. All the family a man could want—assuming you want to adopt us. Why don't you come have dinner with us tonight and make up your mind about us? You won't get to meet us all, of course. A couple of the girls are away at college, one lives out in Los Angeles with her husband, and Seth's in the navy, stationed on the east coast. But I can rustle up a couple of the gals and their husbands, and my youngest is still at home."

Rafe hadn't expected to be welcomed so easily or so rapidly. He was far more accustomed to being treated with suspicion and had been subconsciously prepared for it. Nate's ready acceptance of his story left him feeling off balance.

"Um, thanks," he said. "But it's such short notice, and your wife—"

"Will be thrilled to meet you," Nate interrupted. "Marge has a strong sense of family. She'll welcome you lickety-split. But if it's too soon for you…"

It was. He'd had more time to prepare for this than Nate, yet he was the one balking because it seemed too sudden. He just plain didn't feel ready to be smothered in family.

"Tell you what," Nate said, apparently reading Rafe's hesitation correctly, "let's just take it slow. How about you and me and Marge get together for lunch at Maude's diner tomorrow? Then we can decide where to go from there."

"Sounds good to me."

"I think you and I have a lot of catching up to do, son. A lot of missed ground to cover. I'm looking forward to it."

Rafe wasn't sure he could say the same. Now that he'd finally gone ahead and taken the step, he felt reluctance bordering on total resistance.

What the hell was wrong with him?

Angela was in the kitchen making tuna salad for lunch when Rafe returned with the baby. She heard him come in the front door, heard the baby fussing and the sound of his feet as he climbed the stairs. She hesitated a moment, then decided it would only be polite to ask him if he wanted a tuna sandwich, too.

She didn't really want to face him, but that was ridiculous. She had faced people in much worse situations than this. All they had done was lock horns in a minor fashion, something that should have faded from her mind already.

Except that it hadn't. She felt raw, somehow, and exposed. Vulnerable. And she didn't like the feeling.

The worst of it was that she *was* attracted to him, and it embarrassed her to think he might know it. All those carefully erected walls she had been building against men for years seemed to be tissue thin. No matter how many times she told herself she couldn't have it, and therefore shouldn't want it, she did still want someone to love her.

How weak. How juvenile. She had believed herself stronger than that.

Which just went to show how little she really knew about herself. Somewhere inside this thirty-five-year-old woman was the girl who had believed in love, romance and happily-ever-after. Life had taught her that there was no happily-ever-after, and she had believed that she'd learned her lesson. Ha!

Of course, she didn't know Rafe Ortiz at all, so what she

was feeling was nothing but sexual attraction, which was understandable. It had been a very long time since she'd been with a man, not since her disastrous engagement ten years ago, in fact. Her body was simply reminding her that she was still alive.

Which was something of a miracle, when she considered how poorly she'd been taking care of herself lately. She ought to be rejoicing that she could still feel a healthy attraction to a man.

Instead, she wanted to hide from it. Oh, well. Quitting her job was all the hiding she was going to allow herself to do this month.

With a sigh, she put the knife she was using to slice celery on the cutting board, rinsed her hands and headed up the stairs. Rafe's door was closed, but she could hear him talking to the baby, so she went ahead and knocked.

He answered a few seconds later, the child tucked into the crook of his arm. "Yes?" he said.

"I just wondered if you'd like a tuna sandwich. I'm making one for myself, and I've got plenty of tuna."

"Uh…sure. Thanks. I'll be down in a minute."

She looked from him to the fussing baby. "Is everything okay?"

"Oh…yeah. The peanut's just acting up a little. A bit of diaper rash."

Angela nodded and backed away. She didn't know a darn thing about diaper rash. "I'll be in the kitchen."

Diaper rash. Rafe closed the door behind her and grabbed the baby book from the bed where he'd dropped it. *His fault.* How was he supposed to have guessed that the kid had dumped in his diaper while they were sitting there in the sheriff's office? Hell, he'd been *sleeping.* He'd just been changed not twenty minutes before they got there. Even the peanut usually took longer than that to fill a diaper.

And this stuff was foul. Hardly any wonder that the kid's bottom looked as though it had been burned. Rafe had nearly passed out from the odor when he'd unfastened the diaper.

He didn't have the ointments that the book recommended. Expose the kid to the air? Yeah, that would be fun to clean up after.

He carried Peanut into the bathroom, filled the sink with lukewarm tap water, and gave him an impromptu bath to make sure all the irritating stuff was washed away. Then he patted the kid dry with a nice clean towel.

What now?

Maybe they should go to the doctor?

He stood for a minute, thinking, with the baby wrapped in the towel, then decided to take him downstairs in nothing but the towel. That was about as close to air-drying as he was going to come in somebody else's home. And the darn disposable diapers had that plastic wrapper on them that wouldn't let air in.

Maybe he ought to see about some cloth diapers for emergencies?

He was surprised to realize he was feeling more at sea than at any time since his first few days with the child.

He looked down at his son. "Always something new, isn't it? How does anybody ever get to be an old hand at this?"

Peanut had no opinion on the subject. At least his fussing had stopped.

"Some help you are."

Well, the book seemed to treat occasional diaper rash as inevitable. After lunch, he would dress the kid and go to the pharmacy to get one of those recommended ointments.

Angela had set two places at the kitchen table and directed him to the one with two sandwiches on the plate. "He seems happier now," she remarked as she looked at the baby.

"A bath helped."

"It probably would," she agreed.

"You know much about babies?"

She shook her head. "Not a damn thing."

"Me, either. This is OJT—On the Job Training."

A little laugh escaped her. "It probably is for most people."

"Yeah." She was avoiding meeting his eyes, he noticed,

and that bothered him a bit. What the hell was the matter with him? Why was he letting all these little things bother him? He'd spent years cultivating himself as a man without feelings, now here he was suddenly drowning in them. Damn, he had to get his head turned around straight.

But his head didn't seem to want to cooperate. Instead he found himself noticing just how slender and delicate Angela's hands were as she lifted her sandwich, just how ladylike all her gestures and movements were. She was very different from the women with whom he usually associated, he realized. Very different.

So the warning Klaxon in his head didn't surprise him at all. He knew potential trouble when he saw it. But sometimes he ignored the warning.

Like now. He took a bite of his sandwich and allowed himself the luxury of watching her. She wouldn't look directly at him, so she would never notice. Which gave him time to notice the way her hair teased the nape of her neck. He found himself suddenly wishing he could reach out and touch her there, just the way that strand of hair was touching her. Gently. Lightly.

Damn! He looked down at the sleeping baby in his arms and told himself not to be a damn fool. One kid was more than enough, and thoughts like that had gotten him into enough trouble for a lifetime.

"Great tuna," he remarked. "Thanks."

She gave him a fleeting smile, her eyes not quite meeting his. "Don't thank me, thank the tuna."

"Kinda hard, given his condition."

That elicited another laugh from her, and for just an instant their eyes met.

He felt an electric tingle all the way to his toes. No. No, no, no. With a sense of desperation, he fixed his attention on his plate.

"I've got to go to the pharmacy," he said, trying to find a safe avenue of conversation. "Do you know where the closest one is?"

"On the corner of Main and Fourth."

"I can find it, then."

"I'm thinking about taking a drive up into the mountains this afternoon," she remarked. "It's such a beautiful day."

He grimaced. "After spending the last five days in the car, I don't know that I'm ready for another drive. I think I'll come home after the pharmacy and read a book."

She nodded. "The hard part about vacationing here is figuring out what to do. I like to hike, but..." But she didn't want to be out there alone on the side of the mountain if her blood sugar decided to give her hell.

"That's kind of out of the question for me," Rafe said. "The peanut and all."

"Why do you call him that?"

He looked straight at her, forgetting his resolution to keep his gaze trained elsewhere. "Why not?"

She looked embarrassed. "Sorry. I just wondered if there was a reason."

"Oh." Now he felt like a fool, taking a simple question too much to heart. He had to find a way to shift gears between being on the streets and being in the normal world.

Although, he found himself thinking, this wasn't exactly the normal world. At least, not like any normal world he'd ever experienced before. He had the feeling that he'd somehow stepped out of time into some enchanted place. Everything seemed too peaceful—except his own thoughts, of course.

And he really couldn't afford to allow himself to relax, because Manny might come looking for him, and he wouldn't put it past the guy to actually steal the baby. Molinas had been known to do worse, and this time they would probably feel justified.

A sigh escaped him almost before he realized it.

"Something wrong?" Angela asked.

"That's the third time you've asked me that question."

She pulled back a little and looked away. "Sorry. You're sitting over there looking like gloom and doom and sighing heavily.... Trust me, I won't ask again."

He wondered if he could kick his own butt, because he certainly needed to.

"Look," he said, his appetite gone and his mood turning thoroughly sour, "I'm sorry. I'm jumpy. I admit it. Too much time on the street. Thanks for lunch, leave the dishes, I'll do them when I get back."

Then he and the baby left.

Angela stared after him. Her appetite was gone, too, but unlike Rafe, she had to finish her meal. She'd already taken her insulin, and failing to eat could make her very ill. But the tuna tasted like sawdust now, and the bread wanted to stick in her throat.

All she'd done was try to express some common human concern, and the jerk had bitten her head off. See if she ever made lunch for him again. See if she ever even *talked* to him again.

Reaching across the table, she picked up his uneaten sandwich and hurled it into the sink. Then, feeling better, she managed to choke down the rest of her sandwich with the aid of a glass of milk.

Jerk. From now on, she was going to act as if he didn't even exist.

"This stuff smells like dead fish," the woman at the pharmacy cash register said. "Are you sure this is what you want?"

Rafe looked at the tube of ointment. He supposed if he was a woman, the cashier never would have asked him if he was buying the right thing. He could get resentful, he guessed, but on the other hand, he really didn't want the kid to smell like dead fish. "I thought this was the best," he said finally. "Is there something better?"

"I don't know if it's better, but it doesn't stink. Did your wife tell you to get this? I don't want to get you into trouble."

"I don't have a wife."

The woman's eyebrows lifted; then her gaze became

friendly and genuinely concerned. "So...you're going from the baby books?"

"You could say that."

She nodded. "I did, too, and I learned a whole lot the hard way. Let me take this stuff back and get you something else. Trust me, not only will the baby stink like dead fish, but you'll never be able to get the smell off your hands."

The stink could have advantages, though, Rafe thought. Maybe Manny wouldn't want a baby that smelled like dead fish. The thought almost made him laugh aloud.

The peanut, once again fed, burped and changed, was sleeping contentedly in his carrier/car seat, looking for all the world like an angel. No one would guess the kid's bottom was fire-engine-red right now.

The cashier returned with a different tube. "A little more expensive," she said, "but worth it."

He paid without complaint for the ointment, another dozen cans of infant formula and two more packages of diapers. Then there was nothing to do but go back to the Dalton house, and he wasn't sure he wanted to do that. He hadn't been very pleasant to Angela, and she would probably stare daggers at him. Which was exactly what he wanted, he supposed, but he still didn't like it.

But maybe she'd gone on her drive and he could collapse peacefully on his bed for a snooze to get ready for tonight's round of feedings. Or just read a book. It had been a long time since he'd had the leisure to just sit and read.

Or he could sit and ponder why it was he was getting involved with a total stranger just because the man happened to be his half-brother. He had a feeling that while the baby might have precipitated his action, he wasn't the real reason for it.

He knew that whole chunks of himself were deeply buried, but he had always figured he knew what those parts were. Now he was discovering that he might not know himself as well as he had always believed.

It was a miserable feeling.

On the way home he stopped at the library to get a copy

of the most recent novel by one of his favorite writers. Emma was there at the circulation desk, talking to an elderly man. She gave a little wave as he came in with the baby, and he waved back.

He found the adult fiction section with little difficulty and began to peruse the stacks. Even though he knew exactly what book he wanted, he decided to waste some time. Anything to keep from going back to the house and running into Angela.

He wasn't usually such a coward, but since the kid had come into his life, he was doing all kinds of strange things. No question but what the baby was a bad influence.

By the time he finished, he had chosen three books. He figured if he kept his nose in them, Angela and he could just ignore each other politely, which was the only safe thing to do. He went to check out.

"Oh, that's a good one," Emma said, pointing to the techno-thriller that topped his stack.

"Can I borrow them? I guess I need to get a card. Can I get a card when I don't live here?"

She gave a quiet laugh. "You know the librarian. That's all the card you need." She looked at him. "Are you dying of boredom yet in our quiet little town?"

"I haven't had time. It's a whole different pace of life, though."

"I imagine. I've always wanted to go to Miami."

"Why?"

She laughed again. "The urge usually hits sometime around February or March, when the winter starts to seem too long."

"You and ten billion other people."

"It would be crowded, wouldn't it?"

"It's always crowded," he said. "And in a lot of ways, it's not the nicest town. Listen, you ever decide to come that way, give me a call. I'll make sure you see the best side of town."

"That would be wonderful."

He felt a lot better when he stepped back out onto the street. Angela might be annoyed with him, but his conversation with Emma had somehow made up for it.

Which was probably proof positive that he really was losing his mind.

Late that afternoon, an autumn storm began to work its way across the mountains. As the sun sank lower in the sky, heavy gray clouds approached. The wind took on a sharp bite, and Angela decided that she had to go home.

It was nearing time to test her blood sugar again, and to take more insulin. She might have been able to safely postpone it, but she had promised herself that she was going to adhere strictly to her schedule. She was certainly not going to get herself into trouble simply to avoid Rafe Ortiz a little longer.

When she got back to the house, she found Emma in the kitchen, humming as she prepared dinner. Rafe was invisible, and so was the baby.

"How was your day?" Emma asked.

"Wonderful. I took a great drive up in the mountains."

"It's beautiful up there right now."

"Are we supposed to get snow tonight?"

"Why? Does it look like it?"

"There are some heavy clouds moving in, and the temperature's falling fast."

Emma pursed her lips. "It's possible. Early, but possible. I wouldn't think we'd get much, though."

"I need to go test my sugar. What time is dinner?"

"I figure around six-thirty. Do you need to eat earlier?"

"I'll just put off my shot for a little while. It's no problem. As soon as I come back down, I'll help you, okay?"

"Help is always welcome."

Upstairs, she was relieved to see that Rafe's door was closed. At least she didn't have to face him right now. Driving around had managed to make her feel better, and she was afraid the mere sight of him would irritate her.

Her sugar tested right on the money, and she was proud of herself. It had been a while since she had seen a reading this good at this time of day.

She took a few minutes to freshen up, then went back down

to the kitchen. Gage was there now, and Angela felt her heart lurch as she came upon the two of them. They were locked in a tight embrace, completely oblivious to the rest of the world.

Envy and an ache of longing filled her with sudden strength, and she slipped quickly away into the living room, not wanting to disturb them.

And there was Rafe. He was stretched out on the couch with an open book on the floor beside him, sound asleep. The baby was on his chest, also sleeping soundly, protected by one large hand on his little back.

Angela suddenly had the worst urge to throw back her head and howl. The ache of longing was overwhelming and she wished she could run from it. But there was no escape. No one would ever hold her the way Gage was holding Emma right now, and no man would ever snooze on her couch with her baby in his arms.

That was not for her and never would be, and she thought she had learned to accept it. Instead, all she had learned to do was bury the pain.

She started to hurry blindly out of the living room, feeling almost wild with the need to hide and compose herself before she faced anyone.

As she turned, she came up hard against Gage's chest. He caught her and steadied her. "Are you all right?" he asked.

Behind him she could see Emma, and though she couldn't see it, she could swear that she felt Rafe's gaze on her back. Everyone was looking at her, and all she wanted to do was hide somewhere and lick her wounds until she could face the world again.

"I'm fine," she said thickly, and turned to flee up the stairs.

No one followed her. And never, ever, in her life had she felt as alone as she did right then.

"Angela?" There was a gentle knock on the door, and Emma's quiet voice reached her. "Angela?"

Rubbing her tear-reddened eyes, Angela opened the door. "I'm okay, Emma. Really. Just decompressing."

Emma nodded and stepped inside, closing the door behind her. "You want to tell me what upset you?"

"Nothing, really. I'm just having a hard time…dealing with issues in my life."

"Which issues?"

"I really don't want to discuss it, Emma. Honestly. They're old issues. Sometimes they just reach up and bite me. That's all."

Emma searched her face, her green eyes kind. "I'm here if you need to talk. You know that, right?"

Angela nodded. "I'm sorry, I meant to help you with dinner."

"Don't worry about it. I put Gage to work chopping. He likes it. Says it helps him work out his frustrations."

A little laugh escaped Angela. "Maybe I should chop some things, too."

"Probably. It's great therapy." Emma reached out and touched her shoulder gently. "How about a hug? Those usually help."

Emma's hug did help, Angela thought. Her life had been terribly empty of hugs since her mother died. She wanted to burrow into those arms and cry her eyes out.

"It's okay to feel sorry for yourself," Emma murmured gently. "God knows, I've done it often enough."

She stepped back and sat on the bed, patting the mattress beside her. "Come on, let's talk about it."

Angela sat, but found she didn't want to talk about herself. She was *bored* with herself. Besides, talking about it would do nothing to make anything better.

"Sometimes," Emma said, "I still cry because I can't have a baby."

Angela took a long ragged breath and nodded. "I know. How do you deal with it?"

"I remind myself it wouldn't be good for Gage."

Angela looked at her. "What? Why?"

"Because Gage lost his wife and young children in a car bomb attack. He told me he'd never be able to sleep at night again if he had children to worry about."

"God, that's awful!" And it made her feel small to be whining about her own problems.

"Lately he's mentioned adoption a few times, but I'm not sure if he's just saying that for my sake." Emma shrugged. "All I know is, I'm grateful to have Gage, and I feel awful for wanting any more."

Angela nodded. "I know. I mean…I get so down about my diabetes at times—lately, I've just been wallowing in my own misery—but I have to remind myself that there are lots of people who get diabetes as children who don't live to be my age…or if they do, they're sick and disabled. I've been really lucky. I just need to remember that."

"Easy to say, hard to do." Emma smiled sadly. "Besides, it isn't just luck that got you here. You've always been good about taking care of yourself."

"Until lately." Lately she had been flirting with the possibility of everything from loss of vision to loss of a limb by letting her blood sugar go out of control.

"But you're fixing that now, right?"

"Yes. But you know what? I hate myself. I haven't rebelled like this since I was first diagnosed. All of a sudden I *hate* having to do all this stuff." Angela shook her head. "I'm being childish, and I know it."

"We all get childish at times."

"I feel like such a *failure!*"

"But you're not. You're actually very successful."

"Yeah, right." Angela shook her head.

"I'm not kidding, Angie. It's not your fault that you got diabetes, but it would be your fault if you didn't take care of yourself. You've been very successful in doing what you need to. That's not failure."

After Emma left, Angela laid back on the bed and stared at the ceiling, trying to fight the feelings that threatened to swamp her. Maybe she could call it success that she had lived this long and was still reasonably healthy. Or she could look at the fact that she could die at any moment and therefore couldn't allow anyone to get close to her and call her life a total failure.

Right now, it was looking an awful lot like failure.

Chapter 4

"Wanna go to lunch with me today?" Rafe asked. He and Angela were cleaning up the kitchen after breakfast. Gage and Emma had already gone off to work. The baby dozed in his seat, perched in the middle of the table.

Angela looked at Rafe as if he'd just lost his mind. "Why?"

He shifted to his other foot and studied her with apparent perplexity. Clearly, Angela thought, he wasn't used to being questioned about his motives when he asked a woman out.

"I have to meet the sheriff and his wife for lunch. I just thought you might like to go, too. It beats hanging around with nothing to do."

There was an ulterior motive there somewhere, Angela thought. She wondered what it would take to pry it out of him. Then she decided that the only way she was ever going to know was to agree to go. On the other hand, she could be stubborn when she was feeling manipulated.

"I could just watch the baby for you."

"No, no, I want to take the kid."

"Oh." Why? This sounded like a business lunch. Well, no,

not if the sheriff's wife was coming. Perplexed herself, she looked out the window. "I guess," she said finally, giving in to curiosity. It wasn't the most gracious acceptance she'd ever given.

He didn't seem to notice. "Thanks."

"Sure."

They went back to washing the dishes in silence.

She had cut back her morning insulin, which meant she had to take her run instead of hanging around the house and trying to pry information out of Rafe. Not that he would have told her anything. She was beginning to recognize that he was completely locked inside his defensive walls, even more than she was.

The day was bitingly cold under leaden skies, and from time to time she saw a single snowflake fall. As long as she kept moving, it wasn't too bad. More importantly, running cut her free of all her worries. While she ran she felt good, far removed from the faces that had been haunting her dreams lately, the faces of the people whose dreams she'd had to foreclose on.

She was tempted to run farther than usual but didn't dare allow herself. Her damn blood sugar was like a leash around her neck, restricting her in every direction. Only when she had had it under strict control for a while could she dare press farther to see what happened.

Back at the house, she showered and changed, then made herself a small snack. While she was eating a couple of crackers and a piece of cheese, she heard Rafe come down the stairs. He and the baby appeared in the kitchen a few moments later.

"Listen," he said, "I don't really have any cold weather clothes for the peanut."

She had to smile. "Coming from Miami, I can understand that."

He absolutely astonished her with a smile in response. "Yeah. Anyway, can we leave a little early and go to the department store? I want to get the kid a jacket or something. Actually, I could use one myself, too."

"Just let me finish my crackers."

He hesitated. "You gonna be okay if we do it this way? I mean, I know about your schedule and all. Do you need to come back here and get your insulin before we go to lunch?"

Part of her was reluctantly touched by his concern, and part of her was embarrassed by it. She would have liked to tell him to mind his own business, but that would have been insufferably rude. "I'll just bring it with me. I can take the shot in the ladies' room."

"Okay. I just didn't want you to get into trouble on my account."

He stood there for a minute more, looking as if he wanted to say something; then his eyes grew as cold as the day outside. Angela had the distinct feeling that he'd pulled back into some isolated place inside himself.

"Ten minutes?" he said.

"I'll be ready."

He still didn't move. Finally, in a burst of frustration, she took the bull by the horns. "What's this lunch about, anyway?" She'd already learned that he didn't like questions, so she didn't really expect an answer. She wondered why she even bothered to ask.

But he surprised her. For an instant his face seemed shuttered, then he sighed and said, "I haven't told anybody this, but the sheriff is my half-brother. We just met for the first time."

Angela's frustration seeped away. "Really? That's awesome."

He gave her a half smile. "Awkward as hell, too."

"So you want me there to kind of help out?"

He nodded.

Angela looked down at the cracker in her hand, feeling ridiculously touched that he'd wanted her help. And feeling kinder toward him for having the gumption to admit it. When she looked up, she was smiling. "I'd be glad to help out, if I can."

"Thanks. So eat up and start helping."

She had to laugh.

The trip to Freitag's Mercantile proved to be a lot of fun. Rafe picked out a jacket for himself quickly and with total disregard for anything except whether it fit, but when it came to picking out something for his son, he was a lot choosier. They waded through bunting, snowsuits, jackets, impossibly tiny mittens and caps.

"Heck, I don't know," Rafe said finally. "I just want him to be warm. What's warmest?"

"The bunting. More air space for insulation." Angela pulled a few off the shelves and laid them out side by side.

"Also easier to get him into and out of," Rafe said, eyeing the selection.

"This one has a little hood." It was bright red, warm and fuzzy, with a teddy bear on the chest.

"Let's get that, then. In fact, let's get two, in case he has an accident."

Angela put a red one and a blue one in the shopping cart. "Anything else?"

He said no, but as they were heading toward the checkout, his eye was caught by a cute little yellow jumpsuit with matching booties. He put it in the cart, and Angela felt her heart melt.

After he'd paid, Rafe took the baby into the men's room to change his diaper. When he came out, Peanut was dressed in his brand new red bunting, looking happy and content in his father's arms. Angela had the worst urge to hug them both.

Marge and Nate Tate were waiting for them at the diner. Angela knew the Tates from an earlier visit when she and Emma had had dinner with them, and she was welcomed warmly. Marge and Rafe shook hands when Nate introduced them. Rafe fussed a little, getting the child's carrier seat established safely on a chair beside him, then he settled into his own, and an awkward silence fell.

Maude rescued them by arriving with the menus. "I'm out of blueberry pie," she announced, looking directly at Nate.

"I'll be back in a minute with the coffee, less'n someone here wants tea."

"Just water for me, please," Angela said. "With a slice of lime, if you have it."

"No lime. Got lemons, though."

"Lemon will be great. Thank you."

Maude looked down at the baby. "Cute tyke." Then she stomped away.

Nate and Rafe exchanged long looks, and Marge looked at both of them. It was Marge who broke the silence.

"Nate tells me you're with the D.E.A., Rafe."

He nodded.

"Isn't it interesting that you both went into law enforcement even though you weren't raised together?"

"That *is* fascinating," Angela said, trying to help Marge get the conversational ball rolling. "I never would have imagined there was a cop gene."

For an instant she thought her attempt at humor had fallen flat, but then everyone laughed.

"I read my magazines from back to front," Nate announced.

"So do I," Rafe said.

Marge shook her head. "And here I thought one was enough for the world."

"Well, we'd better go ahead and order," Nate said. "Maude'll just drive us crazy until we do."

Angela opened up the menu and scanned it, quickly realizing that everything there was a diet wrecker. She would probably gain five pounds just from reading it. But given how much she had lost with her diabetes, maybe that was all right.

When Maude returned, they placed their orders. Both Nate and Rafe ordered the steak sandwiches, and Marge and Angela wound up laughing when they both ordered the turkey sandwich.

Maude stomped away without comment.

"I wonder what's wrong with her?" Nate said. "Maude usually has something to say."

Marge shrugged. "Maybe she just won't flirt with you because I'm here."

Nate laughed. "Actually, she's always trying to twist my arm into a piece of pie. Maybe she knows she can't talk me into it with you here."

"I would never deny you a piece of pie."

"I know you wouldn't, honey. But I gotta keep my waistline for you."

Angie watched the way Marge's face softened and the way the two of them looked at each other. After a moment she had to look away, feeling the worst urge to cry again. She found herself looking directly into Rafe's gaze. His dark eyes were smoky-looking, not as hard as they'd been earlier. Was he touched, too, by the obvious affection between the Tates?

But Nate was speaking again, and she turned her attention to him.

"Marva," he began, then looked at Angela to explain, "Marva was our mother. Anyway, she was a sorely troubled woman. What I can't figure was why she never once tried to let me know about you, Rafe. Or just get in touch. Hell, I wrote to her when I was overseas, so it's not like she had reason to think I wanted to disown her."

"I don't know," Rafe answered. "I was too young to think about asking questions like that. She just told me you existed, and that you lived up here. And once she mentioned you were a cop."

"Weird. If she knew I was a cop, she must have checked up on me at least once." Nate sipped his coffee, and the cup clattered as he put it down. He leaned back a little and sighed. "When you think about it, it was a really rotten thing to do, not to let me know I had a brother. I always wanted a brother."

"Me, too." Rafe tilted his head. "It feels strange, though. How do you go about picking up the pieces after all this time?"

"One piece at a time, I guess."

Marge spoke. "What you do is get drunk watching a football game together, then go away for a weekend of fishing."

Before she finished, both Nate and Rafe were laughing.

The humor and laughter were covering the uneasiness, Angela realized. Not only were Nate and Rafe feeling awkward, but so was Marge. It wasn't just the stiltedness of people meeting for the first time, either. She didn't think any of the three of them had difficulty speaking to strangers. Could knowing they were brothers be having this much effect?

"You know," said Marge, breaking the silence that had once again begun to linger over the table, "Nate had a lot to overcome as a child. I imagine you did, too, Rafe."

Rafe looked at her. "In what way?"

"Well," Marge said, "Marva was…" She hesitated.

"She was a hooker and an alcoholic," Nate said bluntly.

Angela's head swiveled sharply around so she could look at Rafe. His face was closed, revealing nothing.

"She gave me the last name Tate, but I'll bet she didn't know for sure who my father was."

Angela caught her breath. Rafe merely nodded, his face expressionless.

"I didn't want to say that, Nate," Marge said gently.

"Why not?" he asked her. "It was true. I try not to condemn her too much, because that's how she paid the rent, but…hell, Marge, if she hadn't drunk so much, she probably could have gotten a real job."

Marge reached out to touch his arm.

"Old story," Nate said gruffly. "The woman had some serious problems."

"Yes, she did," Marge agreed. She looked at Rafe. "Anyway, Nate was a handful himself by the time he was a teenager. Always in one scrape or another. Rebelling, I think. My father didn't want me to date him." She gave a little laugh. "You can see how well I listened. Anyway, I suppose you rebelled, too?"

For a moment Angela thought Rafe was going to refuse to answer. Then he shook his head. "I never did. I learned it was easier to be what people expected you to be."

"Wise man," Nate remarked. "I was always banging my head on brick walls. I still do, I suppose."

"Usually on the county commission's brick walls," Marge said dryly.

"Can I help it if they can't see common sense?" He flashed a smile, and everyone chuckled.

Peanut, who'd been calmly watching the world, chose that moment to start fussing. With practiced ease, Rafe scooped him up and dug a bottle out of the diaper bag. Angela excused herself and went to the ladies' room to inject her insulin. Marge followed her.

"They need a few minutes alone," she said by way of explanation.

Angela nodded and opened her travel kit, pulling out the glucose meter she used when she wasn't at home. It was small enough to fit in the palm of her hand. She would much rather have done this without a witness, but Marge wasn't showing any signs of leaving immediately, and she couldn't wait much longer to take her insulin.

"Oh," said Marge, "you're a diabetic."

"Yes."

"I'm sorry. I have a friend who's been diabetic since she was fifteen. It's not much fun, is it?"

"Frankly, it stinks." She pricked her finger, squeezed some blood onto the test strip, and inserted the strip into the machine. "Ninety. A little too low." She must have exercised harder than she thought this morning and then failed to eat quite enough when she snacked.

"I'll go out and tell Maude we need some orange juice right now."

"Thank you." She gave Marge a warm smile and received one in turn. Marge walked out, leaving her to take her injection in peace. Since she was going to have orange juice, it would be all right to take her insulin to get ready for lunch.

In her travel kit, she carried a pen-style injector that held a little cartridge. It saved her the problem of having to deal with bottles of insulin and hypodermics when she was away from the house.

She took a minute to roll the cartridge between her palms to mix and warm it, then popped it into the pen. Then she pulled down her slacks, rubbed herself with an alcohol swab and injected her thigh.

She was just buttoning her slacks when Marge pushed the door open a crack. "I have your orange juice out here, Angela."

"Thanks, Marge. I'll be right out."

Four times a day, she thought, looking at herself in the mirror. It was the pits.

Then, smothering a sigh, she packed up her kit and went to rejoin the others.

Rafe was gone.

"He went to change the baby," Marge said.

"Again?"

She laughed. "Every time they wake up, and every time they eat, without fail."

Nate grinned. "We swam in a sea of diapers for…how long was it, Marge?"

"I think we went nearly twelve years with at least one child in diapers all the time."

"Wow!" Angela said.

Marge's eyes twinkled. "I felt so liberated when the last girl was potty trained. All of a sudden I wasn't washing a load of diapers every day."

Rafe returned with the baby on his shoulder and slid into his seat. "Do you know a good doctor?" he asked without preamble.

Marge leaned forward. "Several of them. What's wrong?"

"I think we have a little diarrhea."

Marge rose. "I'll go call Dr. Randall for you right now. He can probably see you as soon as we're done with lunch."

"Thanks, Marge."

Angela reached out and touched the baby's hand. At once Rafe Jr. latched on to her, wrapping his little hand around her index finger. His head bobbed a little as he held it up and tried to look at her. "He doesn't seem to be distressed, Rafe."

"No, but...well, I'm new at this gig, so I think I'll get it checked out."

"I would, too," she agreed.

Rafe looked across the table at Nate. "There was one other thing I wanted to ask you about."

"Go ahead."

"My...the baby's mother. Her family are almost all involved in drug importing and trafficking."

Nate nodded. "Great family."

"Anyway, Rocky—Raquel—asked me to get the baby away from them. Unfortunately, the family's not willing to let go that easily. My boss called me yesterday and told me to watch my back. One of them is looking for me and has hired a lawyer."

Nate frowned. "Not good."

"No, it's not." Rafe patted the baby's back gently. Peanut was falling asleep on his shoulder. "Anyway, in case they figure out where I am...could you avoid telling anybody who asks about me where I'm staying?"

"As far as I'm concerned," Nate said, "if anybody asks about you, I'll tell them I don't know who you are. Don't worry about it, son. I'll have my men keep an eye out."

"Thanks. The guy's name is Manuel Molina. Manny Molina. As far as we've been able to tell, he's clean, but..." Rafe shook his head. "So many of the clan are involved that I just don't trust him. And last spring I arrested his brother on trafficking and importing."

"So he has a real ax to grind." Nate nodded and leaned back as Maude approached with their lunches. She put the plates down gently and walked away.

"Maude's definitely off her feed," Nate remarked. "She usually slams the plates down."

"Maybe she didn't want to wake the baby," Angela suggested.

"Anything's possible, I guess." He returned his attention

to Rafe. "I know it's not my place to say anything, but if you've got people like that looking for you, it might be time to consider a new line of work. Especially with a child to watch over."

Rafe turned his head and looked down at his slumbering son. "The thought's crossed my mind," he said quietly.

"You really have a bunch of drug dealers looking for you?" Angela asked Rafe as they drove back to the house.

"Well, I don't know that I'd exactly say that. No one's ever been able to prove that Manny's anything but a legitimate businessman—although I'm pretty sure he got his startup funds from his brother."

"But Manny's got other relatives who aren't so legitimate?"

"Oh, a whole bunch of them. Like I said, the whole family's involved, except Manny. And Rocky."

"Rocky was...your girlfriend?"

He hesitated. "She was the baby's mother, yes."

A strange way to answer, Angela thought. Did he mean he and Rocky hadn't been involved emotionally? That it was just a one-night stand? Had he used the woman to get to her brother?

The thought was unpalatable. Things like that happened in movies and probably happened in real life, but she wasn't sure she wanted to actually *know* someone who behaved that way.

On the other hand...she thought about the way Rafe held his son and took care of him all the time, and decided he really couldn't be so bad. Maybe whatever had happened had been a...mistake. She had heard that men made mistakes like that sometimes.

Maybe that was why he seemed so unwilling to talk about it. Maybe he wasn't proud of what had happened.

But she promised herself one thing: whatever sexual attraction she felt for Rafe Ortiz, she was going to bury it deeply. She didn't want to become another one of his mistakes.

Rafe dropped her off at the house, then continued to the

doctor's office with the baby. Angela stood in the cold wind and stared after him as he drove away, and wondered why she had ever thought coming to visit Emma would be a good break from everything.

Somehow she seemed to be feeling as uneasy and stressed as she had at home. And it was all Rafe Ortiz's fault.

Rafe had never imagined himself standing in a doctor's office discussing the frequency, appearance and odor of a kid's bowel movements, but that's what he did.

Afterward, when he stepped outside, Rafe noticed that the day had grown even colder. The peanut caught his breath and blinked rapidly as the cold air struck his face.

"Yeah, it's a shock to my system, too, little man," Rafe said to the child as they crossed the parking lot. "I can't imagine why anybody wants to live in a climate like this."

In fact, he found himself actually missing the Miami heat and humidity. Man, he'd never imagined himself doing that.

He stopped by the pharmacy to pick up the Pedialyte that the doctor had recommended. When he got back to the house, Angela was nowhere to be seen, and he felt relieved. Being around her made him feel edgy, as though he couldn't fully relax.

The kid wanted to play, so he spread out a blanket on the floor of his room and stretched out beside him. He wondered what the peanut was thinking as he stared into space, making little sounds and waving his arms and legs. He seemed so intent on what he was doing.

But as he lay there with his son, he found his thoughts drifting back to lunch. Nate Tate seemed like a good enough guy, and so did his wife. He had a strong feeling that Peanut would be safe with them.

But he still wasn't comfortable about leaving him. The idea, which had seemed so brilliant in Miami, didn't feel brilliant now, and he couldn't say why. All he knew was that it made him feel distinctly uncomfortable.

And because he was uncomfortable, his thoughts drifted away from Nate Tate and back to Angela.

He didn't know how to act around her, he realized. She wasn't a colleague, and she wasn't a suspect, and his tools for dealing with other sorts of people were apparently very limited.

He didn't make friends. He'd never had any, and he'd always put it down to being too busy. Now he had the opportunity and time to make some, and he didn't have any notion how to go about it. He didn't know how to play the role. He supposed it shouldn't be much more difficult than playing daddy, but he had a whole book to tell him how to do that. There was no book on friendship.

Nor was he really certain that he wanted to make a friend of Angela. She…disturbed him. He couldn't look at her without noting how delicate she was, how soft her skin looked— and how very weary she seemed. He had the feeling she hadn't been well for some time.

To his own dismay, he realized that he kept wanting to reach out to her. Some part of him wanted to hug her and tell her that everything would be okay.

And that wasn't like him at all. Nor was it like him to feel a sexual response to a woman like her. But he did. He kept wondering how her skin would taste and how she would feel beneath his hands.

Really disturbing, that. He had no time or place in his life for a woman, and all his relationships in the past had been as casual as they could be. Even Rocky, who'd managed to get past his guard and get him into her bed that one time. He still hadn't let her get close to him.

And for some damn reason he felt bad about that now. Lying there, looking at the baby they'd made in one blazing moment of passion, he felt awful that there had never been more than that. She'd been a subject, a suspect, a means of getting to her brother. He'd flirted with her to keep her interest, but he'd never intended that it would go that far, and certainly not that it would result in the creation of a life.

He felt despicable. He couldn't imagine how he was going to explain it to the peanut when he got old enough to start asking.

"Well, kid," he could hear himself saying, "I thought your mom was involved in drug dealing, so I made a pass at her...."

Yeah, right. That was one for the movies.

He sighed and rolled onto his back, listening to the soft, happy sounds his son was making, and wondered why the world had gone all cockamamie on him.

He'd never meant to sleep with Rocky, but he had. He'd never wanted to be a father, but he was. He didn't want to be attracted to Angela, but...

Oh, hell, he thought, closing his eyes. He couldn't do anything about the past, but he sure as hell could keep himself from making another major mistake. No matter what he felt about Angela, he decided, he was going to keep it to himself.

He'd already made one mess. He damn well wasn't going to make another.

The Daltons, Angela and Rafe played rummy that evening after dinner, gathered around the dining room table. Peanut, tuckered out from playing so hard that afternoon and apparently content after a bottle of Pedialyte, dozed in his carrier seat.

Angela was finding it difficult to concentrate on the game, because every time she looked up, Rafe's gaze was on her. Every meeting of their eyes made something deep inside her quiver with recognition.

"You know," Emma said after a particularly fun hand that had caused them all a lot of laughter, "it must have been like this before TV."

"What do you mean?" Angela asked.

"What else did people do in the evenings? Talked to their neighbors, read, played cards. It's like when you read a historical novel. You know. After dinner everyone retires to the salon to play cards or listen to someone play an instrument."

"I'd skip the listening to someone play an instrument,"

Gage said, shuffling the deck. They all laughed. "Well, I would," he continued frankly. "Can you imagine how awful it must have been sometimes?"

"Worse yet," Angela said, "imagine having to listen to someone like me sing. I can't carry a tune in a bucket."

"But that's not really the point," Emma said. "Just think what we've lost because of television. People don't socialize the way they used to when they had to entertain each other."

"It's true," Gage agreed. "Like anything else, there are up and down sides, I suppose."

"Well," Emma continued, "I've lived here in this house all my life. I know all my neighbors. I can't imagine what it must be like now for people who move into new neighborhoods and know no one. How can they ever meet if everyone's inside watching the television?"

Rafe spoke. "They probably meet when they're out doing yard work. Or buying dope from the corner dealer."

That elicited another laugh from the group.

"Oh, all right," said Emma, smiling. "I'll stop."

"I guess there are disadvantages to everything," Angela said. "For every achievement we make, we seem to sacrifice something else."

"That's true," Emma agreed. "I wasn't complaining, just thinking about how nice it is to sit here like this talking and playing cards."

"I imagine," Rafe said, "that the great masses of humanity in the past didn't have a whole lot of time left over to be wondering about how to entertain themselves in the evening."

"Probably not," Angela said. "Living hand-to-mouth on a sixty-hour work week would leave you exhausted."

"Oh, stop," Emma laughed. "All right, I was being ridiculously nostalgic for something that probably never existed."

"Except for the privileged few," Rafe said.

"Which means," Angela remarked, "that we're very lucky to be able to sit here and do this now."

Rafe's gaze caught hers, and she saw a smile in his eyes, a smile that left her feeling strangely light-headed.

Gage started dealing the cards. "Back to business, folks. Emma's beating us all."

Emma and Gage retired around ten, and Angela and Rafe were left with each other for company. Then the baby started fussing, and Rafe excused himself to take the child upstairs.

Angela felt inexplicably relieved. Wandering into the kitchen, she made herself a small snack as she had to every night. It was another hour before she could take her insulin, and time was suddenly heavy on her hands.

She'd never felt this way before when she visited Emma. They had always sat up until the wee hours, giggling and talking the way they had all those years ago in the college dormitory. But Gage's presence changed that, and she felt bereft.

Which was ridiculous, she told herself bracingly. She couldn't possibly be jealous because Emma had gotten married.

But she was. In her heart of hearts, she knew she was very jealous. It wasn't just that Gage had taken part of her friend from her, it was that she was jealous of Emma's happiness.

How unworthy. Emma deserved every bit of happiness she found, and Angela wished her well with her whole heart. But she couldn't seem to shut up the little green-eyed monster that wanted the same thing for herself. The little green-eyed monster that said, "If she can have it, so should I."

As with most of the women she knew, Angela had grown up with fairy-tale dreams about romance, marriage and family. Having those hopes dashed on the shoals of her diabetes apparently hadn't made her any less wistful.

She knew that some women with diabetes were able to successfully have children, but her doctor felt she couldn't. Even with the strict attempts she had made at controlling her disease when she became pregnant, she had still lost the child. And the dangers were just too great. Having her blood sugar go out of control during a pregnancy could result in serious deformity to the child, never mind what it might do to her.

And Lance, the man she had been engaged to at the time,

had made it very clear that he didn't want a wife who couldn't have children. Of course, she knew there were men who wouldn't feel that way, but there was something else that held her back.

Her own mortality. She could die at any time, and she knew it. One skipped meal, one missed insulin shot, could kill her. Just because it hadn't so far, didn't mean it wouldn't happen. More than once, stress or misbehavior had landed her in the hospital. And then there was the inevitable effect of diabetes itself. Eventually, if you couldn't keep your blood sugar down, it caused nerve damage. Blindness. Heart disease. Amputation.

How could she ask anyone else to face that with her? It just didn't seem fair to her, and if there was one thing she had a strong measure of, it was fairness.

But that didn't keep her from daydreaming wistfully, and since she'd met Rafe, those daydreams seemed to be back in full force. Why? She wasn't at all sure she liked him. He wasn't always very nice. But when he picked up his son, she saw a whole different side of him.

And that side was overriding all her other perceptions of him.

Sighing, she put together a plate of cheese and crackers, but not too many crackers, because she was taking slow-acting insulin for the night. Maybe she would look over Emma's bookshelves and find something to read. She needed to get away from her own thoughts.

But as if in answer to them, Rafe appeared. "The peanut is back asleep," he announced. "For a couple of hours, anyway."

"Is he still waking you up at night?"

"It's beginning to stretch out a little, but yeah, usually he wants to eat and play around midnight, then again at three. But last night he actually made it from three o'clock until seven."

She smiled, but she could tell it didn't quite reach her eyes. "There's hope, then."

"Apparently so."

"Do you want some cheese and crackers?"

"No, thanks. I'll just get myself a glass of milk. Do you want one?"

"Yes, please."

He joined her at the table, passing her a tall glass of milk.

"How's the baby feeling?" she asked him.

"Seems to be just fine." He shrugged one shoulder. "The doctor said it might just be an upset from all the traveling."

"I guess they're delicate little creatures."

He smiled faintly. "Sometimes it's scary how delicate and dependent they are. At first I was almost afraid to pick him up."

"But they're tougher than we think, too."

"I suppose so. But I don't want to try it out."

She laughed. "I wouldn't, either." And for some reason she wasn't feeling tired any longer, but wide-awake and energetic. "It must be hard to be a single parent."

"I don't know. I never tried it the other way."

She wasn't quite sure how to take that response. His face revealed so little, and she always got the feeling from him that somewhere inside him there was an icy-cold core that nothing touched. Looking into his dark eyes, she felt that she could get frostbite if she got too close.

Trying to find a way to ease the discomfort she was suddenly feeling, she said, "I've never tried it at all."

"It wasn't my plan."

That at least seemed forthcoming, so she decided she must have misinterpreted his expression. He was, she decided, simply a stone face. Then she wondered why it mattered, and why she was bothering to make conversation with him, anyway. There were more constructive things to expend her energy on, such as figuring out what she was going to do now that she had quit her job and wasn't going back into the loan business.

But she was amazingly reluctant to think about that. It wasn't like her, she realized, to avoid thinking about an issue that important. Usually she worried such things to death. Now, for the first time in her life, she was simply drifting, refusing to think about tomorrow or even such important concerns as how she was going to feed herself when she got back home.

Burnout, she decided. It had to be burnout. After she had rested awhile here, she would get back her interest in life.

"Do you ever get burned-out?" she heard herself ask Rafe.

He'd settled back in his chair, sitting at an angle to the table with his legs crossed at the ankle, running his finger up and down the side of his glass. He looked up when she spoke, and she caught a flicker of something in his gaze that was neither hard nor cold. Where had he been? she wondered.

"I don't think so," he said. "I get tired of things the way everybody does, but I wouldn't say I've ever been burned-out."

"I am. I'm so burned-out that I can't even make myself think about what I'm going to do when I get back home."

"Maybe that's a good thing. You wouldn't be resting much if you were worrying."

"That's true." She sighed and forced herself to eat another piece of cheese.

"What are you burned-out about?" he asked. "Your job? Your diabetes?"

"Both, I think."

"That's a lot of burnout."

"No kidding."

One corner of his mouth lifted. "Basically, it's sixty percent of your life."

"More like ninety." She gave an embarrassed laugh. "Listen to me whine."

"Nothing wrong with whining. I do it myself."

"You? When do you whine?"

"I do most of mine on the job." His smile deepened a shade, nearly reaching his eyes. "When I don't like an assignment or a plan of operation."

"That's not whining, to complain about assignments and plans. I'm talking about not liking your *life*."

He was silent a minute, looking at the glass of milk. When

he spoke, he didn't look at her. "I don't particularly like mine, Angela."

She had the feeling he was just coming to that realization himself, and she felt unexpectedly touched that he had shared that with her. He struck her as a man who didn't share much of himself with anyone. "What don't you like?"

He looked at her wryly. "Middle-of-the-night feedings?" But then he shook his head. "No, that's not the problem. Not really. I haven't been on the street since the kid was born. I guess it's giving me too much time to think."

"And that's bad?"

He shrugged. "Keeping busy can be just a good way to avoid thinking."

"I guess it can. Have you been avoiding thinking?"

"Apparently so."

He didn't volunteer any more than that, and she didn't quite know how to ask.

"Or," he said after a few moments, "maybe I'm just growing up. Having a kid will do that, I hear."

"I imagine it would. I've never really had anybody to think about except myself." Except for a brief time when she'd been engaged and pregnant and had made the mistake of making someone else the center of her life.

He flashed an unexpected smile. "I actually find myself doing adult things like worrying about my responsibilities. I probably shouldn't admit this, but I've never thought of life in terms of responsibilities before. It was always something I just *did*. Next thing you know, I'll be worrying about retirement."

She felt a smile lift the corners of her own mouth. "Having kids will do that, too."

"It's sure making me feel old."

"Really?"

"Really. It's hard to feel like a kid when you have a kid depending on you."

Angela hesitated, then asked, "Do you think you have to be a kid to work undercover?"

He thought about it for a minute. "Maybe not for everybody, but for me, yes. I always felt like a kid playing a game."

She noticed he put that in the past tense, and she wondered about it. "A dangerous game."

"Oh, yeah. Very. Never bothered me before."

"And now?"

"Now I'm thinking about it."

She spoke uncertainly. "That might not be a good thing if you go back on the street. I mean…it might make you hesitate.…"

"I've been thinking about that, too. Oh, well."

She wondered how he could dismiss it so easily. If *she* could see the dangers, surely *he* must be able to. "And what about this guy who's looking for you and the baby? Are you worried about him?"

"A bit."

"Well, he'll never think to look for you all the way out here."

"Probably not."

But he would have to go home sometime. Angela heard the thought as surely as if he'd spoken it out loud. "It's an awful mess."

"It could be." He rubbed his chin. "Mess or not, I'm *not* going to let them have Peanut. They may think that because they're related it gives them a right, but I won't have any kid of mine exposed to a bunch of criminals."

"But this Manny might not be a criminal, you said."

"Maybe not, but the rest of the Molinas sure as hell are. Even the kid's grandmother, although to hear Manny tell it, the woman's a saint."

"Really?" The thought amazed Angela. She'd never linked the words *grandmother* and *criminal* in her mind before.

"Hell, yes," Rafe said. "As far as we can tell, she's in on the planning, and she's the one who keeps up the South American contacts. It's *her* relatives back in Colombia who are the other end of the drug pipeline. One of these days we'll nail her just the way we nailed her son. And no kid of mine is going to be in the middle of that.''

"I can see why not.''

"I guess I'll have to get a transfer.''

"Will you miss Miami?''

He snorted. "It's just a place, one I'm not especially fond of.''

"I guess you don't get to see much of the good parts.''

"Nope.''

"That's a shame.''

"Is it?'' His eyes were cold as they returned to her. "What difference does it really make? A place is a place. It's what you make it. My job would probably make any place ugly.''

"That's sad.''

"Somebody's got to do it.''

She nodded, but wondered at his bitterness and cynicism. And his idealism. *Somebody's got to do it,* said a lot about him. He was an odd mix of character traits, and she realized that he fascinated her. She'd never met anyone like him.

"But enough about me,'' he said. "What about you?''

"What about me?''

"You said you're suffering from burnout. Since you can't get rid of your diabetes, what are you going to do about the rest of it?''

"I don't know. It's pathetic, but all I really know is banking. I can't imagine what else I can do.''

"Can't you do something at the bank besides be a loan officer?''

She shook her head. "That's about as high as I'm going to go. Going any higher means getting into bank management. And, frankly, there's something of a glass ceiling and no openings anyway.''

"Try another bank. Unless it's banking in general you're burned-out on.''

"I honestly don't know.'' She crumbled a cracker into dust as she thought about it. "Besides, it all seems so pointless.''

"Pointless? What's pointless?''

She waved a hand and said extravagantly, "Everything."
As soon as she said it, she was embarrassed. It was one thing
to feel that way and another to say it out loud.

"Life, you mean?"

She nodded and looked down, biting her lip. It was awful
to admit just how hopeless she was feeling, and she wished
she'd never said it, especially to this man with the hard eyes.

"Why do you feel that way? Everybody goes through bad
patches."

"Well, I've been going through one since I was eight years
old." The words suddenly burst from her, and there was no
calling them back. "I have a chronic, incurable disease that
could kill me at any time. If it doesn't kill me right off, it'll
probably rot me away in little pieces."

"Have you felt hopeless all along?"

"No...I..." She couldn't stand it anymore. She'd bared her
soul, and he was going to hand her logic? Jumping up, she
fled from the room, determined to go to bed, wondering why
she'd ever been stupid enough to admit what she was really
feeling, hating herself for the weakness of feeling that way.

And ashamed. Deeply ashamed of her illness and her despair. Everything was wrong about her. *Everything*.

She heard Rafe following her, but she didn't dare run up
the stairs for fear of waking Emma and Gage. She walked as
quickly as she could, but knew he was only a couple of steps
behind. Why was he following her? Why couldn't he just leave
her alone?

She threw open the door to her room and stepped inside,
trying to close it behind her, but he pushed his way in without
apology.

She took a ragged breath, fighting the tears that were always
so close to the surface these days. "What do you want?"

"I'm sorry," he said.

"Okay, you're sorry. I just want to be alone!"

He just stood there looking at her, and she had a sudden
wild urge to hit him.

"Look," he said finally, "I've never had a chronic illness,

so I can't imagine how it feels. But I *do* know that I didn't mean anything critical by what I said. I guess I could have asked the question better.''

She didn't answer, just folded her arms so she wouldn't strike out, and stared at him from burning eyes. Her chest felt so tight she could hardly breathe.

"I *do* know," he continued, "what it's like to have death staring over your shoulder. Been there, done that. But I've been lucky. I haven't had to live that way every day of my life.''

She managed to drag in a gulp of air, and her chest loosened a little. "So?"

"So…I'm sorry if you thought I was making light of it. I was just wondering if you felt this way all the time. I can't imagine what kind of hell that would be.''

Sympathy was proving to be worse than what she had mistaken as cold logic. Where before she had been angry, now she was closer to crying than ever.

"I don't think about it all the time," she said finally, her voice thick.

"I don't see how you could. You'd go crazy."

She managed a nod and took another deep breath, trying to steady herself, trying to ease the painful tightness in her throat. "I'll be okay. I'm just…down lately." She wished he would go away so she could have a good bawl and get it all out of her system.

"It's been rough lately, hasn't it?"

His continued sympathy surprised her. This cold man who seemed to want to keep himself at arm's length was surprising her. "Everyone hits rough patches," she said stubbornly. "I'll be *fine*.''

"Sure you will." But he showed no sign of leaving.

"Look," she said finally, "I'm blue, but I'm not suicidal. You don't have to worry I'm going to do something stupid. What I'm going to do is wait twenty minutes, take my insulin right on time, and then go to bed.''

"Sounds like a plan." But he didn't move, and his eyes

were scouring her face as if he were looking for something and not finding it.

"I'm *okay,* Rafe," she said firmly, though she felt far from okay. "Thanks for caring."

He nodded slowly. "It's the caring part that kind of floors me."

"What?"

His lips curved, but the faint smile didn't reach his eyes. His smiles almost never reached his eyes, she realized. Why that should sadden her, she couldn't imagine. "Never mind," he said. "I don't know if I could explain it to myself, let alone someone else." He started to turn away, then sighed. "Oh, hell."

"What's wrong?"

He faced her again. "Me. You. Hell, I don't know." Then he reached out for her, wrapping her in his arms and snuggling her face against his shoulder.

She was astonished at how hard yet welcoming his body felt, and how surprisingly good it was to have her face nestled against a man's shoulder while his strong arms hugged her. She was surprised, too, by how good he smelled, like soap, and man, a heady mixture she'd almost forgotten. That and the faint smell of baby....

"If you need someone to talk to, just wake me up," he said roughly. "I know what it's like. There've been plenty of nights when I could've used an ear."

She tilted her face up, trying to see his expression, but all she succeeded in doing was bring her mouth to within inches of his. He took it as an invitation, and she was almost shocked to realize that she wanted him to.

The touch of his mouth wasn't what she had expected. From someone who looked so hard, she expected a touch equally hard. Instead she got the butterfly brush of lips, a warm caress that made her knees go weak. When he lifted his mouth an inch away, she thought she might die from the loss of contact. God, she hadn't realized just how hungry she'd become for human warmth.

"I'm not good at this," he whispered unsteadily.

"At what?" She whispered, too, afraid of shattering the tenuous moment.

"At comforting. I've never comforted anyone before."

That was probably the saddest thing she could imagine a human being saying. Forgetting her own problems, she reached up and touched his cheek gently. "You're doing just fine."

He closed his eyes tightly, as if her touch was causing a violent storm of emotion inside him. "Yeah?" he finally asked, a mere breath of sound. His arms tightened around her, and his mouth found hers again, a little harder this time, but still gentle, almost questing, as if he were seeking her approval.

She responded in kind, hoping that somehow, even in her miserable state, she could offer him some of the comfort he was giving her.

But as soon as she responded, he stiffened. Then he let go of her and stepped back.

His eyes were open now, dark windows on some dark place inside him. "This isn't wise," he said.

Then he turned sharply on his heel and walked out, closing the door quietly behind him.

Angela stood frozen, feeling as if her universe had been rocked to the core by a simple human touch. A maelstrom of feelings whipped through her, feelings she couldn't even name, making her want to cry, making her feel more alone than she had ever felt in her life, except when she lost the baby and her fiancé.

And when they passed, she felt empty. Exhausted. Raw.

He was right, she thought. It wasn't wise at all.

But how was she ever going to forget that it had happened?

Chapter 5

At four in the morning, feeding a hungry baby in a room dark except for a single lamp, and silent except for the soft little sucking sounds the baby made, Rafe found himself rediscovering loneliness.

It was something he hadn't thought about in a long, long time. Not since he'd been taken from his mother and discovered that a foster home, no matter how kind, couldn't replace the comfort of being near the one person who had held you and cared for you since birth.

Of course, Marva's care hadn't been the best in the world, but it had been *care*. Whatever her other failings, Rafe had never doubted that she loved him, not even when she was too drunk to wake up to tell him what to have for supper.

The state of Texas had taken that away from him, and he'd been lonely until he learned to bury the feeling forever.

Until tonight.

Maybe it was the kid, he thought. His son was tucked against his bare chest, little fingers curling and grasping, looking up at him with those amazingly serious and intent infant eyes. The touch of those little hands had an emotional intimacy that was getting to him despite all his barriers against feeling. He was getting seriously attached to the kid.

Which would be a bad thing. If he couldn't keep the kid, would the baby spend the rest of his life missing what his father had missed ever since the state of Texas had intervened in his life? He hated the thought.

What the hell had Raquel been thinking of? She could have signed the kid over for adoption even before it was born. Why had she wanted *him* to have this kid? She must have known that she didn't mean anything to him.

Or maybe not. Something in his chest ached with a feeling he hadn't had since he was ten years old. Sitting there feeding the baby, he found himself remembering Rocky's incredible vulnerability.

She hadn't been at all what he expected, not when they got in bed. He'd thought her a passionate, fiery, hot-tempered La-tina who knew what the score was. Instead, once they'd fallen into bed, he'd discovered that was all a front. The real Rocky had been lonely, and wide-open to hurt.

And he'd hurt her. He'd betrayed her. He'd jailed her brother. How could she possibly want to give him her child? Some stupid notion that he was the baby's biological father and would care?

Or had she been getting even in the most devious female way possible?

It was certainly a possibility, he thought. And if that was what she had intended, she'd succeeded. He couldn't look at his son without remembering how he'd betrayed her. Without feeling that he was going to spend the rest of his life trying to make up for being such a damned jerk.

A sigh escaped him. At the same moment, the peanut decided he'd had enough to eat. Rafe set the bottle aside, moved the kid to his shoulder and began to pace the room, rubbing the little back gently. The floor creaked beneath his feet, and he hoped his footfalls weren't disturbing Gage and Emma.

Peanut made a little cooing sound, apparently enjoying his

ride around the room. What went on in that little head? Rafe
wondered. People might think infants were a blank slate, but
when he watched *this* infant, he was convinced there was an
entire world inside that small brain.

As he paced, waiting for the gas bubbles to escape the
baby's tummy, his thoughts strayed back to Angela and what
had passed between them.

That had been a serious mistake. And he could find no
excuse for his behavior. He didn't just grab women and kiss
them like that. He didn't reach out emotionally to *anyone* that
way. Yet that was what he had done, for a few moments
making himself more vulnerable than he'd ever been in his
life. Worse, he'd let Angela know he was vulnerable.

Every instinct he had warned him against the danger in that.
He tried to tell himself that Angela wasn't a subject in a case,
so how could it matter? But it did. And just as dangerous was
the way her vulnerability was reaching out to him.

Just the way Raquel's had during that one wild night. The
difference was that the next day he'd gotten what he needed
to nail Eduardo Molina and had never needed to see Raquel
again. He was going to see Angela every day as long as he
stayed in this house.

Maybe he should move back to the motel. But that wasn't
the best environment for the child. He thought about taking a
risk and going back to Miami, but as long as Manuel Molina
knew where he was, he was at risk and so was the baby. God
knew how many people Manny might have told where Rafe
lived. One word in the wrong ear and poof! Peanut would be
an orphan.

So what options were left? Dumping the kid on Nate Tate
and hightailing it back home himself?

That had been his original plan, but for some reason he
couldn't bring himself to seriously pursue it. Nate wouldn't
want the kid, anyway, he told himself. The man was a grand-
father now. Why would he want to start another family?

But that was just an excuse, and he knew it. He had the

strongest feeling that if he asked, Nate would say yes without hesitation. But he couldn't bring himself to ask.

God, what a mess!

Thoughts such as those kept him up long after Peanut went back to sleep, until the sun rose and he heard Angela stirring.

Until the baby awoke again, a little later than usual, and started demanding his morning feeding. Which meant that Rafe had to go downstairs to face whatever there was to face from Angela after last night. He figured she would probably be mad at him.

But the baby wasn't going to wait. He changed the crying kid, tucked him against his shoulder, and went downstairs shirtless and shoeless, feeling as if he had grains of sand behind his eyelids.

Gage was just going out the door as Rafe came into the kitchen. Emma and Angela were sitting at the round oak table nursing cups of hot coffee, and Angela was eating scrambled eggs and toast.

"Mornin'," he said, and headed straight toward the refrigerator.

"Let me get you some coffee, Rafe," Emma said. "Would you like me to make you some breakfast?"

"I'm not hungry, but thanks." He found a clean bottle and nipple, opened the Pedialyte, and set about preparing the kid's breakfast with one expert hand.

"How is he doing?" Emma asked.

"No more diarrhea," Rafe responded.

"That's good."

"Yep." He thought about heading back upstairs, but Emma had put out a fresh cup of coffee for him, and the aroma drew him. Giving in, he sat at the table with the women, feeding and holding the baby one-handed while he sipped his coffee with the other.

"You're good at that," Emma said wistfully.

He shrugged a shoulder. "Desperation's a great teacher. What I could really use is another arm." He avoided looking at Angela.

No one had any more to say, and for that Rafe was grateful. He'd had about three hours of sleep, all told, and the sound of other voices was grating on his nerves. *Angela* was grating on his nerves, he realized. Sitting there, staring into her scrambled eggs as if she was terrified that a look from him would turn her to stone.

But what really grated on him was knowing he was responsible for it. He should *never* have touched her. The woman had some serious issues to deal with, and he didn't have the time or inclination to get involved with them. He never had the time or inclination to get involved that way, so what the hell had he been thinking of last night?

The peanut was kneading his chest, and he looked down, meeting those serious dark eyes. Hell, it was getting bad when staring at a baby could absorb him this way. But he didn't stop himself, just kept looking down into Peanut's eyes as if nothing else in the world mattered.

And maybe it didn't.

Emma rose eventually, excusing herself to get ready for work. That left Rafe and Angela together in a silence that was suddenly fraught with unspoken words.

Finally Angela spoke. "When..." Her voice cracked and she stopped, then tried again. "When do you put him back on formula?"

"Later today. I've got to get some distilled water to mix with his formula, thin it out and put him back on it slowly."

"Oh. But isn't distilled water unsanitary?"

"I have to boil it first."

"Oh."

Silence fell again. He kept his gaze pinned to the baby as firmly as if it was tacked there. He didn't want to look at her, didn't want to see her terrible vulnerability.

Angela rose and went to rinse her dishes and put them in the dishwasher. "I'll watch the baby while you go out for water, if you want."

He wanted to refuse, but for the kid's sake, couldn't.

"Thanks," he said reluctantly. "The doctor thinks all the bouncing around might have unsettled him."

"I can see how it might. Well, I've got to go get ready for my run. Inflexible schedule, you know."

She said it airily, as if it didn't matter. But he knew it did, and knowing made him look up. Their eyes met for the first time that morning, and what he saw made him catch and hold his breath.

In his day he'd seen people in all kinds of pain, but he couldn't remember ever seeing the kind of haunted hurt he saw in Angela's gaze. Before he could think what to do or say, she'd left the room.

And with a sense of relief he went back to being a father. That was a role he knew how to play, a role that was becoming increasingly comfortable with practice. With Angela, he didn't know who to be, what to say, what to do.

She put him off balance, and he didn't like that at all.

Up in her room, Angela changed from her robe and night-gown into her jogging sweats and shoes. The cold look was back in Rafe's eyes, she thought. The look that had vanished last night when he'd tried to comfort her was back this morning like the stark gray walls of a fortress.

She'd been stupid to think anything had changed between them. Not that it mattered. She couldn't afford to get any closer to him, because he was dangerous to her peace of mind.

Sitting there this morning, trying not to watch him feed the baby, trying not to notice his powerful bare chest, had only served to remind her of how dangerously susceptible she was right now. Her loneliness and current misery were making her too easy a touch for anyone who evinced the least concern for her.

And worse, she was rediscovering herself as a sexual being. Rafe was awakening yearnings she'd tried to cut off years ago, reminding her that she was a woman.

If she had to get the hots for someone, why did she have to choose a man with hard eyes and a cutting edge? Why couldn't she have chosen someone safe and comfortable? Why did she have to get the hots at all, come to that? No man in his right mind would want her, and she wasn't built to have a casual affair. It just wasn't in her.

It was a relief to step outside into the brisk morning air and start trotting down the street. The run would clear her head. It always did—as long as she didn't give herself low blood sugar by pressing too hard.

She passed the sheriff's office on her way out and her way back every morning, but this morning, as she went past on her return lap, Nate Tate, wearing his khaki uniform and a blue jacket, fell in beside her, keeping pace.

"You're not wearing running shoes," she remarked, surprised by how nice it felt to have him join her.

"Combat boots. They'll do. I'm assuming you can't just break off your run and have coffee with me?"

"Sorry." She shook her head. "I adjusted my insulin to compensate for this."

"I thought so. I usually take my run in the evening."

"I do, too, when I'm working. It's a beautiful morning, though."

"It sure is."

They covered another block in companionable silence, but Angela was sure there was a point to Nate's joining her. He had never struck her as a man who did pointless things.

"What do you think of Rafe?" he asked.

The question surprised her. Emma had always said that Nate Tate never gossiped. Of course, this wasn't exactly gossip. He was asking her opinion. "He seems like a hard, lonely man."

"That's what I thought." He sighed, a ragged puff of air as his feet hit the pavement. "I can't imagine why Marva didn't tell me about him."

"Maybe she knew you'd want to take him away."

He didn't say anything for another half a block. "You might be right. I didn't think about that. But that woman was a lousy mother. If Rafe's experience was anything like mine, he raised himself."

"You didn't do such a bad job, Nate."

A chuckle escaped him. "There's some who wouldn't have agreed with you when I was in my teens. The army straightened me out a lot."

"Rafe doesn't seem to be doing too badly," she lied.

"Really? I would have seen it differently. I've rarely seen a man so alone...." He trailed off and fell silent as they rounded a corner onto Front Street, where Emma's house was. "That's not true. I've had some friends who were like him. Walled in solitude. If life beats you up enough, you stop letting anything get close to you."

When they reached the house, Angela invited him in. "You can talk some more with Rafe. I won't be in the way. I need to eat something and shower."

"Thanks."

They found Rafe sound asleep on the couch, the baby tucked in his arm. He'd showered, shaved and dressed in a shirt and slacks, but hadn't put on any shoes. The sight of his bare feet touched Angela somehow, as did the sight of the baby snuggled against him.

"Let's go make some coffee," she whispered. "He might wake up."

Nate nodded and followed her to the kitchen. Angela made a fresh pot of coffee, then pulled her obligatory snack out of the fridge, choosing a piece of fruit. Nate declined food.

"The older I get, the harder it is to keep my weight down," he told her. "It's become a real chore."

"I'm having trouble keeping my weight up." When the coffee was done, she poured him a cup, then excused herself to go shower. "I won't be long."

"No rush, sweetpea. I'm enjoying the peace this morning."

Rafe knew they'd come into the house—he would have been lousy at his job if he hadn't been able to wake at the slightest unusual sound—but he hadn't wanted to let them know he was up. He listened to their voices coming from the kitchen, but only when he heard Angela go upstairs did he get up, carrying the baby tucked in the crook of his arm, and go to the kitchen.

Nate's back was to him as he stepped through the door. Without turning, Nate said, "I figured you were awake, son. I take it you're avoiding Angela."

Rafe stood where he was, surprised by the man's perception, and annoyed that Nate could read him so well. Most people couldn't read him at all.

"I just needed a minute to wake up," Rafe said. He crossed the kitchen, poured himself a cup of coffee, then leaned back against the counter and looked at his half-brother. "Did you want to see me?"

Nate leaned back in his chair, crossing his legs loosely and sipping his own coffee. "It was an impulse. I figured since we were brothers, maybe we ought to take a stab at getting better acquainted."

"It's an accident of birth."

Nate nodded slowly. "That's true. But I figure you must have some reason for wanting to meet me after all this time."

Rafe met Nate's gaze steadily, even as his heart lurched uneasily. What was the man, a mind reader? "The kid got me to thinking about family, that's all. He needs some family besides me, and the Molinas don't count."

"Fair enough." But Nate's expression remained thoughtful. "So why don't you and the baby come over for dinner Friday evening? You can meet a couple of your nieces, and I know they're dying to see the baby."

Rafe nodded, sure that backing away—even though that was what he suddenly wanted to do—would make Nate even more suspicious. "Thanks. I'd like that."

"Bring Angela, too," Nate said, rising. He carried his cup to the sink. "Gotta get back to work. See you tonight."

After Nate was gone, Rafe looked down at his son. "How the hell did I get myself into this, Peanut?"

Bring Angela. Right. She was probably going to like that idea about as much as he did.

But Angela surprised him. Whatever had been troubling her

this morning seemed to have vanished when she returned downstairs, freshly showered and dressed. She agreed readily enough to go with him to the Tates', and seemed happy when he turned the child over to her while he went to the store.

Somehow he found the change in her even more discomfiting than her earlier uneasiness.

Lack of sleep, he told himself. He was suffering from lack of sleep. There could be absolutely no other reason why everything in the world seemed to be irritating him to death today.

But it wasn't lack of sleep when he was checking out at the pharmacy and happened to look across the street toward the courthouse to see Manny Molina standing there. He would recognize that jerk anywhere. In an instant he was back on alert, the way he was when he worked the streets.

He looked at the cashier as he accepted the change. "Is there a back way out of here?"

She looked at him as if he were crazy.

"Just tell me," he said more insistently. "Can I get out the back?"

"I guess...." She pointed. "Through the door at the back by the pharmacy counter. Is something wrong?"

"Not yet."

He grabbed the bottled water and headed toward the back of the store. A minute later he was in an alley. His car was out front, but he decided to leave it.

What now, dimwit? he asked himself. How had Manny found him? And what if Manny was as dangerous as Eduardo? He'd led the man to this town, and maybe to Gage and Emma...and Angela.

Hell! He stood there for a couple of minutes, then headed home through alleys and back streets.

Rafe Jr. was in a playful mood, so Angela spread a blanket on the living room floor and sat cross-legged beside him as he waved his arms and legs and cooed at the world.

She was fascinated with the baby. Watching him absorbed

her as few things had lately, and from time to time she just couldn't resist hugging him.

Reaching out, she let him grab her index fingers, then lifted him just an inch or so above the floor. What a grip! His strength amazed her, and even when she lowered him back, he didn't let go immediately.

She heard the back door open and close, and wondered if Emma had come home early. Then Rafe appeared in the living room doorway.

"Manny's in town," he said.

Angela felt her heart skip. "Are you sure?"

"I'd recognize that guy anywhere. I saw him when I was checking out of the pharmacy. I went out the back way. Listen, I'm going to call Nate and Gage. Why don't you lock the front door?"

"Okay."

She rose at once and went to do as he asked, feeling frightened, because he seemed to consider this so serious. She could hear Rafe talking on the phone in the kitchen and the baby cooing from the living room. Such normal sounds that it was nearly impossible to believe anyone could be in danger.

She wasn't used to thinking in those terms. In her life, the dangers that lurked were things like foreclosure and loan denial, or emotional pain. She couldn't imagine living in a world where people might actually try to harm you physically.

But that was Rafe's world, and apparently he'd brought it along with him. He was definitely a man to avoid. She didn't want his world impinging on hers. Hers was already difficult enough. She thought about going back home rather than staying around for this mess.

But then she stood in the living room doorway and watched the baby playing, and realized that that innocent child had been dragged into Rafe's world, too. The baby needed all the protectors he could get.

She scooped up the child and carried him out to the kitchen. Rafe was just hanging up the phone.

"Nate's going to keep an eye on the house," he said.

"Gage is out on an investigation, but as soon as he gets in, Nate is going to send him home."

She looked at him, clutching the child tightly to her breast. "Do you really think that's necessary? Is that man going to kidnap the baby?"

"I don't know. I don't know what's on his mind. And I don't like that. I especially don't like the fact that he managed to find me, and that he followed me all the way here. That's a little more than wanting occasional visitation."

Angela wished she could argue with him, but she had to agree. Why wouldn't this Manny person just assume that Rafe would eventually come home with the baby? "Maybe you should call your boss and let him know what's going on."

Rafe leaned back against the counter and folded his arms across his chest. "I don't think that would be wise."

"Why not?"

"Because somebody had to tell Manny where I am."

"You think your boss did?"

"I don't know who it was. I'm not inclined to suspect Kate, but somebody else in the office might be an informant. First there was Manny finding my apartment. He said he had me followed. Maybe. But now this. I don't like it at all."

"You live in an ugly world, you know?" The words burst from Angela, a protest against the uneasiness that was filling her, born of concern for the child in her arms. "How can you bring a child into a world like that?"

"Believe me, lady, that was never my plan!"

"Well, you don't plan very well, then."

His face became as hard as she had ever seen it, and his dark eyes grew sharp enough to sting her. "You don't exactly live in a pretty world, either, Angela. At least I don't take away the homes of innocent people."

He couldn't have stunned her more if he had slapped her. She stood gaping at him, aware that her heart was suddenly thudding hard.

"I go after crooks, lady. People who hurt other people. You see that little kid you're holding? I'd really, *really* like it if by the time he went to school I could be sure there wasn't some dealer somewhere standing on a street corner thinking up new and improved ways to give him a drug habit. I go after people who import drugs so they can get rich on the ruined lives of thousands of people. I go after people who break the law. Who do you go after? Farmers? People who've been honest and hardworking all their lives, only to have a couple of bad years through no fault of their own? To my way of thinking, you aren't a whole lot better than the people I go after."

She couldn't even breathe. Her heart hammered so hard and rapidly that there didn't seem to be any room left in her breast for air.

"Take—" Her voice broke. "Take the baby. I don't want to drop him...."

At once his face changed. He crossed the room like a shot and took Peanut from her. Holding the child in one arm, he reached out with the other, putting his arm around her shoulders, steadying her. "What do you need?" he demanded roughly. "Orange juice?"

She hadn't eaten enough after her run, she thought. Maybe she had taken too much insulin...or maybe it was just the adrenaline that was surging through her right now.... She was feeling dizzy, weak, cold sweat beading her brow.

"Sit down," he said. "Right where you are. Just sit down...."

She felt herself sinking to the floor, sitting on the tile, leaning against the cupboard, all of it seeming far away. Closing her eyes, she let her head fall back and willed the weakness to pass.

"Here."

She opened her eyes and saw a glass of orange juice, felt the hard edge of the glass touch her lip. She opened her mouth, felt the cold juice pour in. Swallowed.

When he took the glass away, it was empty. "What else?" he said, his voice almost ragged. "What can I do?"

She managed to shake her head. "The baby..."

"He's right here, counting the floor tiles. Angela, what else do you need? Tell me."

"I'm...okay."

Orange juice took longer than candy, but now that it was in her system, the weakness would pass soon. She just had to wait it out.

Rafe swore quietly and sat cross-legged beside her on the floor. "Does this happen every time you get mad?"

It was too much effort to answer. She didn't even bother to try. She just let her eyes close.

"Hey," he said almost gently. "Don't go away from me. Keep your eyes open."

She didn't want to look at him, but she opened her eyes, anyway. "My sugar must have been low to begin with," she said, the orange juice beginning to work.

He gave her a crooked smile. "So this doesn't happen every time you get mad?"

"No...no..." And now she was starting to get embarrassed. She wanted to crawl into a hole and hide, but she didn't have the energy yet to find her way upstairs.

He reached out, surprising her, and brushed a lock of her hair back from her forehead. "You're looking better," he said decisively. "Not a whole lot, but some. Boy, did you scare me."

"Sorry."

"No, *I'm* sorry. I shouldn't have struck out at you like that. It wasn't fair, and it wasn't true."

"It was true, all right. If it hadn't been, it wouldn't have hurt."

Little by little her body was coming back to her. She no longer felt as if she and it were at opposite ends of a long tunnel. The floor felt hard now, as did the cupboard behind her.

"No," he said, "it wasn't true. I just...well..." He looked away, then gave her a rueful shrug. "You got under my skin, Angel. You have a way of doing that."

If she'd been herself right then, she probably would have

gotten up and fled. She didn't want to get under his skin, didn't want to get any closer to this dangerous man. But she wasn't herself, so she just sat there dumbly and wondered where this was all going to lead.

He looked at her a minute longer, then leaned over and picked up the baby.

"Here," he said, settling the child in her lap. "Your legs are softer than the floor. You going to be okay for a minute?"

"I'm getting better," she assured him. "Really."

"Good. I'll be right back. I just want to take a quick look out the windows."

The threat was back. He brought it back with those few simple words. But instead of getting upset, Angela just sighed wearily and looked down at the child lying on her thighs. "We'll be okay," she said. Since they were already on the floor, there was no risk of dropping the baby, and she could tell the danger of her passing out was over.

The peanut was getting tired, she noticed. His eyelids were looking heavy, and he was sucking on his fist. "Doesn't he have a pacifier?"

"No. Maybe I should get him one. Back in a minute."

She didn't look up to watch him go. What was the point? She had a feeling she would be watching him leave countless times until he finally went for good.

An ineffable sorrow filled her. She tried to tell herself it was just her hypoglycemia, that it would pass when the juice fully hit her system, but deep inside, she knew it was something more. It was looking at a baby in her lap, something she could never have for her own. It was thinking about a world where people could say such hurtful things to each other with perfect truth. It was thinking about a hard-edged man who could be so amazingly gentle that he utterly disarmed her without warning.

It was thinking about all the things she could never have, as if her diabetes had built a glass wall between her and the rest of the world.

It was self-pity, and she tried to force it from her thoughts.

Time to get on the stick, she told herself. Time to start thinking about the future, instead of everything that was wrong with her present. Time to stop wallowing.

Rafe came back a few minutes later. "There's an unmarked car across the street, and no sign of Manny." Bending, he took the child from her lap, then reached down with his free hand to help her up and to a chair.

"You sit down," he said. "You still look pale. I'm going to take the kid upstairs and put him down for his nap. Be right back."

She didn't know if that was a good thing, but she was feeling too whipped emotionally to do anything except what he said.

He looked over his shoulder just before he disappeared. "Do you need your test kit?"

She nodded. "Thanks. It's in the black leather case on my dresser."

"I'll get it."

A glance at the clock told her it was already time for her next insulin dose, and almost time for lunch. But now she was out of whack again. God, how weary she was of this, weary to the bone with fighting a battle she didn't seem able to win. She was doing everything right. Everything. And yet still she'd made a fool of herself, needing help from someone else for something she should have been managing on her own.

Life was the pits sometimes. And she didn't see any end in sight.

Rafe returned with Angela's kit and put it on the table in front of her. "What exactly do you have to do?" he asked, sitting across from her.

She sighed and decided she was silly to be so sensitive now, after he'd had to help her through an attack. "Prick my finger, squeeze a drop of blood on a test strip, put it in the machine and take a reading."

"Would you be more comfortable if I left the room?"

"What difference does it make?"

"None to me."

She chose a finger than wasn't too sore from all the repeated prickings and did the test. "Still a little too low," she said.

"So what now?"

"A few crackers." Then more insulin. Then eating again a half hour later. Then the same thing, over and over and over...

He got the crackers for her. "You want milk, too?"

"That might be too much. Just water, please."

He returned with a glass of water and sat. "So what happened, Angela? Help me understand. You seemed okay one minute, then the next you were out of it."

"I guess my blood sugar was a little low to begin with. Being diabetic, I try to keep it just a little high, because it's so easy for it to drop. Anyway, I was probably low normal, then, when I became angry, I had an adrenaline rush that drove my level even lower. If I hadn't been a little low to begin with, it wouldn't have bothered me at all."

He nodded slowly. "I get it."

She put the kit away and nibbled on a cracker.

"I'm sorry," he said. "I shouldn't have struck out at you like that."

"Why not? I deserved it. And appearances to the contrary, I'm not *that* fragile."

"Yes, you are, Angela. You're very fragile."

She didn't know if she liked that, but when she looked at him, there was something in his gaze that made her feel warm all over, so she didn't argue with him. Uneasy, she looked down at the cracker she was holding. "It's embarrassing," she said finally.

"Why? People sometimes have illnesses. I don't see what's embarrassing about it."

"You've never had to be carried out of work on a stretcher because you passed out at your desk."

"Ah."

"That happened to me three times in the last couple months I was there. You don't have doctors who look at you and say, 'You've got to pay more attention to yourself. You've got to be better about your schedule. You ought to know better than this.' "

"No, but I've got bosses who say pretty much the same thing sometimes." One corner of his mouth lifted. "But I will admit I don't get carried out on a stretcher unless I get shot."

"Have you been shot?" The thought gave her a pang.

He shook his head. "Not yet. I've been attacked with a knife a few times, but nothing that needed more than a few stitches."

"That's awful."

"No more awful than what's happening to you."

"What's happening to me is caused by my own carelessness."

"Same here. I only get hurt when I slip up. But you…Angela, you can't predict everything that's going to happen in your life. I can see how it gets out of control every now and then."

"I just need to be more careful."

"Ditto." His half smile blossomed into a full smile. "Don't be so hard on yourself. Life has a way of taking us by surprise."

Gage arrived then, coming in the back door. "Hey, gang," he said as he stepped in. "So the bad guy is in town?"

"I saw him when I was at the pharmacy. My car's still down there."

"Want me to get it for you?"

Rafe shook his head. "I don't know if Manny knows my car. I suspect he does. Besides, the Florida plates will stick out."

"Then we'll leave it." Gage pulled out a chair and straddled it. "Nate's got an unmarked car parked out front."

"I saw." He hesitated. "It's just a little obvious, Gage."

"The car's going to move every half hour or so, and we've got a couple of guys who'll switch off."

"You don't know the Molinas. They can smell a cop at a hundred yards."

A grin flickered over Gage's face. "All right, I'll ask Nate to pull him."

"I just don't want to put a neon sign out front. It would probably be better if I left."

An instinctive protest rose to Angela's lips. She might not like the idea of some criminal stalking Rafe and the baby, but even less did she like the idea of Rafe and Peanut wandering from town to town like some ghastly version of the Flying Dutchman. "No," she said.

"I agree with Angela," Gage said. "You can't go on the run for the rest of your days because of some jerk."

"I don't want to put anyone here at risk."

Gage dismissed it with a wave of his hand. "How on earth is this guy gonna know where you are? You lie low here with the baby. If there's any need to take the child out, Emma and I can do it, or Angela. Regardless, Emma and I are agreed that you're not going to leave for our sakes. If it becomes apparent it's necessary for the child's safety, we'll figure out something. But for right now, let's just watch this guy."

"Is someone tailing him?"

"Not yet. But in this town a stranger sticks out like a sore thumb. Especially one who's asking questions. People won't tell him a thing, but they'll mention him to Nate, you can be sure. Just relax. There's no way he can hide around here, and sooner or later he's going to have to find a place to sleep. There aren't too many of those around."

"One, as I recall."

"That's the only motel. There are a few people who have rooms to let, but we're not exactly a major convention center. We'll know where he is by midnight tonight."

Rafe nodded. "Okay. I'll lie low and see what develops."

"And if he tries anything, he's going to have to deal with the Conard County Sheriff's Department. Nate takes a dim view of people like Manny Molina."

One corner of Rafe's mouth quirked upward. "A little frontier justice, hmm?"

"Let's just say that anybody who wants to mess with Nate Tate's brother is apt to find life getting extremely difficult."

"Well," said Angela brightly, "I don't know about you two, but that makes me feel a whole lot better."

Gage laughed, and after a moment, a reluctant chuckle escaped Rafe.

"Messing with Nate," Gage said, "is a risky proposition, Angela. The man's a lion when someone he cares about is threatened."

"But," said Rafe, "Nate doesn't know me from Adam."

"He knows enough. So relax and enjoy an enforced vacation. Let the local law deal with this guy."

Rafe looked at Angela. "So I guess I get to play a lot of solitaire."

"We'll find a way to pass the time," she said impulsively, even as she wondered why she was including herself.

Rafe stood and walked over to the kitchen window, looking out. "I'm not used to spending so much time on my duff. In a couple of days I'll have a king-size case of cabin fever if this keeps up."

Gage spoke. "You can get out of here, if you want. Angela can drive you and the baby out of town. You'll just have to keep down until you get safely away. Or I can take you. Take a long walk in the mountains. Go fishing up on Spirit Lake. I don't think Molina will be looking for you there."

"I'll think about it." He sighed and turned around to look at them. "I don't mean to be a complainer. I just can't figure out how that guy found me, and it's making me as uneasy as hell."

"You want me to call your boss? Ask around about the Manny problem without letting her know where you are? I can call in my official capacity and mention that the guy has turned up in town, and I'd like to know whatever she has on him."

Rafe shook his head. "Thanks. But I can't be sure word won't get into the wrong ear."

"Ah…" Understanding struck Gage. "I didn't think of that."

"You know how secretive the D.E.A. is about its agents, Gage. First the guy found my apartment, and then he found me all the way out here. Somebody is talking."

Gage nodded. "What about your boss?"

Rafe hesitated. "I think Kate is clean. She was the one who called to warn me Manny was considering legal action. But I don't know who else at the office might have found out where I was going. The D.E.A. may be secretive when it comes to talking to outsiders, but secrets are general knowledge all over the office. It's assumed that everyone who works there is trustworthy. You know how that goes."

"Yeah, I do." Gage sighed. "Somebody found out where I lived…" He trailed off, his face darkening. Then he shook himself. "Well, we'll see how Molina feels when he learns his reputation has preceded him."

"What do you mean?"

"Nate is thinking about making the guy seriously uneasy. He may think no one here knows about his drug-running family, but he's about to find out differently."

Rafe nodded. "That might work."

"Nate's hoping it will. In fact, we're hoping it might scare him right back to Miami."

"But what then?" Angela asked. "Rafe can't go back to Miami at all, can he?"

Both men looked at her, but neither offered a response. The question hung in the air, unanswered and unanswerable.

Chapter 6

Rafe went to sleep easily that night. Near midnight, Gage had reported that Manny had checked in at the Lazy Rest Motel. So the guy wasn't trying to hide out or escape detection, Rafe thought. That was a good thing...unless he got to wondering too hard about what Manny might be up to. He decided not to. Manny had never been the brightest of the Molina crop.

But then Peanut didn't wake for his usual 4:00 a.m. feeding. Rafe woke up exactly fifteen minutes past the usual time, panic jarring him out of bed and across the room to the baby's portable bed even before his eyes opened. Rafe Jr. was sleeping soundly, breathing normally. In short, the kid was okay.

Rafe settled back on his heels, suddenly weak with relief. Minutes ticked by while the baby slept on and the strength came back to his limbs. Finally he decided to go downstairs, get himself a drink and fix a bottle for the peanut just in case. No way was the child going to sleep until seven without a feeding.

On the way to the kitchen, he stopped by the front windows

and looked out. The street appeared peaceful. Nothing was moving out there in the moonlight. The unmarked car was still there, but much farther down the street now. If anyone was in it, he couldn't tell from this distance.

So Manny was probably enjoying whatever dreams he was having at four in the morning. Sighing, Rafe turned for the kitchen, afraid that if he didn't get that bottle upstairs soon, the baby would wake and rouse the entire household.

The kitchen was dark, but the instant he stepped in, he realized that he wasn't alone. A shadowy figure stood in the corner by the back door. His heart slammed into high gear. "Who's there?" he asked hoarsely, prepared to jump back at the slightest indication that something was wrong.

Angela's voice came out of the darkness. "God, you scared me!" She stepped into the moonlight that poured through the café curtains. "I aged ten years!"

"Sorry." He allowed himself to relax, muscle by muscle. "Why are you standing in the dark?"

"I thought I heard something outside."

His heart, which had just started to slow down, sped up again. "Where?"

"Out by the garage. I'd just come down to get a glass of ice water when I heard it."

Emma and Gage had a detached garage. It occurred to him that if Manny was looking for a car with Florida plates, he might well check the garage. In which case, Manny hadn't noticed Rafe's car parked on the street in broad daylight.

No, he couldn't believe that. Florida plates in Wyoming at this time of year were probably as rare as dodo birds. His car would have stuck out like a sore thumb, parked across the street from the courthouse square. In fact, that might have been why Manny was standing there in the square when he saw him.

So maybe someone had innocently told Manny where he was staying? Rafe didn't have as much confidence in the local closed-mouth policy as Gage did. Why would anyone around here care about protecting a stranger?

"You stay here," he said to Angela. "Watch from the window and shout for Gage if you see anything. I'm going out to check."

"No!" The word burst from her, and she crossed the kitchen swiftly, laying her hand on his arm. "No, Rafe! He might have a gun!"

"I don't think Manny's that stupid." But he thought of his own gun up in his bedroom and considered going up to get it. Then he decided against it. If Manny was out there prowling, he wanted to catch him at it, not give him a chance to get away.

"I'll be okay. He won't be expecting me."

"You can't get out the back door without it creaking, Rafe. You know that."

"I'll go out the front."

He covered her hand briefly with his, then left her, thankful that he hadn't been able to read her face in the pale moonlight.

It was cold outside. The night air struck him like an icy slap as he slipped out the front door. He was wearing nothing but a pair of jeans, and his Florida-thinned blood was shocked by the unaccustomed chill.

He ignored it. Moving silently on bare feet, he crept down the porch stairs and slipped around the side of the house toward the garage. The moonlight was brighter outside, bright enough that he could see every detail. What he couldn't see was inside the garage.

Creeping toward it, his every sense on red alert, he scanned the surrounding bushes and the shadows beneath the trees. Nothing.

He stepped on a piece of gravel, bruising the arch of his foot, and paused as a wave of pain shot through him. But he'd long since learned to keep quiet even when something hurt, and no sound escaped him. He was uneasily aware of how visible he must be, standing frozen in a puddle of moonlight between the trees.

But nothing happened. No one suddenly leaped out of the

shadows; no gunshot ripped the night silence. There was no sound except the rustling of the wind in the trees.

He reached the garage door in another couple of steps. Checking the lock, he found that it was tight. No sign of tampering. The only other way to get in was through the side window.

Moving carefully, he crept alongside the building until he reached the garage window. Here the moonlight aided him, pouring through the window, illuminating the interior.

The window was tightly closed, and nothing was out of place inside the garage. Emma's car was tucked in there, leaving little room for anything else. Someone could be hiding behind the car, he supposed, but he would have to wake Gage up to get the key to check.

He tried the window; it didn't budge. Examining the frame, he couldn't see any sign that it had been tampered with.

Turning, he leaned back against the side of the garage, away from the window, and listened for any sound of movement from within.

A minute passed. Then another.

Then, without warning, a brilliant light blinded him.

"This is the police," said a voice over a loudspeaker. "Put your hands up and don't move."

Rafe didn't know whether to laugh or swear. He was pinned by the spotlight beam from a police car on the street, mistaken for a prowler. Lifting his hands, he faced the car and waited.

Angela came flying out the back door of the house, robe flapping around her, giving the whole world a view of long, graceful legs. Rafe no longer wondered if he should swear or laugh. He started laughing.

"It's all right," Angela called to the police officer who was climbing out of his car. "We heard a noise. He was just investigating!"

Lights were beginning to turn on in the houses next door and across the street. Any minute now this was going to turn into a circus, Rafe thought, laughing again.

"I don't see what's so funny," Angela said, standing on

the sidewalk beside the house, hugging herself against the cold. The deputy didn't turn off the spotlight, though. He approached them, his hand on his nightstick.

He was a huge man, Rafe realized as the cop came closer. At least six-five, with long inky hair and an exotically chiseled face.

"Hi, Micah," Angela said, shivering. "It's okay. This man is a houseguest of the Daltons."

The deputy paused, looking him over from eyes so dark that the spotlight didn't even seem to reflect in them. Then he looked at Angela.

"Angela Jaynes?"

"That's right. We met at Nate's house a few years ago."

The deputy nodded, then scanned Rafe from head to foot one more time. "You must be Ortiz."

"That's me." Rafe put his hands down. "Angela heard a noise from the garage. I was checking it out."

"Seems like you've got more important things to be protecting," the deputy said levelly. "Next time, pick up the phone and call us."

Then, without another word, he walked over to the garage and shone his flashlight in through the window. "Better get Gage," he said to Angela. "We need to look inside."

But almost before he finished speaking, Gage emerged from the house wearing nothing but jeans and his boots.

"What's going on?" he asked. "Howdy, Micah."

"Gage." The big man nodded. "Noise from the garage. Got a key?"

"Just a second."

Micah's gaze drifted back to Rafe. "This department doesn't have anything more important to do right now than make sure you, your kid and the Daltons stay safe. You follow?"

Rafe nodded. "Sorry. I didn't want him to get away."

Angela stepped closer to Rafe, wanting to defend him but not knowing how. "It's my fault. I should have called. I just wasn't sure what I heard, and I didn't want to raise an unnecessary hullabaloo.''

Micah's granite face cracked just a little bit. "Really." He waved toward the neighborhood where a crowd was collecting. "Seems like we raised more than we would have if you'd just called.''

Rafe started laughing. "Sorry," he said. "It's...ridiculous.''

At that, even Micah smiled. Gage appeared with the key in one hand and his pistol in the other. He'd donned his bullet-proof vest.

"Let's check it out," he said.

He was just unlocking the garage door when Emma stuck her head out. "Rafe? The baby's crying. Want me to get him?''

"If you wouldn't mind, Emma. He probably needs a change and a bottle.''

"I think I can handle that." She disappeared back inside, and Rafe looked at Angela.

"Next time," he said, "I *will* pick up the phone.''

A laugh escaped her. "But this isn't funny. There might be someone in the garage.''

"I seriously doubt it. Go inside, Angela. You're shivering.''

She shook her head. "I started this. I'll finish it.''

It took Micah and Gage only a minute to check out the garage. They found no one in there. Gage locked up again, and he and Micah rejoined Rafe and Angela.

"Whatever you heard, Angela," Gage said, "must've come from someplace else.''

"I guess. I'm sorry about all this uproar.''

"That's what we're here for," Micah said, touching a finger to the brim of his cowboy hat. "Good night." Then he went to reassure the gathered neighbors.

A few seconds later the spotlight turned off and night resumed its reign.

"I feel like such a jerk," Angela said.

"That makes two of us." Rafe took her arm and guided

her back into the house. "We're all on edge. Jumpy. It's okay."

"Better jumpy than sorry," Gage said as he held the door open for them. "But considering you're the target, Rafe, I'd be obliged if next time you'd wake *me* up to investigate."

"You're right. I'm too used to acting alone."

Emma was sitting at the table with the baby, feeding him a bottle. "We don't know that anybody's a target," she said reasonably. "Not in the sense of being in physical danger."

"The problem, sweetheart," Gage said, "is we don't know *what* the threat is."

"Exactly," Rafe agreed. "Manny Molina is a big question mark. I have no idea how to predict what he might do. I hate that. Here, give me the kid so you can go back to bed."

"I'm enjoying this," Emma said with a smile. "I'll turn him over to you when he's done…as long as you don't mind?"

"I don't mind."

Angela got her glass of water and joined Emma at the table. Rafe sat beside her. Gage leaned back against the counter, loosening the tapes on his bulletproof vest.

Angela spoke. "But didn't you say that Manny isn't involved in criminal activity?"

Rafe's dark eyes settled on her. "Not as far as we know."

"But," said Gage, "we don't know what lengths he might go to get the baby. Or whether he wants revenge on Rafe for arresting his brother. Just because the guy isn't involved in the drug trade doesn't mean he isn't capable of some pretty bad stuff when motivated."

Angela nodded and looked at the baby. "Poor tyke. He's too little to be involved in all this ugliness."

"I doubt he's aware of any of it," Rafe said.

And indeed, the child appeared oblivious to anything except the pleasure of sucking on his bottle. But Rafe felt a twinge of guilt, anyway. This sure as hell was no way to raise a kid. He was going to have to figure out some way of dealing with the Molinas so they didn't become a permanent problem.

Emma turned the baby over to him a few minutes later, then headed back to bed with Gage. With the baby on his shoulder, Rafe paced slowly. "Things can't continue like this," he said.

"No, they can't," Angela agreed. Now that the excitement had passed, she was feeling tired. Maybe too tired? She rose and got herself a couple of crackers.

"You okay?" Rafe asked.

"I'm fine."

"The problem is, I don't really know what Manny is after, or what he'll do to get it. If it were his brother, I'd know exactly what I'm up against, but Manny is a cipher."

"Maybe he really does just want visitation."

"It's possible." He mentally replayed the scene with Manny back in Miami.

"But you can't quite believe that."

"No, I can't. I mean…why not just wait for me to come back to Miami?"

"Maybe he thinks you won't ever come back."

"Possible, I guess." Extremely likely, given the way he'd left town. "But given the nature of my work, I get seriously bent when someone tracks me down like this."

"I can understand that." A small sigh escaped her. "Do you *have* to do this kind of work? I mean… Oh, I don't know what I mean. I'm tired, and it's none of my business. Good night, Rafe. I'm going upstairs."

Did he have to do this kind of work? The longer he was off the street, the less desire he felt to go back to it. The problem was, he didn't know how to do anything else. He supposed the agency could find him a desk job somewhere, but the thought of being tied to a desk didn't exactly appeal to him, either. And unless he dealt with Manny Molina, all these questions were going to be moot, anyway.

Damn, he couldn't have this guy following him all over the world no matter what he was after. Maybe he ought to just go over to the motel right now, roust the guy and have it out with him.

But if he did that, he would never be sure exactly what Manny had come here intending to do. Better, he decided, to just watch and wait. In fact, he'd better call Nate first thing in the morning to tell him not to confront Manny.

Let the man play out his hand. It was the only way they could ever know what he was up to.

Then, as he was climbing the stairs to put the peanut to bed, he found himself remembering the nice view he'd had of Angela's legs when she'd come outside earlier.

Man, he really didn't need *that* right now. But the image wouldn't go away. It followed him into sleep, where he had erotic dreams of running his hand up those smooth, lovely legs.

Angela awoke late the next morning. Far too late. Before she even opened her eyes, she knew her blood sugar was low. Irritation filled her. She threw back the blankets, pulled on her robe and stalked downstairs ready to bite someone's head off.

Not that it was anyone's fault. But she was so damn sick and tired of this! She hardly noticed Rafe as she stomped into the kitchen, yanked open the fridge and poured herself a glass of juice with a trembling hand.

Rafe didn't say anything. He was sitting at the table, reading the morning paper, the remnants of his breakfast on a plate beside him. The baby sat in his carrier seat on the table, waving his arms and talking to no one in particular.

Realizing that she'd just burned up even more sugar with her nasty little mood didn't make Angela any less irritated. She sat at the table, feeling the early weakness in her limbs, and tossed down the orange juice like an alcoholic after a long dry spell. Now her entire medical schedule for the day was screwed up and she would be struggling to keep everything in balance until she could get back on track.

"Bad morning?" Rafe asked mildly.

"I slept too late."

"Most people don't get upset about that."

Her tone was acidic. "Most people aren't supposed to take their insulin and eat at eight a.m."

"Oh."

"Yeah, oh."

He rustled the pages of the paper, turning to the editorials. "So," he asked in the same mild tone, "does getting low blood sugar make you crabby?"

She wanted to snarl at him. She settled for more acid. "Just slightly. But what makes me even crabbier is knowing my schedule is all out of whack again, and I've got to figure out some way to keep things in balance until I can straighten it out."

He nodded. "So how do you do it?"

"Do what?"

"Adjust your schedule?"

"I change the proportions of fast-acting and slow-acting insulin."

"Do you know how to do that?"

"Of course!"

"Then I guess you know how to take care of it."

Now she *really* wanted to snarl at him. Couldn't he see what a miserable way this was to live? Of course not. *He* didn't have to deal with four shots a day, four blood tests, blood sugar that was out of control, not being able to sleep late, not being able to...

Her angry thoughts stuttered to a stop. Maybe the orange juice was hitting her system, or maybe she was just seeing herself clearly. Whatever it was, she decided she didn't like herself very much right then.

"I'll be fine," she said, no longer wanting to eat him alive with a side order of hash browns.

"Of course you will. You've been dealing with this for nearly thirty years, right? It seems to me that you must be pretty good at handling it." He smiled at her then.

The urge to kill him came back. How dare he smile at her like that, making her feel warm and beautiful and somehow special?

"Actually," he continued, "I think you're pretty remarkable."

He had no right to say things like that to her, she thought. No right to make her feel this way. No right to make her want to throw herself into his arms until his smile was wrapped all the way around her.

"So go take your insulin," he said. "I'll make your breakfast. Do you want your usual amounts, or do you need to adjust that, too?"

She couldn't think. Measuring her food was the last thing she could focus on right now. "Um...the usual."

"I'll take care of it."

Somehow she found herself on her way back upstairs. Away from him, she was able to think more clearly about how to adjust her dose, but her thoughts kept going back to his strange reaction to her.

He had refused to allow her to wallow in self-pity, but he'd been nice, almost gentle about it. Then he'd commended her for being so knowledgeable about how to take care of herself. This guy ought to run for president. He could charm the socks off a cat.

When she went back down, she was dressed and feeling fresher.

Rafe put her breakfast in front of her at the table. "No running this morning?"

"Thank you. No...everything's too out of whack. I'll just focus on getting back on track for now."

"Good idea. After you eat, how about the three of us take a drive up into the mountains? It's a beautiful day out there."

Which was how she found herself driving out of Conard City toward Thunder Mountain on a beautiful autumn day full of sunshine and chilly breezes. The man should definitely be a politician. Or a nurse. He'd been the one who remembered to bring her travel kit and some food in addition to the diaper bag. The way her head was working today, she would have just waltzed out the door without a thought for them. It was one of the dangers of being diabetic. Even after all these years, she could still *forget*.

Rafe ducked down in the back seat until they were safely out of town; then they stopped, and he joined her in the front.

"Did anything happen with Manny?" she asked.

"I asked Nate to let it lie until we find out what he's up to. Better to know what his plan is. But let's not talk about him, okay?"

"Fine with me." There certainly seemed to be no reason to ruin this beautiful day with thoughts of Manny Molina. She stole a glance at Rafe and saw he was sitting with his head back against the headrest and his eyes closed, washed in the sun that poured through the car windows.

He was so handsome, she thought almost wistfully. No, not handsome, exactly. His face was too hard, and lined from the Miami sunshine. He didn't look like a model or a movie star. But attractive. Very attractive. Hispanic and Anglo blended perfectly in him, giving a dusky tint to his skin and strong features.

She stared down the road ahead of them as the mountains grew closer, but all she could see was Rafe Ortiz's face against the rising wall of blue splendor ahead of her.

The mountain peaks were dusted white with snow, and as they climbed higher she needed to turn up the car heater. When she glanced at Rafe again, she found him staring at her, his obsidian eyes inscrutable.

"Don't stare at me," she said on an uncomfortable laugh.

"Why not? You're the prettiest thing around."

The compliment left her feeling almost breathless. Why would he say such a thing?

"I usually go for dark hair," he remarked, his voice almost drowsy. "But your hair...did you know it's got an almost silvery quality? Like fairy dust..."

She didn't know how to respond to that. But she could feel her cheeks pinkening, and her heart hammered quickly.

"You can't tell it in the house," he said as if he was discussing wallpaper. "But out here in the sun...you've got amazing hair."

"Thank you." The words sounded husky.

"Cute nose, too," he added, a smile in his voice. "Tiny little nose."

"It's not tiny!"

"No, it's just right for you. Not big like mine."

Automatically, she looked at him and found him grinning. "Stop it!" she said, starting to laugh. "You're making me uneasy. And you don't have a big nose."

"I imagine I'd look stupid with a smaller one," he agreed. "Sorry. Am I making you uncomfortable?"

"Yes."

"Didn't mean to. I'm having this problem."

She noted how he looked away from her and realized he was being serious. "What kind of problem?"

"I don't know how to relate to you."

"Why don't you just relate to me like anybody else in the world?"

"That's the problem."

"What do you mean?"

He sighed and closed his eyes. "I relate to types, not individuals."

She thought that over but couldn't make sense of it. "I don't understand, Rafe."

He shook his head a little, then sat up higher in his seat. "It's hard to explain. Don't worry about it. I'll quit embarrassing you."

He'd closed himself off again, and Angela felt a burst of frustration. Every time she started to feel she might actually get to know him, he backed away. But what could she do about it? And what did it matter, anyway?

They found a turnout that announced a hiking trail and decided to stop there.

"We won't be able to go far," Rafe remarked. "Too much to carry, and no convenient way to carry it."

"That's okay." She shouldn't exert herself too much, anyway.

She carried the blankets and her kit; Rafe slung the diaper

bag over his shoulder, took the baby in his arms and picked up the plastic bag holding the food.

It was a perfect day for hiking, cool enough that movement kept them warm rather than make them hot. Sun poked through the pines, dappling the path, and late-season wildflowers poked up here and there, adding color.

A quarter-mile down the path, Rafe pointed out a clearing off to the side, where the grass was thick and the sun bright. "Let's stop there. I wonder if it's okay to build a fire."

"I don't know."

"Maybe I'll skip that, then. Better safe than sorry."

They spread a blanket on the grass and sat on it with the baby. Peanut seemed enthralled by all the colors and cooed happily.

"He's staying awake a lot more," Rafe remarked. He leaned back on his elbow so that he was only a foot from Angela but could still watch the child. "It's kind of neat. When I first got him, he slept so much, it was like he was always a stranger. Now he's awake more and showing definite signs of personality."

"I think kids are born with personality. Not that I'm an expert on kids. But it seems to me that if we were all blank slates when we were born, brothers and sisters would grow up to be a lot more similar than they do."

"You might be right. Nate and I were raised apart, but were both in law enforcement, after all."

"And you both read your magazines back to front."

He laughed and looked up at her. "That's a real kick. Imagine a gene for something like that!"

They'd already had this conversation, and Angela realized they were both stumped for something to say. They were falling back on what they knew to be safe. It was as if there was a brick wall between them.

And Rafe had built that wall, she thought. Then, immediately, she realized that wasn't fair. She had her own defenses, particularly when it came to men, so she kept this wall of reserve between herself and Rafe, not trusting him.

She sighed a little and tipped back her head to let the sun kiss her face. From somewhere she could hear running water and the whisper of the wind in the pines. A perfect day on a perfect planet. The only thing not right was her. And a lot of that was her fault.

She spoke, taking her courage in her hands, needing to cross that wall of reserve. "What you said about reacting to people as types?"

"Yeah?"

"I do the same thing."

"How so?"

"I don't trust men."

He paused a moment before answering. "That might not be so dumb, Angela. I don't think most of us are really trustworthy when it comes to women."

"Really?" She looked down at him. "What about Gage? And Nate? They seem trustworthy."

"They're exceptions. Believe me."

"You don't have a very high opinion of yourself."

He laughed, but the sound contained no mirth. "No, I'm just honest. That little kid lying there proves it. I unzipped my pants at the wrong time, under circumstances that were wrong, and I knew it. I wasn't thinking. And what came out of it? A child I didn't even know about until his mother died. That doesn't really make me trustworthy, does it?"

"But you're taking good care of him."

He shrugged and looked away from her. "It makes me a good actor. Give me a role and nobody can do it better. The kid needs a dad, so I'm being one."

"You're not acting, Rafe. I've watched you with the baby."

"No? Then I'm doing a great job. Living the role of Dad. Just the way I live the role of D.E.A. agent."

"That's not a role. That's what you do."

"Same difference. You know how I see myself, Angel?"

That was the second time he'd called her Angel, and this time she didn't dismiss it as a slip of the tongue. The word settled uneasily into her heart, touching her in ways that frightened her. She couldn't allow that. But she couldn't prevent it, either.

"How do you see yourself?" she asked, feeling suddenly reluctant to pursue this conversation any further. Walls were a good thing, she realized suddenly. And tearing them down was dangerous.

"I see myself as an angel of justice."

She didn't know how to take that. Her response was cautious. "Really?"

"Yes, really." He gave her a sardonic smile. "Sounds stupid, doesn't it? But the thing about angels is that they can't allow themselves to feel anything. Because if they felt anything, if they felt any sympathy for human hopes, dreams and desires, they couldn't do what they do."

"I never saw angels that way."

"Think about it, Angela. Angels are dispensers of celestial justice and wrath. Do you think they could do that if they *cared?* Do you think I could have done what I did to Raquel if I *cared?* I'd never have been able to arrest her brother. I'd never have—" He broke off sharply. "Never mind."

Angela was suddenly finding it hard to breathe. His words were striking her painfully, hitting her in places that she hadn't realized were becoming vulnerable. "I...don't think you're as hard as you believe."

"Really?"

"I've seen genuine feeling in you."

"Don't delude yourself, Angel. Don't trust me. I'm a great actor."

Her chest was tight, her throat growing tighter. She looked away from him at the baby and tried to beat back the dark emotions that were fluttering around the edges of her mind like the wings of bats. She should have left the walls high, she realized. She never should have tried to breach them.

She sat there listening to the breeze in the trees and the aching silence in her heart and reached desperately for equilibrium.

Peanut made some fussy sounds, and Rafe sat up like a

shot, picking up the child, checking his diaper, then changing it with swift practiced motions. Peanut didn't like the cold air on his bottom and began to cry. When Rafe finished buttoning him up into his bunting, he settled down a little, trying to suck his fist. Rafe got out a bottle and began feeding his son.

Angela looked at the two of them, at the gentle way Rafe cared for his son, and couldn't quite believe it was just an act.

But that didn't mean Rafe was capable of caring for anyone else, she reminded herself.

He spoke. "Do you need to eat something?"

It was hard to believe his concern for her was also just an act, but maybe it was. Maybe he figured she needed a caretaker and was fitting himself to the role. The thought angered her.

"I can take care of myself."

"Sure." He kept his gaze pinned on his son. "Just don't wait on me. It wouldn't be polite to have a low sugar attack out here in the woods."

That was blunt enough to take her breath away. "Don't be such a beast!"

"Why not? I am."

She fumed, reluctant to argue any more with him. His nastiness, she had a feeling, might know no bounds at all. And he knew enough about her now that he could cut her to the quick.

Reaching for her kit, she tested her blood sugar. A little low. Making the adjustments was nearly automatic now, though. She could take her regular insulin and eat a full meal.

Ignoring him, she got out her injection pen, walked off behind a bush and gave herself a shot. When she came back, she opened up the bag and took out a sandwich for herself. He could damn well get his own food.

If she hung around with this guy too much, she thought bitterly, she was never going to get her sugar under control. He kept messing it up with all this anger.

When she finished eating, she lay back on the blanket and closed her eyes, listening to the quiet sounds as he cared for his son, then ate his own lunch.

No more talking, she decided. Keep everything on a super-
ficial level, where it was safe for both of them. Apparently
when he started to feel vulnerable, he struck out. And when
she was vulnerable, his striking out hurt her. Bad combination.

The baby apparently went to sleep. She heard Rafe move
but didn't look to see what he was doing. Little by little, the
sun on her face and the silence began to make her feel drowsy.
She felt herself drifting gently. Sleep beckoned, and she was
ready to follow it.

Then something blocked the sun. Her eyes flew open, and
she discovered Rafe lying beside her, propped up on his arm,
looking down at her.

"Sorry," he muttered. "I didn't mean to wake you."

"I wasn't sleeping." Nor was it likely she would now, not
the way he was looking down at her. He had such an intense
gaze; it seemed to bore right into her and touch her in places
she didn't want anyone to touch.

"I'm sorry I snapped at you," he said. "I've been irritable
lately. Must have something to do with my whole life being
turned on end."

She didn't say anything. She wasn't going to talk to him,
she reminded herself. Every time she did, she wound up feeling frozen, cold and alone.

"Don't talk to me," he said finally. "I don't blame you. It
must be like dealing with an angry rattlesnake."

"It's not exactly easy."

He shook his head. "No. It never has been. I've been hearing all my life how hard I am to deal with. Basically, I'm not
like other people."

He said it without any hint of self-pity, as if it were a statement of fact. Perhaps it was that which overcame Angela's
resistance to getting into it with him again. "Who tells you
that?"

"Everyone. My mother. My foster parents. My co-workers.
Raquel."

Raquel. Angela was beginning to hate that name. "What
did she say?"

"That I was a monster. That no real human being could sleep with a woman, then arrest her brother. She was right."

Angela didn't know what to say to that, but she could imagine what a burden it must be for him, especially now that Raquel was dead and he could never rectify what he'd done.

"She was angry," Angela said.

"Yeah, she was angry, but she was also *right*."

"You couldn't be expected not to do your job because you...because you slept with her."

"That's what I thought. Priorities and all that. The damn job always comes first. My mission. My reason for being." He shook his head and sighed. "But she was still right. Not about arresting her brother, but I never should have slept with her. I can't figure out why I did."

"She must have been attractive."

He nodded. "Very. But there are a lot of attractive women in the world. I don't sleep with them."

He was really troubled by this, she realized. For all that he said he was an angel who couldn't feel a thing, he was feeling an awful lot about Raquel and the way his child had been conceived. She had no idea what to say that might comfort him.

"Anyway," he said, "I messed up royally. I wasn't using my brain."

"How did Raquel die?"

"Drive-by shooting."

"My God!"

"She wasn't even the target. She got caught in a gang disagreement when she went to visit a sick friend. They caught the perps. None of them knew her from Adam. Disgusting, isn't it?"

"It's terrifying!"

"There are places in this country," he said slowly, "where hopelessness breeds barbaric behavior. Drugs make it a lot worse, but drugs aren't all of it. There's a resentment of society at large, a feeling of alienation, that leads to the formation of smaller societies. And some of those societies preach a culture of power and death. Tribalism gone bad, I guess. But it would sure help if we could get the drugs off the street. Then there wouldn't be so many kids with the money to buy a gun.''

''It's such a bleak picture.''

''Yeah. It is. Kids want so badly to belong, and they're easy targets for gangs.'' He closed his eyes a moment. ''Once they get in, they find it isn't so easy to get out. One sixteen-year-old that I know of wanted out, so the rest of the gang nearly beat him to death. His family had to go into hiding. Anyway, that's what cost Raquel her life. A damn turf war between two gangs, a dozen kids who are still wet behind the ears. The shooter isn't even old enough to be charged as an adult.''

''I'm sorry.''

''So am I. And I don't want to raise my kid in that. Or anywhere near it. And I certainly don't want him with the Molinas. It's not just their drug smuggling I'm worried about. They have gang affiliations, use some of them to control the streets for drug traffic. Money and drugs can buy a whole lot of influence on the streets.''

''But Raquel wasn't involved in that, was she?''

He shook his head. ''Not with the gangs. Not with the kids whose warring got her killed. When she was younger, she used to be a mule.''

''What's that?''

''She carried drugs from South America into Miami. She was lucky and never got caught. Then she started to grow up, and she backed out of active participation, at least as far as I could tell.''

Angela felt utterly shocked by this glimpse of a world she couldn't even begin to understand.

''It was the Molinas who found her killers. They used their street connections to force the kids to turn themselves in. That wasn't pretty, either. Those kids had to surrender to the law or face street justice.'' He shook his head. ''What a choice for a twelve-year-old—prison or death on the streets.''

''So…you don't really want to go back to Miami?''

''The longer I'm here, the worse it sounds, actually. But

cities are no different anywhere, Angel. They all have these problems.''

"They're not all bad, either.''

His smile was bitter and didn't touch his eyes. "No, not if you're lucky enough to live in a better neighborhood.'' He sighed, then shook his head. "I'm sorry. I'm being a downer.''

"That's okay.''

"No, it's not. We came out here to get away, not worry about problems we can't fix.''

"It's been my experience that trouble follows us wherever we go.''

A short laugh escaped him. "Ain't that the truth.''

Then he lay beside her, clasping his hands behind his head. "I'm glad we came up here. It's easy to forget all the ugliness when everything is so beautiful.''

The minutes slipped by on the buzzing of an insect and the occasional call of a bird. Drowsiness began to steal up on Angela again, and with it came flashing images.

Images of Rafe leaning over and kissing her, that same gentle kiss he'd given her the other night. But in those imaginings, the kiss deepened, became something more than comfort.

Everywhere the sun touched her skin, she tingled, but a deeper tingling began, a delicious, almost forgotten feeling. In the safety behind her closed eyes, she indulged it, letting the images grow and develop until she was on a pinnacle of sexual anticipation, half wishing he would roll over and take her in his arms and half hoping he wouldn't move a muscle.

It had been a long time since she'd allowed herself to feel these things. As much as she might ache for the man beside her, she knew better than to think reality could possibly measure up. Reality always shattered illusions.

So she lay there, imprisoned in a silky web of delicious, nearly forgotten feelings, torn in two directions, and unwilling to open her eyes and shatter the fantasy that she was a whole woman some man might actually want.

But then a shadow darkened her face, and Rafe's voice said, "Angela?''

Reluctantly she opened her eyes. He was leaning over her, a frown creasing his brow.

"You okay?" he asked.

Then, as if someone else owned her body, she reached up and twined her arms around his neck. And she didn't care if it was the biggest mistake she had ever made.

Chapter 7

Angela felt an instant of resistance from Rafe, but before she could drop her arms and release him, he closed his eyes and kissed her.

It wasn't the gentle kiss he had given her before, not at all. This time his mouth settled demandingly over hers. Hungrily. Realization that he wanted this as much as she did exploded in her brain, unleashing all her yearnings like a wind hitting a banked fire. Embers burst into flames.

His chest settled against hers, crushing her breasts in the most delightful way. His hands clasped her head, holding her for his kiss, and she relished the feeling.

His tongue found its way between her lips, past her teeth, meeting hers in teasing strokes that caused her to go weak with longing. The only thought in her head was a single word: yes…

He was drinking from her as if she held a life-saving nectar, with hunger and single-mindedness unlike anything she had ever known. The world faded away, until he was the sum of her universe. He and the feelings he was stoking in her, the sparkling, sizzling flares of desire that were igniting everywhere inside her, sensitizing her every nerve ending to his merest brush against her.

She felt him move, felt him lie over her, between her legs, and she accommodated him, needing his weight on her as desperately as she had ever needed anything. His hardness pressed against her, and she reveled in it.

When he pressed against her again, she rose to meet him, driven by the hard ache between her legs, by a heaviness that needed more heaviness, each movement feeding her hunger for more.

One of his hands slipped between them, finding her breast through the fabric of her shirt and bra, squeezing gently, finding her hard nipple, brushing against it, sending more sparks running through her to join the conflagration at her center.

She ached for him, burned for him, felt everything inside her spiraling downward to the knot of aching need between her thighs. She lifted herself, pressing harder against him. Clutching at his back, she felt the play of muscles, and it only fueled her need.

He was man, she was woman, and nothing else in the world seemed to matter. He swept her higher and higher, reminding her that she could reach the stars if only she would stay close enough to him.

And then the baby cried.

It was just a single whimper, but it acted like a pin on a balloon. In an instant, the two of them froze. Their eyes met, and Angela felt shame pour through her. Rafe squeezed his eyes shut for an instant, then rolled off and away from her, sitting up and reaching for his child.

Angela stared at the sky overhead, wrestling with a maelstrom of emotions ranging from anger and disappointment to shame and fear. How could she have acted this way? How could she have let herself become so wanton?

"I'm sorry," Rafe said over his shoulder.

She didn't want to talk about it. The last thing on earth she wanted to do was add reality to what had just happened by holding a post mortem. "Forget it," she managed to say, her voice thick.

Jumping up, she walked off into the woods, needing the space. Not to see him. Needing not to hear him.

How could she have been so foolish? The man was poison. And even if he weren't personally a bucket of trouble waiting to happen, she knew better than to give another man a crack at her.

Finding a boulder, she sat on it in the dappled sunlight and tried to feel the peace of the forest around her. The wind was becoming chillier, though, and a few moments later the sun disappeared behind the mountain, leaving her in a strange twilight. Without the sun, the day was even colder, and she had no choice but to go back to the clearing. She zipped up her jacket and headed back with a heavy heart.

When she arrived, she found Rafe had packed everything up.

"Time to go," he said, as if nothing had happened between them. "From here on, the temperature will keep dropping."

She nodded and picked up the blankets. They walked back to the car in silence, neither of them making a sound. They were, thought Angela, even further apart than they had been a few short hours ago. And it was her fault. She should never have reached for him.

"I'll drive most of the way back," Rafe said. "If you don't mind."

"No, that's fine." At least she could keep her eyes closed. She passed him the car keys, trying not to let her skin brush his. She failed, and was dismayed when another electric crackle passed through her. She did *not* want to notice how warm and dry his skin felt, how enticing.

When she climbed into the passenger seat, she promptly buckled up and closed her eyes, signaling that she didn't want to be disturbed.

Rafe had other ideas, however. After they'd been driving awhile, he said, "I'm sorry."

She shifted irritably in her seat. "And I said forget it."

"Not until I've said my piece. I shouldn't have let things get out of hand like that. I know better."

"So do I. It just happened. Let's forget it."

He sighed but didn't say anything for a few more minutes. Just as she was beginning to relax, thinking he was going to drop it, he spoke again. "I'm sorry I made you feel bad."

She couldn't imagine how she could safely answer that.

"Hell, I made us both feel bad," he said. "It's never fun to taste something you can't have."

That pretty much summed it up, she thought. "It's okay," she said, deciding she was acting like a child rather than an adult. "I understand why you don't want me."

He spoke impatiently "Do you? That's interesting, because the problem isn't that I don't want you."

"You don't have to be nice to me, Rafe."

"Who said I was being nice? Are we on different wavelengths here?"

Irritation surged in her again. "I guess we must be."

"Apparently so." He fell silent again, and she was relieved to let him.

When they approached town, they switched places, Rafe hunkering down in the back seat. At the Daltons' house, she pulled into the driveway near the back door and climbed out, looking around.

"It's clear," she said, opening the back door of the car. Rafe and the baby disappeared quickly inside, leaving her to carry the blankets.

She pulled the car back out on the street, so Emma could get into the garage, parked it, then went inside by way of the front door.

Rafe and the baby were nowhere to be seen, for which she was grateful. She'd had enough of that man, she decided. If she never set eyes on him again, it would be too soon.

Emma came home early from work, complaining that she felt as if she were coming down with the flu.

Rachel Lee   145

"It's awful," she told Angela, who was reading in the living room. Rafe hadn't come out of his bedroom all afternoon.

"Well, you just go to bed," Angela said, instantly concerned. "Can I get you anything? Aspirin? Chicken soup?" Emma looked awful, she thought, pale, with a fevered look to her eyes.

"I just took some aspirin. I feel like I've been beaten all over and my chest is tightening up."

"Do you need some cold medicine?"

"I have some, I think. I just hope I didn't give this to the baby."

"Can babies that young get the flu?"

Emma shook her head. "I'm the wrong person to ask."

"Well, don't worry about anything. I'll make dinner. Just let me know if you need anything."

"It's better if you stay away from me," Emma said. "You know what happens to your blood sugar when you get sick. I'm just going to curl up under a stack of blankets and feel sorry for myself. I have some chops thawing in the fridge. If you can't find anything, just ask."

"I'll manage, Em. You know that. Did you let Gage know you're sick?"

"I called him before I closed the library. He'll be home at the usual time."

She tottered off to bed. Realizing it was nearly five, Angela went to scope out the kitchen.

Gage arrived a few minutes later and headed straight for the bedroom to check on Emma. Angela couldn't help but think how nice it must be to actually have someone worry about you when you were sick.

"Did I hear Gage come in?"

Angela almost jumped at the sound of Rafe's voice. She whirled around, feeling herself tense at his nearness. "Emma's sick with the flu and went to bed. He went to check on her."

"The flu?" He looked down at the child in his arm. "Oh, great."

"Can babies that young catch it?"

"I don't know. Maybe I'd better keep the peanut upstairs."

"I can bring your dinner up if you want."

His dark eyes settled on her. "No, I don't want you waiting on me. The kid usually naps through dinnertime, anyway."

"Why don't you ever call him by his name? Are you afraid of getting attached?" As soon as the words were out, Angela realized how accusatory they sounded. She braced for his response.

"Actually," he said slowly, "it just doesn't feel right somehow. So I call him Peanut. What's wrong with a pet name?"

"Nothing."

He kept right on staring at her. "Obviously it bothers you, for some reason."

"It's none of my business. But Raquel must have loved you a whole lot to name the baby after you."

His face hardened, and he turned his back. "Actually," he said, "knowing Raquel, I think she was trying to manipulate me." Then he left the kitchen.

God, he was a piece of work, Angela thought. The woman had been dying when she named the child. It was difficult to believe that under those circumstances manipulation had been very much on Raquel's mind. Well, he wasn't *her* problem.

Upstairs, Rafe settled on a blanket to play with the baby and wondered what the hell was up with Angela. Why had she acted as if he was doing something wrong by giving the kid a pet name? And why did she have to say that Raquel must have loved him very much to have named the child after him. That was ridiculous!

He and Raquel hadn't known each other well enough to fall in love. They'd been in lust. That was all. Period.

Naming the kid after him…that had been an attempt to get him to do what she wanted, namely, raise the peanut.

Which was fine. The baby wasn't that much trouble, and frankly, he wouldn't give any child to wolves like the Molinas, let alone his own. She could have called the kid Cuthbert and he would have done the same thing.

But she hadn't loved him. No way. He'd seen the hatred

and anger on her face when he'd arrested her brother. If she'd ever fancied herself in love with him, that fancy had died right then and there.

But Angela didn't believe that, and he couldn't tolerate the thought. God, this was all difficult enough without believing that Rocky had loved him.

Forgetting the baby for a few minutes, he lay back with his hands behind his head and tried to deal with his roiling emotions, most of which were extremely unpleasant. Lately, he realized, he hadn't been liking himself very much, and it all started with the night in the hospital.

The way the doctor had looked at him when she realized he hadn't even known Rocky was pregnant. The way her face had changed when he said he hardly knew Rocky. It was a reflection of how he felt about himself, now that he thought about it.

He had a very strong notion about what a father owed a child, and it certainly wasn't what his own father had given him—which was nothing but life. He'd always hated his old man for skipping out that way.

But—and this was gnawing at him, too—hadn't he been proposing to do pretty much the same thing when he'd come up here? Would it really be any different for him to give the kid to Nate and head back to Miami? Sure, he'd planned to visit often, but the peanut would probably feel every bit as abandoned as he had.

Oh, it was an *ugly* picture he was getting of himself.

Closing his eyes, he listened to his son's murmurs and coos and thought about what kind of man he would like that child to grow up to be. It was. uncomfortable to realize that he wouldn't want his son to emulate him in any way.

He wanted his son to be a better man.

Rolling onto his side, he looked at the baby and felt his chest squeeze tight with something nameless and painful.

Rocky had wanted the boy to be better, too. And there wasn't anybody in the whole world who could undertake that task with more determination than he could.

* * *

Dinner was quiet that evening. Emma stayed in bed, and Gage stayed with her. Rafe and Angela faced each other over pork chops, mashed potatoes and spinach. Rafe seemed reluctant to look at her, and Angela couldn't really blame him. She'd been out of line when she had spoken about Raquel. What did she know about the woman, after all, or about what had happened between her and Rafe? But she couldn't think of a single thing to say that would erase what she had said.

Her appetite was poor, and she had to force herself to eat. One of the downsides of her condition was that she couldn't indulge her moods when it came to food. She couldn't skip meals when she wasn't hungry, and she couldn't binge on double-chocolate mocha ice cream when she got blue.

But the thought wasn't self-pitying this time, it was wry. Wry, too, was the realization that coming here to escape stress hadn't worked. Sitting silently across the kitchen table from Rafe wasn't exactly stress-free.

The kitchen windows rattled suddenly in a gust of wind. She looked toward them, wondering if the weather was changing.

"What's it like this time of year in Florida?" she heard herself ask.

"Hot." He dipped a piece of his chop into the potatoes, then looked at it as if he wondered what he was doing. "Well, not as hot as summer. We're generally in the mid-nineties in the summertime, but right about now we're seeing temperatures in the mid-eighties. Sometimes even lower."

"Sounds good." She was beginning to feel chilly, as if that gust of wind had sucked the warmth from the house. The windows rattled again, and this time she could hear the unmistakable moan of the wind. "We must be getting a front."

"I wouldn't mind seeing some snow. When I was a kid in Killeen, we used to get light snow sometimes in the winter. I can remember maybe a half dozen times. I wouldn't mind seeing some of the real stuff."

She couldn't imagine a life without snow. A life without

winter and all its attendant discomforts and chores. "I hate driving on it," she remarked.

"Then don't go to Texas. Folks there don't begin to know how to handle the stuff. It's dangerous."

"We northerners have to learn all over again every winter."

A short laugh escaped him. "You get a lot of snow where you live?"

"An appreciable amount. I've always wanted to visit Florida, though. When they start showing the ads in the winter, it looks so good, all those palm trees and people in shirtsleeves."

"I can't argue with that."

Another silence fell, disturbed only by the occasional gusting of the wind. Angela looked down at her plate and tried to psych herself into eating some more.

Rafe spoke. "If you ever decide to come to Miami, let me know. I'd be glad to show you around."

She lifted her head and looked at him, surprised. "Thank you. That's a very generous offer."

He shrugged. "I'd enjoy it. You know how it is. When you live in a place you never have time to see the sights. When you have somebody to show around, you enjoy it more."

She nodded. "Thanks."

Gage appeared, carrying his dinner tray.

"How's Emma doing?" Angela asked.

"Not too bad, considering. I need to go out and get her some fruit juice. We're almost out." He rinsed his dishes at the sink and started putting them in the dishwasher. "Great dinner, Angela."

"Thanks. Listen, if you want, I can run to the store."

"Nah. I'll do it." He flashed a quick smile. "Gives me a chance to take care of her."

Angela felt a twinge of wistfulness. "It must be nice having someone to look after."

"It is. It makes life worthwhile." He grabbed his jacket and headed for the back door. "Back in a few."

There was no mistaking the frigidity of the air that blew in during the brief moment the door was open.

"That *feels* like snow," Angela said. She started to get up, to go look out the window, when Rafe stopped her by reaching out and covering her hand with his own. Electric sparks shot through her, so unexpected that she yanked her hand back. Her gaze met Rafe's, and she saw something dark and lonely in his face.

"Eat, Angela," he said quietly. "You know you've got to eat."

"I was just going to look out the window."

"After you eat. You're picking at that like a bird, and you're going to make yourself sick."

She wanted to be irritated with him, wanted to tell him that she could take care of herself. But the truth was, it felt good to have someone care about her, even if it was only the passing concern of a mere acquaintance.

So she remained in her seat and resumed her meal. Rafe rose and walked to the window, looking out. "Weather report," he said. "There are definitely snow flurries."

"Really?" She jumped up and went to stand beside him, pulling back the café curtain to look. Snowflakes whirled everywhere, emerging from the night to sparkle in the light pouring through the windows of the house. "Oh, it's beautiful! It looks like one of those little globes filled with artificial snow."

"It's fantastic."

His tone, she realized, was almost reverential. But before she could puzzle that out, he turned to look at her. "You're not eating," he said sternly.

"Okay, okay." She tried to sound grumpy, but instead it came out on a laugh. And for some reason, she realized that her appetite was returning. She went back to the table and dug in. A minute later Rafe rejoined her.

"How about coffee after dinner?" he asked. "I'll make it."

"Sounds good."

He wasn't at all awkward in the kitchen, she thought as she watched him. But he hadn't been awkward with the baby, either, or anything else she had seen. Rafe Ortiz was a man who excelled at anything he chose to do.

She admired that in people, even if she wasn't that type herself. She tended to be more of a screwup, she thought. She couldn't remember any time in her life when she'd ever made the grade completely.

Gage returned while they were washing up. He stuffed bottles of juice into the fridge, then excused himself to return to Emma's side. "I'm reading to her," he said "It helps get her mind off her fever."

Rafe and Angela looked at one another. "That's nice," they both said at the same time.

Gage laughed and left the room.

"He knows how to love," Angela remarked.

"Yeah." Rafe looked at her. "I'm not sure I do."

The honesty and vulnerability of the remark surprised and touched her. "You love your son."

His eyes widened a little, as if he were surprised, but then he said, "Yeah...maybe I do."

It seemed like a strange answer, but Angela refused to pursue it. She'd spoken out of turn enough for one day. They took their coffee into the living room, turned on the TV and settled on the couch while the wind blew around the corners of the house.

Aware of Rafe only a few inches away, Angela found it difficult to concentrate on the television. It would be easy, too easy, she thought, to lean over a little and touch him. The mere thought made her heart pound, but no amount of telling herself she was being silly would banish the thought.

She had felt his kiss earlier today, had felt his body hard and firm against hers, had felt the rush of sexual excitement she'd nearly forgotten, and apparently neither her brain nor her body was going to allow her to forget it again.

Every muscle in her body seemed to be heavy, and the narrator's voice on the TV was nothing but a string of incomprehensible syllables. Every bit of her attention was focused on the man beside her and what he could make her feel. The memory of that afternoon was so vivid, suddenly, that she could almost feel the kiss of the sun on her skin.

It was both a relief and a disappointment when they heard the baby cry. Rafe jumped up immediately and headed up the stairs, leaving Angela to try to get a grip on her runaway imagination. It was almost embarrassing to realize how aroused she had become simply by thinking about him. She was just grateful that there was no way he could have known what was running through her head.

It had been a long, long time since a man had affected her this way, and she wanted to resent it. The things she dreamed of could never be hers for more than a few passing nights. She knew that. Lance had *proved* that. And even if her illness wasn't a major obstacle, Rafe would be heading back to Miami shortly, and she would be heading back to Iowa. Anything they did now would be no better than a fling.

She didn't want that. She didn't want to use or be used. So what she needed to do was build her defenses as high as she possibly could, as quickly as she possibly could.

Rafe brought the crying baby into the living room. "Would you hold him while I make his bottle?"

"Sure."

Holding a squalling, angry child was a little more intimidating than she had expected. The baby was pushing hard at her with his legs, as if he wanted to squirt himself right out of her hold.

Rafe returned with the bottle, but when he reached for the baby, she reached instead for the bottle. "I'd like to," she said, popping the nipple in the peanut's mouth. He clamped on it instantly, quieting. "This is the only chance I'll ever have."

He sat beside her, bending his leg so he could face her, resting his arm over the back of the sofa. "You really can't ever have kids?"

She shook her head. "Probably not. The risk is just too great, for me and a baby. It seems foolhardy. If I had better control of my diabetes, that might be different, but..." She shrugged and made herself focus on the child's face.

"I'm sorry. I know that's important to women."

"But not to men?"

"Maybe to some. It wasn't something I ever thought about...before."

"It's important to some, all right." The bitterness slipped past her guard and was out before she could stop it.

"What happened?" he asked.

She told herself it would be best to tell him, because she could give him all the reasons he should avoid her, and that would help her keep out of trouble as much as anything she could do.

"I was engaged," she said. "His name was Lance, and he seemed cool with my diabetes. Of course, my control was pretty good at the time we got together. I guess he didn't really understand what it could be like."

She took a shaky breath.

"And then?" he asked.

"Then I got pregnant. It was a nightmare almost from the beginning. I had to start seeing a doctor every week, my blood sugar started going crazy, and finally one day I wound up in the hospital, unconscious in diabetic ketoacidosis—that's what happens when the blood sugar gets really high. I lost the baby. The doctor said he didn't think I should try again. And Lance...well, Lance said he couldn't handle it. He wanted a normal wife and normal kids."

"The bastard."

She shook her head. "No. Really. He was just being honest. And he was right. Being married to me would be like living on a hospital ward. Shots four times a day, meals at regular intervals, no impromptu behavior because it might be dangerous. I mean...I couldn't blame him. I couldn't sleep in on Sunday morning, or decide on a whim to stop and have doughnuts after a movie, or any of that stuff. It was like we were living on opposite sides of a glass wall and couldn't quite get together."

"That's one way of looking at it, I suppose." Almost absently, he reached out and touched a wisp of her hair where it caressed the nape of her neck. The light touch made a shiver of longing run through her. This wasn't working the way she had planned.

"But there's another way of looking at it," he said after a moment.

"Yes?"

He nodded, and this time all four of his fingertips touched the sensitive skin of her neck in a soft caress. "How about that he could have adjusted to your schedule? How about that he could have savored getting out of bed early on Sunday morning to spend the time with you?"

"Are you a romantic?"

He shook his head. "No. Not at all. Just…realistic. Your schedule is inflexible. It *has* to be. So why couldn't some guy turn it into an advantage? Early breakfast over the paper on Sunday morning. Out on the patio, maybe. Bacon and eggs for two. Gourmet coffee."

Almost in spite of herself, she smiled. "You make it sound so nice."

"It could be."

She shook her head. "But I can't have children. That's why most people get married."

"If it is, then most people are stupid."

She didn't argue with him; she didn't have the heart. Instead she looked down at the child in her arms and found herself understanding why people considered having children to be so important. To go an entire life without holding a baby like this…without holding one's own child like this… Her throat tightened with an unbearable ache, and she forced herself to take a deep breath.

"Hey, I didn't mean to make you sad."

She looked at Rafe and saw that his expression was concerned and…almost gentle. "You didn't." She managed a weak smile. "I'm fine."

But he didn't look as if he believed her. His fingers continued to stroke her neck gently, and she found comfort in the touch. When the baby finished eating, she felt a loss for more reasons than one.

Rafe took the child from her. "I need to go change him."

Deciding she couldn't face Rafe again that evening, she went upstairs and closed herself in her bedroom. Never in her life had she felt more alone.

Friday night dinner with the Tates was a pleasant affair. Three of Nate's daughters were there, Krissie, the youngest, who was still in high school, Carol, who was a nurse and married, except that her husband was out of town, and Wendy, also a nurse, who worked in the county's emergency medical services with her husband, Billy Joe Yuma. Rafe was made to feel welcome by everyone, but there was a certain stiltedness to the evening, anyway. Families, Rafe found himself thinking, didn't grow overnight.

He hardly got to hold the peanut, though. Everyone wanted a turn with the baby, including Marge Tate, who told him she would be happy to baby-sit anytime. It was a nice offer, but one he didn't expect to be around to take advantage of.

It would have been the perfect opening to ask Marge and Nate to take the child while he went back to work, but the words never passed his lips. Somehow they had become locked up in his heart, like the memory of something bad.

Later, after the older girls had gone home and Krissie had gone to bed, Rafe, Marge and Nate retired to the den with the baby and cups of coffee.

"Is Emma feeling any better?" Marge asked.

"She was up and around a little bit today, but she's still pretty weak."

"And Angela? I'm sorry she didn't come with you."

"She was feeling a little peaked herself."

"I hope she's not getting sick."

"Me, too." The truth was, Rafe thought, Angela didn't want to spend another minute in his company. She'd been assiduously avoiding him for the past two days. Not that he could blame her. He never should have touched her.

Nate was holding the baby now, and Rafe noticed how safe and secure his child looked in the man's arms. Maybe he could do a lot worse by his kid than leaving him here. But as soon as he had the thought, he battered it down. No. That wasn't going to work. It wasn't fair to the child.

"Well," said Nate, his voice a deep rumble, "I found out what Manny Molina wants."

Rafe felt his pulse speed up. "What?"

"You'll have a deputy serving papers on you sometime in the next few days. I haven't made a big point of saying where you are, but I can't keep it a secret forever, and neither can Gage."

"Papers for what?"

"Custody."

"Oh, for crying out loud!"

Nate smiled faintly. "Exactly my thought."

"He can't possibly expect a court to give the child to *him.* Not with his family. Besides, the courts here don't have jurisdiction. I don't live here."

"He's apparently claiming you moved here with the intent of depriving him and his family of access to the child."

Nate patted the baby's bottom thoughtfully for a minute, then said, "Maybe this is just an attempt to flush you out."

Rafe's adrenaline was now pumping furiously through him, making it impossible for him to remain seated. He stood and started pacing the room. "He can't do this."

"He's doing it. The thing about courts is, they can make your life hell for a long time, until things get resolved. I'd recommend you get a good attorney and try to quash this thing right off. You can probably do that on the jurisdictional issue, if nothing else. But you'll probably have to face it all over again when you get back to Miami."

"Hell." He stopped pacing right in front of the bookcase and stood staring blindly at the titles. "I can't believe that jerk."

"Either way, son," Nate said slowly, "you might want to start examining your life-style, because one court or another is sure as hell going to."

Nate took him and the baby home, but this time there didn't

seem to be much reason to hide in the back seat. One way or another, Manny was going to find out where he was. And since the man had filed a custody suit in the local court, it was unlikely he would come hunting Rafe with a gun. It would be too obvious, and Manny would be too easy to find.

But he could still make life miserable for Rafe.

He was not in the best frame of mind when he entered the house. He desperately needed someone to talk to about all the crazy things he was feeling, but it was late, and everyone was in bed already, even Angela, who still needed to take her eleven o'clock injection, if he remembered correctly. Which meant she must be awake in her room.

He put the baby to bed, then walked down the hall to Angela's room and knocked on her door. When she didn't answer, he figured she still didn't want to talk to him. Reluctant to knock again, he started to turn away just as the door opened.

She stood there, wrapped in her bathrobe, her hair tousled as if she'd been lying down. "What's wrong?" she asked.

"Me," he said. "I need to talk."

She hesitated.

"We can go downstairs if you'd be more comfortable."

But as if his comment made her feel silly, she stepped back. "Come on in." She waved him to the armchair in the corner, closed the door and sat cross-legged on the bed. "What happened?"

"Manny's filed for custody of the baby."

Her jaw dropped; then her blue eyes sparked with anger. "I can't believe the nerve of him!"

"Me neither."

"It's not his child! *You're* the father."

"Yep. I'm sure of that. I had a DNA test."

Her face changed subtly. "What would you have done if it was negative?"

"Hell, I don't know." He rubbed his eyes, then planted his elbows on his splayed knees. "I don't even remember what I was thinking back then. I was shocked. Disbelieving. I mean, she could at least have sent me a note telling me she was pregnant!"

"That's true." She regarded him cautiously, sensing he was on an emotional edge. She had no idea what this man might be capable of when he blew up.

He shook his head. "On the other hand...I figure she planned to raise the baby herself. She didn't want me involved. Not until she was dying and there was nobody else she wanted to have the kid."

"That could be."

"Of course it could be," he said impatiently. "There's no other way to explain it. She hated me. I know she hated me."

"Not entirely."

"Oh, cut it out, Angela. I don't need that crap. She hated me."

"Maybe it's easier for you to believe that."

He swore. "You can be a bitch, you know?"

"So can you!"

He astonished her with a wry smile. "That's *one* name I've never been called before."

She flushed.

"I guess I woke you up, huh? You're not in a very good mood."

She sighed. "I'm in a rotten mood, but it's my own fault. Ignore me."

"You just can't get over this thing with Raquel, can you? You can't believe that the woman hated me, not when she slept with me and had my baby. You can't believe a woman is capable of that, can you?"

"Taken all together, it stretches my imagination a little." She looked down, then spread her hands. "Okay, I've had a sheltered life. Maybe it was possible for her to hate you. Maybe she did."

"She did. And you know what? That kills me more than if she had loved me."

Her eyes widened as they searched his face. "Why?"

"Because if she had loved me, she would have made some

attempt to get in touch with me after. And things wouldn't have turned out like this.''

"Would you have married her?"

He looked off into space. "I don't know. But I know I would have taken her away from there. I know she wouldn't have been someplace where she could be shot.''

Which, he realized miserably, was tantamount to admitting he had cared about Raquel, something he'd been steadfastly denying for a year now. Oh, it was not at all a pretty picture of himself.

"You cared about her, didn't you?" Angela said softly.

"Yeah." He swallowed some indefinable emotion, and cleared his throat. "Yeah. A little." He didn't want to admit it to her, but he'd never been much for lying, except to himself, apparently.

"So why didn't *you* get in touch with her afterward?''

"You make a habit of asking impossible questions?''

She shrugged a shoulder, as if she didn't care. "You want to talk about this, I'm not going to pull punches. Your call.''

He sighed and raked a hand through his hair. "Okay. Hell, I guess somebody ought to ask tough questions. God knows, I've been avoiding them for too long.''

"So why didn't you get in touch with her?''

"Because she hated me. I saw the look on her face. There's no way on earth we could have had anything together, not after the way I betrayed her.''

"Are you sure she didn't betray *you?*''

He stared at her, trying to read her expression, feeling slightly disoriented by the direction of her questions. "What do you mean?''

"Well, she turned on you after you arrested her brother. But didn't you tell her at the outset you were a D.E.A. agent?''

"She didn't believe me.''

"How can you be sure of that?''

He almost gaped at her. This woman's thought processes seemed to be leaping all over the place. He almost got up and

walked out in disgust, but curiosity overrode his other feelings.
"What are you talking about?"

"Well, knowing you were a D.E.A. agent, she shouldn't
have been surprised that you arrested her brother. She must
have *known* you were going to do the right thing."

"With the Molinas, the right thing is always standing by
your family, no matter what they do. Even if she believed me,
she must have thought I wouldn't arrest her brother."

"Hmm." Angela shook her head slowly. "Let's try this
from a different angle. Keeping in mind, of course, that family
solidarity couldn't be *everything* to Raquel, considering that
she gave her son to *you,* not her brother."

That statement hit him with all the force of a blow. The
inconsistency in Raquel's behavior suddenly seemed as obvious to him as if it were painted orange. A few minutes passed
before he could bring himself to speak. "Where does this get
me?"

Angela tucked her robe more tightly around her legs.
"Well...what occurs to me first is that she believed you were
D.E.A., and that she was using you to break away from her
family. Maybe she wanted out of the whole drug-running mess
and saw you as a lifeline."

He thought about it and didn't like the way it made his gut
twist. "Then why was she so angry when I arrested her
brother?"

"Maybe it was an act. Or maybe she'd been hoping you'd
arrest *her.*"

"I doubt that, Angel. Do you have any idea what a federal
trafficking sentence looks like? She'd have been signing away
the rest of her life."

"So maybe she was just pretending to hate you so nobody
else in the family would see how relieved she was. I'm guessing what you did put paid to the Molinas' business."

"For now, at least."

"So she was out of it. And maybe that's what she wanted.
And maybe she used you to achieve that, then betrayed you

by turning her back on you once you gave her what she wanted.''

He was feeling stunned. This woman had taken everything he thought he knew about the situation and twisted it around into a whole new landscape. Had he been duped? Had Raquel really been that calculating? He couldn't believe it.

But he couldn't dismiss it, either.

"I don't know,'' he said finally. "I don't know.''

"Well, I could be all wet. It's just that what you've been saying didn't add up for me. And I keep remembering what you said about Raquel not wanting her baby to be raised by her family. That sounds like a woman who wanted out.''

He nodded slowly, absorbing the ideas she had presented a little at a time. He had been so sure…and now he wasn't sure of anything at all.

But he hadn't been sure of anything at all since he'd found himself holding a newborn son he'd never expected. Everything that had been secure and solid in his life had, in that instant, become shifting sand.

Rising from the chair, he walked over to the window and pulled back the curtain, staring out at the darkness.

"Should you do that?'' Angela asked. "Manny might see you.''

"It doesn't matter. Since he filed the custody suit, he's the last person I need to be afraid of. He's too obvious now.'' Which for some reason didn't make him feel any better. There were all kinds of threats, and Manny's latest action was a threat that seemed bigger than looking down the barrel of a gun. He couldn't say why—or maybe he didn't want to.

"Parents have rights that exceed those of other relatives,'' she said in a reassuring tone.

"Except when the parent is unfit.''

"You're not unfit!''

"No?'' He dropped the curtain and turned to look at her, a grim smile on his face. "How is it going to look in court when it comes out I never even knew the kid's mother was pregnant?''

"You couldn't know if she didn't tell you."

"But *why* didn't she tell me? All kinds of suppositions can be made about that. And then there's this whole trip up here. At least one person could be called to testify as to my reason for looking up Nate."

"He's your brother."

"You know why I came up here, Angela? It wasn't just to find my missing brother. No. The reason I came was because I figured I could dump the kid on Nate and get back to my real life."

She looked shocked. Her blue eyes grew huge, and her mouth tightened. He'd seen that look before, on a doctor's face. There must be something to it, he thought. Two women had now looked at him with that same disapproval. One, he might dismiss, but two made a trend.

"And now you can testify to the same thing," he said. He didn't know what he expected her to say, or if he expected her to reply at all. He didn't wait around to hear. A moment later he was out of her room, closing the door behind him.

Well, he thought, he'd put her in her place. She wouldn't give him any more of those yearning looks that were grating along his nerve endings.

But that didn't make him feel any better, either. Back in his room, he sat in the chair beside the portable bed, and watched his son sleep.

Manny might get the kid. And if he did, Rafe had no idea what he was going to do.

Chapter 8

Morning dawned gray and cheerless, with occasional snow-flakes falling from an angry sky. The wind had a raw bite to it, and after her run, Angela was relieved to come indoors. Emma had felt well enough to go to the library that morning, and Gage had gone with her, apparently not as convinced as Emma that she was back up to par.

The house seemed to echo with silence. Rafe was up in his room with the baby. She hadn't seen him this morning at breakfast and had the feeling he was avoiding her after last night.

Not that she could blame him. She'd said some things that couldn't have made him feel very good, and he'd admitted something that she strongly suspected made him ashamed.

She had the worst urge to make him feel better, but she had no idea how to go about it. She'd been shocked last night when he'd said he'd planned to give up his son, and even though she was sure he no longer intended to do that, she was still horrified that he'd even thought of it.

Which wasn't really fair, she told herself as she sat in the kitchen munching on crackers and sipping hot tea. Just because she wanted a child so badly that she ached with the longing didn't mean everyone else had to feel the same way. In all fairness, Rafe had had a stunner dumped on him. It wasn't really unreasonable that he'd sought some way to avoid giving up everything he'd worked for, especially when he was still trying to get used to the idea. And he would have been a saint if he hadn't felt some resentment when it happened.

Sighing, she looked out at the bleak gray day and thought of the man and child upstairs. They were, she thought, more alone than anybody she'd ever known. They had no friends, and even the blood relationship with Nate would have to be hammered out over time before it could offer the kind of security most people took for granted in familial relationships—or even in friendships.

It wasn't her problem, she reminded herself, but she'd always been one to worry about other people, even people she didn't know very well, like her clients at the bank. God, she'd spent so many nights sitting awake trying to figure out a way one family or another could avoid losing their farm. Her boss had kept telling her it wasn't her problem, except to clear the bank's books, but she couldn't look at it that way.

She sighed again and put away the crackers. It did no good to think about it. It was behind her, and now she needed to focus on making a new, better life for herself.

But instead of thinking about her options, she found her thoughts turning back to the man and child upstairs. Bad as her situation might be, Rafe's was worse.

The phone rang, and she answered it. "Dalton residence."

"Hi, Angela," Emma's warm voice said over the phone. "How's it going?"

"Just fine, Emma. Are you feeling okay?"

"Fit as a fiddle. Gage is hovering, and I'm enjoying it." She laughed. "Listen, I was just thinking, we haven't really done anything interesting since you arrived. How about a trip into Casper on Monday? I've got the day off, and we could do some shopping."

"Sounds great to me."

"Good! That makes me feel even better. I haven't done any girl shopping in ages. Gage tries, but the whole mall thing bores him after a while."

"Well, wear your track shoes. I haven't been to the mall in ages." She hadn't felt like it in months. It had seemed like too much effort.

"Just what I had in mind. Well, I've got to get back to work. This weather has got people interested in books again. Oh, could you take the two steaks out of the freezer and thaw them?"

"Sure."

After she hung up, Angela pulled the steaks from the freezer and set them on the counter. Then her thoughts rolled back around to Rafe. He had to be feeling awful. But maybe he was just asleep? He might have been up really late last night, worrying.

It was nearly eleven, and she decided to risk it. First she showered and changed into jeans and a sweatshirt, then she knocked on his door.

He answered it, wearing nothing but a pair of sweatpants that looked as if they'd seen better days many years ago. His dark hair was tousled, and his eyes were puffy.

"I'm sorry," she said. "Did I wake you?"

"I was just getting up. Something wrong?"

Now that she was facing him, she didn't know what to say. Coming up here to cheer him up had seemed like a great idea until she was actually faced with talking to him. He was so imposing, and the bare expanse of his chest prodded her thoughts in directions she did *not* want to go.

"I was, um, just concerned about you."

"I'm fine."

The response seemed to close the conversation, so she started to turn away, but he reached out and touched her shoulder, stopping her. "Could you do me a favor?"

She managed a smile. "Sure."

"Would you take Peanut downstairs and get him started on his feeding? I really need a shower."

Carrying the baby felt so good, she thought as she took the child downstairs. The little body, dressed in a fresh playsuit, fit beautifully into the crook of her arm, and the little face was bright and alert. Peanut, at least, was glad to be alive this morning.

He also seemed more interested in observing his world this morning than actually eating, although the minute she offered him the bottle he latched onto the nipple as if starved.

She moved to the rocking chair in the living room and rocked gently as she fed the baby, sinking into a rare contentment.

When he was done with the bottle, she put him on her shoulder to burp him, still rocking gently, still feeling more useful and real than she could remember having felt in a long time.

Babies, she thought, had a way of cutting through all the crap. This was what really mattered in the world.

Rafe joined them twenty minutes later, but he didn't seem in any hurry to take the child from her. Instead, he sat across from them, watching as Angela propped the baby on her lap and let him look around.

"He's alert this morning," she remarked.

He nodded. "Bright-eyed and bushy-tailed."

"It seems hard to believe he could be at the center of so much trouble."

"Well, he's not the cause of it. I am."

"You're being rather hard on yourself."

He shrugged. "Just being honest."

"You don't…you don't still want to give him up, do you?"

He shook his head. "No. And certainly not to Manny."

"I don't see how they could find out that you meant to give the baby to Nate. Who else besides me knows that?"

"My boss." He rubbed his chin, a quick, almost irritable gesture. "She thought it was a good idea. I can't work the streets with a baby."

"No..." But they'd already discussed this. "Did she push for it?"

"She pushed me to find a resolution one way or another."

"Have you?"

"I don't know. I can't give up the kid, but I don't want to give up my job, either. Oh, hell, it's a mess. I guess I just need to resign myself to a tame future."

"Is that so bad?"

"I don't know. I haven't exactly led a tame life. I can already feel myself rusting."

She couldn't help it. A soft laugh escaped her. "You don't look rusty."

"Trust me, I can hear my brain cells squeaking." But he smiled faintly as he said it. "Nah, it's not that bad, really. But it's as if the focus of my entire life has shifted. I'm more absorbed in that child than I ever would have imagined I could be."

She looked down at the dozing baby in her arms and nodded. She knew exactly what he meant.

"Let me take him up and change him," Rafe said abruptly. "I'll be back down in a little while. Maybe we can find some way to amuse ourselves on a cold, gray day."

She watched him leave and waited for his return, but the minutes ticked away, and finally she gave up and went to look outside. The flurries were falling faster now, and she felt cold and barren to her very soul.

Life could be so damn lonely.

Gage returned home midafternoon, stepping inside with a blast of cold air. Rafe had waited to come back downstairs until he heard Angela go into her room.

That was the best thing, he thought. She was getting too close to the private places in his soul, and he was beginning to feel as though he'd been hanging his laundry out in the breeze for her inspection. He much preferred it when people didn't know much about what went on inside him. Giving them knowledge only gave them ways to hurt him.

After he had left her to go change the baby, he had realized just how much he was exposing himself and wanted to put a distance between them again. Making her mad at him seemed the easiest way to do it.

But then Gage showed up and blew his plan out of the water.

"How's Emma?" Rafe asked when Gage had closed the door behind him.

"She's fine, just a little chilled. I came home to get a sweater for her. How's everyone here?"

"Asleep, except for me."

Gage smiled. "Well, you can give this to Angela when she wakes up, then." He reached into his leather jacket and pulled out a white business envelope. "It came in the mail today."

Rafe took it. "Sure." Which meant he was going to have to talk to her again, and lately, talking to her had become an orgy of self-recrimination and self-exposure. He wanted to sigh.

Gage went to get the sweater, and two minutes later was on the way back to the library, leaving Rafe to contemplate the depth of silence in a house where two people weren't speaking to each other, and the third one was sound asleep in his travel bed.

His apartment had never seemed this empty or this silent in the days before Peanut arrived. He told himself he was just getting used to all the noise and activity of having a baby.

Except that wasn't true, and he knew it. He was getting dangerously addicted to having someone to talk to. To having Angela around.

He sat in the silence for a few minutes, listening to the hum of the refrigerator and the occasional moan of the wind around the house. The snow flurries had lightened again, but occasional big flakes were still falling. He should have found the sight magical, but he somehow found it as lonely as the silence.

With a sigh, he gave in and took the envelope upstairs. Whether or not he wanted to talk to Angela, he didn't feel right about sitting on her mail, especially an envelope from a bank.

Upstairs, he knocked on her door. She answered almost at once, giving him a guarded look.

"Gage asked me to give this to you," he said. "It came in today's mail."

She took the envelope and looked at it. "My ex-employer. Thanks."

She didn't close the door or turn away, so he hesitated to just leave. Then she ran her thumbnail under the flap and opened the envelope.

Inside, instead of a business letter, was a sheet of notebook paper covered with spidery writing in blue ink. Angela unfolded it, read for a moment, then gasped and dropped it on the floor. She turned away quickly, covering her mouth with her hand.

Without considering the propriety of his action, Rafe picked up the letter and scanned it.

Dear Ms. Jaynes,
You probably don't remember me, but you foreclosed our farm last spring. I want you to know I'm grateful for how hard you tried to prevent it. But I thought you should know, my husband killed himself two weeks ago. I'm not rightly sure what the kids and me are going to do..."

Rafe dropped the letter and reached out for Angela, pulling her into a tight hug. She wasn't making a sound, but he could feel hot tears dampen his shirtfront as he held her. Something inside him seemed to be cracking wide-open, letting pain for her pour through into his awareness, letting it out of the dark place where he kept all his feelings so tightly locked.

"It's not your fault," he heard himself saying huskily. "It's not your fault...."

But still her tears scalded him. When she started to shake like a leaf in a hurricane, he eased her over to her bed and got her to sit. He never took his arms from around her but sat beside her, letting her cry it all out.

"They shouldn't have forwarded that letter, the bastards," he said quietly. "They shouldn't have done that to you...."

"Why not? It's my fault...." Her voice broke on a sob.

"It's not your fault. My God, Angel, you didn't make the rules of that game. The *bank* did. Their shareholders did. You didn't make the drought, or the fall in crop prices, or anything else that led to this. And you didn't make that man kill himself. You didn't hand him a gun or a noose. You can't blame yourself for this. You *can't*."

She lifted her wet face and looked at him. "I do. I had a hand in it. Maybe I could have found some way of preventing all this."

"That woman said you did everything you could. Even *she* knows it. Angel, you didn't deal these blows. Life did."

"I remember the kids," she said brokenly. "I still remember those kids...." She buried her face in his shoulder, and he held her, rocking her gently, waiting for the storm to pass.

He thought about how unfair life could be. Angela didn't deserve to feel this way. She had been no more responsible for that foreclosure and its outcome than he had. She was as much a victim of fate, the elements and bank policies as the family that had lost its farm. Not that he blamed banks for what happened, either. All they had done was bet alongside the farmer that he would have a good crop. The only difference between them was that the bank, unlike the farmer, had a way to collect when the crop didn't deliver.

He tried to express this to Angela but wasn't sure if she heard him. She grew quieter, though, as if she didn't have the energy to cry anymore.

After a while she said thickly, "I need to eat. All this stress..."

"Tell me what you want. I'll bring it up here."

"I have some candy on the dresser."

He was reluctant to let her go, but he went to the bag of

hard candies and unwrapped a piece for her. She popped it in her mouth, sucking on it as she wiped her eyes.

"Are you gonna be okay?" he asked. "Physically, I mean."

She nodded. "I just need to get my sugar up...." Her voice trailed away; then she turned from him and hammered her fist on the pillow. "God, I'm so sick of this!"

He didn't ask what she was sick of. He had a pretty good idea. Between her disease and this damn letter, she had every right to feel that way. He rubbed her back, wishing he could do more to make her feel better.

It was almost a relief when she finally turned to him again and came into his arms. Outside, the wind howled a mournful tune, the perfect counterpoint to what they were feeling in this bedroom. The sound was as lonely as a train whistle at night.

She wasn't crying anymore, and the anger she had been feeling had apparently eased. Her body was soft in his embrace, pliant and relaxed as if she had found a haven. He hoped she had.

And much to his own surprise, he discovered he liked comforting her. It made him feel useful in a way he had seldom felt, useful on an emotional level. Even the baby didn't make him feel this way. The infant was dependent on him for everything, but it wasn't the same as having someone turn to him for comfort.

Which revealed to him a quirk in his own psyche. For the first time in his life, he considered his deepest motivation and realized that what he needed most of all was to be needed. His work with the agency had merely been a form of that, causing him to become one of the best undercover operatives they had. Causing him to make himself nearly irreplaceable.

It was part of what appealed to him about Peanut, too. Nobody else could replace him; he was the child's dad.

Now this. He supposed Angela could replace him with any number of other friends who could comfort her, but right here and now she had turned to *him*.

And that made him feel damn good.

It was also making him feel something else, he realized as

he noticed his body's stirrings. A warm languor was beginning to fill him, thick and sweet as honey. His heart began to beat heavily, and he closed his eyes, savoring the moment.

He had always loved women but preferred to keep them at a distance, ever since he had learned how much they could hurt him, a lesson he had received early in life. But Angela was already past his emotional barriers, already inside with him, and what he was feeling now seemed like the most natural extension of that. It was, he realized dimly, the exact reverse of the way his relationships with women usually worked.

Alarms should have been sounding, but if they did, they were so muffled he didn't hear them. All he knew was that holding Angela felt better than anything in his life had ever felt.

And she seemed to feel the same way. She relaxed into him more and more, and he dared to start stroking her back. Then a thought occurred to him, and though he was reluctant to shatter the mood, he had to ask, "Are you okay? Do you need more candy?"

"I'm fine," she murmured. She started to pull back, as if she realized how much she was leaning on him, but his hold on her tightened, keeping her where she was. She didn't fight him, giving in with a quickness that told him she was enjoying this embrace as much as he was.

And it was she, finally, who tipped her head to look up at him, bringing their mouths into close proximity.

Her eyes were still puffy from her tears, but she was no longer crying. Her lips were slightly parted, as if she were about to speak, but she didn't say a word. She moved not a muscle, hardly even breathed, as if she were feeling exactly what he was feeling.

And what he was feeling suddenly blossomed into full-blown hunger for her. He wanted her over him, under him, all around him, wanted to drive himself into her warm moist depths and forget that anything else existed. His heart jumped to a faster rhythm, and he could feel himself pulsing with yearning. The world began to recede. Even the wind's moan sounded as if it were far away.

Nothing existed except Angela and her soft pink lips only a few inches away. Nothing existed except this woman and her soft, warm body pressed against his.

Time seemed to halt. Dimly he was aware that he was breathing more rapidly, but so was she. The air around them seemed to shimmer, and, faint but distinct, he could smell the sex odors as their bodies awakened.

As his mouth lowered to hers, he realized that he hadn't learned a thing. He was about to make a huge mistake. And he didn't care. He *needed* her.

Her mouth was warm, still tasting of cherry candy. The minute his lips found hers, she opened to receive him, apparently hungering for him as much as he hungered for her. The realization fueled the heat growing in his groin, and he was perfectly willing to take the invitation. His tongue dipped into her mouth, finding hers and stroking it with sexual promise.

He felt her shiver, and she responded in kind, her tongue darting against his, her hands suddenly clutching at his back as if she was afraid she would fall.

She ought to be afraid, he thought hazily. And so should he. This was dangerous for two people who were so vulnerable right now. Dangerous for two people who had so many reasons not to get involved.

But he was already involved. In a week or so, he would leave and go back to all his problems in Miami, alone. So being involved didn't matter.

It was as good a rationalization as any for what he was about to do. Distance would make him safe in the end, so he could take the risk now.

Somehow they were now lying side by side across the bed, wrapped in each other's arms, kissing with a hunger and desperation that crumbled the remaining barriers. He felt her pelvis press against him, heard her little moans of eagerness, and in response his own heat became blinding.

There would be time later for finesse, but right now there

was no time for anything except getting rid of clothing as fast as possible.

He tore at her sweater, pulling it over her head. He hardly noticed the athletic bra she was wearing; he was too busy clawing at the fastening on her jeans.

And she was tugging just as eagerly at his sweatshirt. He helped as much as he could while he fumbled at her jeans. He kicked his own shoes off while he pulled her jeans down. They caught on her ankles, and he gave them a mighty tug. When they came free, they continued to sail across the bedroom. In one swift movement, he rose to his feet and shoved his own pants down and away, along with his briefs.   .

He was naked at last, and never in his life had being naked felt so good or right. It was as if this moment had always been meant to be.

He paused an instant, just an instant, to look at her lying there in her white bra and panties. She was still a little too thin, but she was beautiful anyway, with curves in the right places and a vulnerability that tugged at some place deeply inside him.

Bending, he tugged her panties off and bent to press a quick kiss on the curly mound of blond hair he had revealed. Then he lay beside her and pulled off her bra.

She caught her breath, and her blue eyes opened a little, looking at him with a sudden uncertainty that moved him.

"I can stop," he whispered huskily. "I can still stop." But he didn't want to. With the small creamy mounds of her breasts only inches away, with the warm, moist depths of her center within reach, stopping was the last thing on earth he wanted to do.

But he owed it to her, if that was what she wanted.

There was a heart-stopping moment when she didn't respond; then she reached out for him, pulling him to her. A sigh of relief had barely escaped him before warm skin met warm skin, setting off explosions of desire in every nerve ending.

Now! The word seemed to explode in his brain. He ought

to take his time, ought to savor every moment, but he couldn't. The need that was driving him was greater than any he had ever known. He found her breast with his mouth, sucking deeply on her already-erect nipple, feeling triumphant when she moaned and arched toward him.

He slid over her, pulling her knees up until she was completely open to him. Reaching down, he felt her delicate folds with his fingers, stroking them gently while he continued to tease her breast with his lips and tongue. She was wet and eager, arching toward his fingers with an unmistakable demand.

He was glad to oblige. He found her opening with his shaft and an instant later was buried inside her. Where he belonged.

For a few moments neither of them moved, as if the sensation was too exquisite. Then, propped on his elbows and knees, he began to move, slowly at first, then more rapidly, as she met him thrust for thrust.

He opened his eyes a little and looked at her, looked down at them joined together, then at her face. Her head was thrown back, her eyes closed, her lips parted and swollen, and soft, delicious little moans escaped her.

They were together in the most intimate way two people could be. Even as passion drove him on an ever-tightening upward spiral, he realized that he had never felt as complete as he did right now.

Then his last thoughts vanished in an explosion that seemed to rise from his very soul, and he heard his own cry echoed as Angela joined him in bliss.

The baby was crying. The sound roused Angela from a place so warm, languorous and deep that it seemed to come from a long way away.

She felt Rafe move, felt him lever himself off her until he sat beside her.

"I'm sorry," he said. She felt him brush a kiss against her lips. "I'll be right back."

She didn't move, didn't open her eyes, listened to the sound

of him padding across the bedroom floor and down the hallway.

His departure left her feeling raw. Embarrassed. Ashamed.
Unwanted. Twisting around on the bed, she crawled under the
covers and buried her face in the pillow, trying not to cry.

This was a serious mistake. She had done what she had
promised herself never to do again. And instead of savoring
the afterglow, she was achingly sad, empty, and angry at herself. And so very alone. More alone than she had been in her
entire life.

He wouldn't come back, she thought. The baby was just a
good excuse to do what he wanted to do—get away from her.
Then she wondered why she was reacting so emotionally. She
had *known* there could never be anything between them but
sex, but she'd gone ahead and made love with him, anyway.
What was she blaming *him* for? Her own stupidity?

"You okay?"

She nearly jumped out of her skin when she heard Rafe's
voice. Turning her head quickly, she saw that he was standing
naked beside the bed, holding the baby and a bottle.

"Sorry I was gone so long," he said, as if he could read
the raw emotions she was feeling on her face. "Peanut was
hungry."

She managed a jerky nod and pressed her face into her
pillow again. She heard the bedsprings creak and felt the mattress dip as he sat. A moment later he was beneath the covers
with her, and the baby was tucked between their naked bodies.
She looked, and found Rafe lying on his side, propped up on
his elbow, feeding his son and looking at her.

This was too intimate, she thought, the baby between their
naked bodies. Too intimate. This was a place visited only by
married couples who shared a deep commitment. This
was...this was something she had thought she would never
know.

But she knew it now, and almost in spite of herself, she
rolled onto her side and let herself feel the baby against her
bare skin. He was wearing his playsuit, but that didn't matter.

He was a baby, and as if he were her very own, she was holding him against her breast.

A shaft of unanswerable longing ripped through her, leaving her bleeding in her very soul. But she couldn't make herself move away. Couldn't make herself destroy this perfect intimacy.

"I'm sorry," Rafe said again.

"For what?"

"Leaving you like that. It was bad timing. But one thing I've discovered is, babies are born with bad timing."

Almost in spite of herself, she smiled. Something about the child against her was making her feel at peace again, as if somehow this would all be right in the end. And right now, she didn't want to think about any other possibility.

What she wanted to do was lie there and pretend she had a right to this. That this was her baby, her husband, her life. For just a little while, she wanted to live in a fool's paradise.

"Yes," she said, "they have bad timing. But they're so absolutely perfect, anyway, aren't they?"

He smiled back at her. "I kinda think this one is."

Peanut finished his bottle, then wanted to play for a little while. They lay on either side of him, pushing back when his little feet shoved against their hands, letting him grab their fingers, listening to him coo his sheer delight in life.

"I hope he can always be this happy," Angela remarked.

"He *is* a happy kid, isn't he?"

"He certainly doesn't cry as much as some babies I've seen."

"No, he's never done much of that. A little when he wants to be fed, or when he needs changing, but otherwise, he seems pretty content with life."

"Don't you wish you could be like that? I do."

His smile deepened. "Maybe we'd be like that if we spent our waking hours lying on our backs and cooing, instead of doing all the other stuff we do."

She had to chuckle. "Yeah, I guess. Earning a living and all that kind of stuff kind of takes the glow off, doesn't it?"

"Sometimes."

Peanut grabbed her finger and hung on to it, jerking it around in the air as he waved his arms. He was looking so intently at her that she finally bent and kissed him on his soft little forehead.

"You'd make a good mom, Angela. You know that."

There was a husky note in Rafe's voice that made her look at him. But before she could fully read his expression or ask what he meant, he rolled out of bed and picked up the sleepy baby.

"I'm putting him back to bed," he said, and disappeared.

Too close, Angela though. They were getting too close, and he felt as unhappy about that as she did. Suddenly furious at him, at the whole damn universe, she jumped up from the bed, picked up his clothes, tossed them out into the hallway, and closed and locked her door.

Then, grabbing a piece of candy to suck on, she thought about just how rotten life really was.

When Rafe found his clothes in the hallway outside Angela's closed door, he didn't know whether to laugh or get mad. "Damn prickly pear," he muttered, then felt a bubble of laughter rising from the pit of his stomach.

God, she was a case. But so was he. And he supposed she had even more reasons to be wary of him than he had to be of her. After all, she'd lost her fiancé and her baby, and she'd listened to him talk about how he had treated Raquel. That closed door, and his clothing scattered in front of it, was about what he deserved.

Well, he thought, it wasn't the first time in his life he'd been a jerk. He just hoped that he hadn't made Angela pregnant, because the last thing on earth he ever wanted to do was put her through another loss like that.

Grabbing his clothes, he pulled them on. Despite the central heating, the house was drafty and cool, and getting draftier as the day outside grew colder. He went downstairs to make a pot of coffee.

He and Angela, he thought, kept getting close, then pulling away as fast they could. Earlier it had been his fault, when he hadn't come back downstairs. In retrospect, that had been as-inine, regardless of his reasons. Maybe he needed to stop being quite so skittish. But even if he did, he doubted it would make Angela less so.

Why bother, anyway? This relationship was scarcely born and bound to go nowhere. But he was still annoyed at himself for giving in to the urge to make love to her. Considering how upset she had been beforehand, by now she probably figured he had taken advantage of her tears.

And maybe he had. Maybe he really was the user that Ra-quel had called him. Maybe he took from people what he wanted, then moved along unscathed.

Maybe he was just about the most disgusting slug a person could be.

He was just pouring his cup of coffee when a hammering summoned him to the front door. He went to answer it and found a deputy standing there.

"I'm looking for Rafael Ortiz," he said.

"That's me."

The deputy handed him a thick envelope. "Service of court papers, sir." He nodded, turned and walked down the steps and back to his car.

Rafe stood in the open doorway, letting the icy wind blow around him, looking down at the envelope in his hand. The rage that filled him knew no bounds.

"Rafe?" Angela's tentative voice came from behind him. "Rafe, what is it?"

He turned, slamming the door behind him. "That son of a bitch Manny. I've been served."

"Nate told you this was coming."

"I know." He tossed the papers across the foyer. "But somehow, actually getting served made it real. That son of...I'm going to have his *cojones* for this."

"They'd probably taste pretty good with some salt, pepper and catsup."

The remark came at him sideways, and he gaped at her for a moment before a bark of laughter escaped him. "Yeah. Mustard, too. No, better yet, some really spicy salsa." He swore, but he wasn't quite as angry as he'd been a minute ago.

"Maybe you should read them," she said, indicating the envelope. "Just in case. So you know what you need to do."

"I know what I need to do. I need to get me the best lawyer I can find in this forsaken little burg and get the whole damn thing thrown out."

Her eyes widened. "Can you do that?"

"Sure. I don't live here. I'm just visiting." But he wasn't as sure as he sounded. Inside, the doubts were eating him alive. What he knew—all he knew—was that he couldn't let Manuel Molina take his son from him, not if he had to kill him to prevent it.

"I…" Angela hesitated. "I, um, I'm sorry I threw your clothes out like that. I don't know what came over me."

"I do. That was the smart thing to do, lady. I'm poison for everybody I meet."

Then, grabbing the envelope, he went to the kitchen, leaving her standing at the foot of the stairs, staring sadly after him.

Chapter 9

After a weekend of flurries, snow finally fell. When Rafe woke on Monday morning, two inches of it covered the ground. The sky still looked heavy and gray, and he wondered if there would be more snow before nightfall.

He had expected to be thrilled with the sight, but he hardly noticed it. His mind was focused on one thing and one thing only: dealing with Manny.

By nine-thirty he'd found a lawyer who would talk to him. Not that there were a whole lot to choose among. One said he was representing Manny, and the other said he never did family law. In a town this size, it was surprising that any lawyer wouldn't do everything. Which left Constance Crandall, whose secretary promptly made an appointment for eleven.

And that kind of worried him, the quickness of that appointment. In Miami, he would probably have had to wait days to be seen. So this Crandall woman wasn't all that busy. Which might not be a good thing.

But what else was he going to do?

When Angela returned from her morning run, her cheeks reddened from the cold, he swallowed his pride and asked her to watch the baby while he went to the attorney's office.

"I can drive you," she offered.

He shook his head. "It's only a couple of blocks, and I don't want to take Peanut out in this if I can avoid it." He hated the way her face softened when he said that, as if he were doing something special. He wasn't doing anything special, just being practical.

And how was he going to deal with all this crap when he got back to Miami? Where was he going to find someone who could baby-sit at the drop of a hat? Someone he trusted the way he trusted Angela?

But he couldn't think about that now. Right now he had to think about keeping the baby so he could deal with all the problems the kid was going to create. What was wrong with this picture?

Feeling crabby, he dressed as best as he could for the cold, then stepped into the freezer that Wyoming had become. He supposed it didn't seem all that cold to the locals, but he felt as if his skin was going to freeze. His feet even got cold through the soles of his shoes as he walked over the dry, powdery snow. And his pockets weren't deep enough to keep his hands warm. Why would anyone want to live like this?

Constance Crandall's office was in one of the big houses near Front Street. When he stepped inside, the warmth of the central heating made his cheeks burn. The secretary, a middle-aged woman with a no-nonsense attitude, offered him coffee. He accepted it gratefully, needing to get warmth any way he could. When the coffee came in a ceramic mug instead of a foam cup, he wrapped his frigid fingers around it gratefully. Miami had never looked so good.

Ten minutes later he was ushered into the attorney's office, a pleasantly appointed, large room with stacks of papers and books everywhere. What he liked most was the fireplace, where a fire was burning cheerfully, heating the room.

Constance Crandall was a young woman with a mane of

dark brown hair and bright green eyes that looked at him from behind thick lenses. Her youth unsettled him.

"How long have you been in this business?" he asked bluntly.

"A year." She didn't seem to take the question amiss. "I passed the bar a year ago."

"You feel up to this case?"

"I concentrated on family law in school, and I've handled six custody cases in the past year."

Six didn't sound like a whole lot. On the other hand, what else could he do? He passed her the papers he'd received. "This guy is my kid's uncle. He wants to take the baby away from me."

"The law tends to uphold the rights of the parents over the rights of other relatives, Mr. Ortiz."

"Hmm."

She read through the papers more quickly than he had. He didn't know if that was good or bad. But maybe she knew what was important and what wasn't.

She looked at him. "He lives in Miami. What about you?"

"I live in Miami, too."

"Well, Wyoming doesn't have jurisdiction, then. Jurisdiction in these matters is decided by the child's home. But that will just move the problem to Miami. How do you feel about that?"

"Six of one, half dozen of another," he admitted reluctantly. "I guess I'd just like to get this mess out of my hair."

"Let's talk about it, then. Maybe we can figure out a way to deal with it right now. Is there any way you could reasonably say that this is the child's home, rather than Miami?"

Rafe hesitated. "Would it be to my advantage to do this here?"

"Any more advantageous than doing it in Miami? That depends. It'll get done faster—our dockets aren't as full, I'd imagine. And folks around here tend to be pretty strong on parental rights. But if you could give me some reason why a local judge or jury would instinctively want to favor you over the plaintiff, we might be getting somewhere. Do you have relatives here?''

When he hesitated yet again, she said, ''Remember, anything you tell me is covered by attorney-client privilege. I *can't* tell anyone else.''

''Nate Tate is my half-brother,'' he said. ''That's why I came here to visit. I thought he could take the baby…until I get my job sorted out.'' Which was shading it a little, but what the hell. He couldn't face what he had originally intended to do without having a guilt attack bigger than Wyoming.

That was when she started to smile. ''Nate Tate? Oh, you couldn't have said anything better, Mr. Ortiz. Yes. It would definitely be to your advantage to pursue this here. Now tell me everything you know about Manuel Molina.''

When Rafe got back to the house, he found Angela sitting in the living room playing with the baby. Peanut was fixated on Angela's face. She was whistling softly. And every time she whistled a note, Peanut puckered up and imitated her, making a little whistle.

''Did you see that?'' Angela asked, laughing. ''He's such a smart boy, aren't you, Peanut?''

Peanut made a gurgle that sounded almost like a chuckle.

For a minute Rafe forgot all his concerns, watching with pride and delight as his son whistled again and again in response to Angela.

He also noted how happy Angela looked, how absorbed she was in the baby, and he felt a warm tug in the vicinity of his heart. He also felt strangely envious, wishing she would look at *him* that way.

Finally, she did. Holding Peanut in one arm, she looked up at him. ''How did it go?''

''Pretty good, I guess. It's *cold* out there. If you want to come to the kitchen with me, I'll tell you all about it while I make some coffee.'' Constance Crandall had warned him not to discuss his case with anyone, because they wouldn't be covered by attorney-client privilege, but he somehow felt his secrets would be safe with Angela. He'd never felt that way about anyone before.

In the kitchen, she and Peanut sat at the table while he made the coffee.

"Basically," he said, when he finished and sat across from her, "I told the lawyer all about Manny and Nate."

Angela caught her breath. "Even the part about leaving Peanut with Nate?"

"Even that part, although I shaded it a little, saying I was only thinking about leaving him with Nate until I got my job sorted out. Which is true enough now, because I couldn't possibly leave the kid with anyone any longer than it takes me to get my life organized."

She nodded, but he noticed she was holding the baby even closer, as if the thought of leaving the child anywhere was unthinkable to her. He could identify with that.

"Anyway, she thinks I ought to fight it out here, because any judge and jury in the county would give custody to Nate, or to Nate's brother, in a heartbeat before they'd give it to the brother of some drug dealer from Miami."

Angela smiled, then laughed. "Oh, that's so true! People around here think Nate walks on water. If he says you ought to have the kid, nobody else on earth will stand a chance. Nobody."

Then she noticed he wasn't laughing, and she sobered. "But?" she said. "I sense a *but* coming."

"Well, yeah. I mean, I need to talk to Nate about this whole cockamamie idea I had. You know, it sounded great in Miami, but ever since I got here, it's been looking worse and worse. I don't even want to mention it to him." Crazy as it seemed, he suddenly didn't want his newfound brother to think poorly of him.

Angela's face softened. "I think Nate will understand, Rafe. He's a very compassionate man."

Rafe shook his head. "He'll think I was crazy. Give my kid to a stranger? I *was* crazy."

She looked down at the baby, then back at him. "Do you want *me* to talk to Nate for you?"

He sighed and shook his head. "No, this is one I've got to do myself."

"Well, then, call him and get it done. I don't know about you, but I can't stand having stuff like this hanging over my head."

"Me neither," he admitted. He got up, poured himself a cup of coffee, and was just reaching for the phone when a knock sounded on the front door. "What now? More papers?"

He went out to answer it, and Angela followed into the foyer. When Rafe opened the door, she saw a small, slightly plump, Hispanic man standing there.

"Manny!" Rafe said surprised.

"Rafe. You gonna invite me before I become a Popsicle?" Without waiting for an invitation, Manny pushed past him into the foyer. Rafe gave in and closed the door behind him.

"There's my nephew," Manny said, pointing at Angela and the baby. "Look at that! I knew it! Some father you are! Already the baby's in a stranger's hands. I thought we could work it out, but if you're going to be giving my nephew to strangers—"

"I'm not a stranger, Mr. Molina," Angela interrupted.

"No, she's not," Rafe hastened to agree.

"Then who the hell is she?"

Rafe looked at Angela, and she at him. Then, astonishing them both, Rafe said, "She's my fiancée."

"Your fiancée?" Angela had dragged Rafe into the kitchen, while Manny stayed in the foyer, claiming she needed help with the baby's bottle. "Are you crazy? My God, you're fast with the lies!" She was whispering, albeit angrily, to keep Manny from overhearing.

"I'm used to working undercover. I lie like a snake. I've spoken ten lies for every truth I've ever told." He whispered, too, but she couldn't tell if the spark in his dark eyes was anger or humor.

"You said you always tell the truth."

"Not if my life or the life of someone I love is on the line."

She glared at him. "God. I don't believe this."

"Look, it's just until we get rid of him, okay? Will that kill you? This isn't about us, anyway. It's about the baby."

She looked down at the child. After a moment she said, "We'd better make him a bottle. I don't want to give that worm any excuse to think we're crazy."

He fixed the bottle swiftly and handed it to her. "I'd take him, but I want both my hands free, in case."

She didn't ask what he meant by *in case*. She would rather have his hands free, too.

Manny was still waiting in the foyer, and the look he gave them was sharp. "Lovers' tiff, huh?"

"No," said Rafe flatly. "And I don't think I should be talking to you. In case you've forgotten, we're involved in a lawsuit."

Manny waved a hand. "My lawyer says the judge is going to throw it out and we'll have to take it back to Miami. So who *is* she? Some tramp you picked up?"

Angela's arms tightened around the baby. Rafe, she thought, looked as if steam were about to come out his ears.

"Don't you talk that way about my fiancée. And it's none of your business who she is. What's more, *my* lawyer says the judge *isn't* going to throw this case out. So get your butt out of here, Manny, and talk to my lawyer."

Something changed in Manny's gaze, as if he hadn't expected this response. "Being tough, huh?" he said after a moment. "Well, let me tell you, dumping my nephew on strangers ain't gonna help you in court. Any court."

Rafe didn't say anything. He simply pointed to the door. After a few seconds Manny turned, muttering, and left.

"What an obnoxious man," Angela said when he was gone.

Rafe turned from the door and looked at her. "I was never very fond of him."

"I can see why."

"Listen, about this engagement..."

"There *is* no engagement."

"We both know that, but can we keep that to ourselves?"

She hesitated, looking guarded. "I won't lie under oath."

"I'm not asking you to. We're a long way from anyone swearing to anything, anyway. Just...if Manny believes that, he might be even more reluctant to fight this issue to the bitter end."

Angela had no idea whether she agreed more because of the baby or because of Rafe. Probably a combination of both, but finally she said, "Okay. Now, if you'll take the baby and excuse me, I need to go take my afternoon insulin."

He smiled as he took Peanut from her. "Thanks, Angel."

"Don't thank me. I'm beginning to think I need to be committed."

He watched her go up the stairs and felt a sudden ache in his groin as he watched her hips sway and remembered Saturday afternoon. He wanted her again, desperately, but he didn't dare touch her. How in hell did he get into these messes, anyway?

No answers were forthcoming.

Wanting to cry wasn't going to help a damn thing, Angela told herself as she checked her blood sugar and prepared her insulin. Being angry wasn't helping anything, either. Her blood sugar was way too low again. Damn it.

She grabbed a candy from the dresser, popped it into her mouth and debated whether to take the insulin right now. This entire trip had been arranged to give her some peaceful time to get her diabetes under control, but all it seemed to be doing was putting her back on the blood sugar roller coaster.

Too much stress. Rafe was driving her nuts. She needed to avoid him as much as possible. Imagine him saying she was his fiancée! Of course, that would be the only way he would ever say such a thing, under duress. It was the only way any man would ever say such a thing about her.

She wanted to strangle him. For some reason, just hearing him say that had turned her emotions into a maelstrom.

And if she took her insulin now she would need to head right downstairs and eat, which would mean seeing him again. She didn't want to see him again. Ever.

Liar.

Okay, she was exaggerating. But she didn't want to go downstairs right now and see him. She needed time first. Time to collect herself and get past this need to either cry her eyes out or kill him.

What a set of options!

But one thing was not optional. She needed to take her insulin now, then eat a meal, or she was going to be off schedule for the rest of the day. Giving in, she injected herself, then headed downstairs.

Rafe was in the kitchen, baby in his arm, talking on the phone. With Nate, she presumed. She tried not to listen but couldn't prevent herself. Moving around the kitchen, trying to be quiet, she started to prepare lunch for herself. She refused to make any for him. He could damn well take care of himself.

She noticed her legs were shaky, and she was feeling a little light-headed, but she didn't really pay attention to it. She was listening to Rafe, trying to piece things together. Something about the meeting this afternoon…something about Manny….

She fumbled as she tried to peel a few leaves of lettuce off the head she'd taken from the refrigerator. It fell from her hands, and she watched it roll across the floor. Her legs were shaking, and she reached out for a chair…

The next thing she knew, she was lying on a gurney, wrapped in blankets, snowflakes falling right on her face. Oh, God, she'd done it again. Then Rafe's face hovered over her. "You're going to the hospital," he said. "I'll be there in a few minutes…."

She thought he kissed her forehead, but she wasn't sure. The ambulance doors closed, and she was gone again.

Inside the house, Rafe tore through Angela's purse, looking for her keys. He found them. Damn, he had to get his car out of the impound lot, where he'd let them tow it to keep it out of Manny's sight. He should have done that Friday. Hiding from Manny hadn't accomplished a thing, and now he was without wheels when he most needed them.

God, she'd been so pale. And when she keeled over like that, his heart had stopped. What if she'd been alone when that happened? He couldn't bear to think about it.

The baby. He hated to take Peanut to the hospital with him, but there was no choice. He bundled the child up in winter clothing and set out, scared to death....

Scared to death. The last time he'd gone to a hospital it had been to get the news that Raquel was dead and he was a father. He had a sudden flashback to standing at Raquel's grave with the baby, but his mind played a trick and showed him Angela's name on the tombstone, instead.

"God, Rocky," he heard himself say, "we can't handle this again."

We. He and the baby. Neither of them could sustain another loss. And realizing it, he understood that Angela was closer to the child than Raquel had ever had a chance to be. The baby would probably always miss his mother. They said babies knew their mother's voices and their heartbeats even before birth. But now Peanut was attached to Angela....

He didn't want to think about the psychological problems this kid might have from all this loss. He didn't for one minute believe that babies didn't know such things. After all, he'd been missing his dad his whole life. A man he couldn't even remember.

Which was why it never paid to get attached, right? Right. Peanut was going to have to learn the same hard lesson.

But, attached or not, whether they ever saw Angela again or not, he couldn't stand the thought of her dying.

"She's not going to die," he heard himself saying to the baby. "She's not going to die."

He didn't know whom he was trying to comfort more, himself or his son.

Nate was already there, in the emergency room waiting area. He reached out and took the baby from Rafe so Rafe could unzip his jacket. "They've got her inside," he said. "Doc Randall is working on her."

"Was she awake?"

Nate shook his head.

Rafe took his son back, clutching the child to his chest. He hadn't even brought a diaper bag, he realized. Some dad he was. But the small warm body in his arms was a comfort beyond his ability to describe.

They sat together, the two stranger-brothers. Peanut seemed content to doze in the crook of his father's arm.

"Doc says this won't take long to sort out," Nate said. "I hope not."

"Yeah. I'm not very patient about things like this."

Nate reached out and put a comforting hand on Rafe's shoulder. "It'll be okay, son. She got here fast."

Rafe closed his eyes a moment. "She just fell over. Like a tree falling. And her face was so white...."

"What happened?"

"I don't know. I mean, Manny showed up at the house. I guess it was stressful. She took her run earlier this morning, but as cold as it was..."

Nate nodded encouragingly, so Rafe continued. "I don't know much about this disease, but I'm wondering if the cold didn't make her sugar lower than she expected. Then we had this little argument, and she went upstairs to take more insulin. Then she came down and was making lunch and...bam!"

"I have a feeling that even with the best efforts in the world, this disease gets out of control sometimes. Don't blame yourself."

Rafe looked at Nate, surprised the man had read him so well. "I've got plenty to blame myself for."

"We all do. Which is why we shouldn't go around taking on guilt over things that aren't under our control. What did you want to talk to me about, anyway?"

For an instant Rafe couldn't even remember. Then, in a burst of self-loathing, he told Nate the whole sordid story, leaving nothing out. "Well," he said, "you might as well know the worst. The whole reason I came up here was because I wanted to discover what kind of person you were.''

''Hardly surprising. I'd have done the same thing myself if I'd known about you.''

Rafe shook his head, suddenly hating himself more than he ever had. ''I never would have, except for the kid. I couldn't handle the baby and work the streets, so I thought...I thought...''

''That maybe if your brother was a decent, upstanding person, he might take the baby?'' Nate asked the question, his tone revealing nothing at all, except that the idea didn't surprise him.

Rafe looked away. Hearing his own unforgivable thoughts on Nate's lips didn't make them sound any better.

Nate spoke again. ''But you don't want to do that anymore, do you, son?''

Rafe shook his head, decided he was worm sludge. Lower than snail tracks.

Nate took his hand from Rafe's shoulder, and Rafe felt the absence painfully. Now Nate would tell him just what a bucket of sewer sludge he really was, and he deserved every word of it. He waited for the ax to fall, looking down at the son he couldn't believe he had ever wanted to give away.

Nate spoke. ''Years ago, back when I was still a kid, I got Marge pregnant. I didn't know it.''

Rafe's ears pricked up.

''Anyway,'' Nate continued, ''I went off to war before she knew about it, 'cause I promise you, if she'd told me, I'd've married her then and there if I'd'a had to hold her daddy at gunpoint to get him to agree. But I didn't know, and when she found out, her daddy sent her away to live with a cousin. She was only sixteen, and back then nice girls didn't get pregnant out of wedlock.''

Rafe managed a nod, listening intently.

''So, anyway, her dad threw my letters away, and the ones she wrote to me never got to me, probably because her dad and her cousin were throwing them away instead of mailing them—which is why I still hate her cousin to this day. But that's neither here nor there. I was reported dead, Marge never got any letters from me...so she gave the baby up for adoption.''

Rafe turned to look at Nate, forgetting his own misery for a moment. The older man's face was shadowed with old pain, and he wanted to reach out, but he didn't know how.

"Marge never told me about the kid. Even when I got home. Even after we got married. Her dad told her not to, because there was nothing I could do about it. It would only cause me pain, he said. And Marge couldn't see that it would do any good at all.''

"But you found out."

Nate nodded. "One day, some twenty-seven years later, this young man showed up on my doorstep, looking for his birth parents. That's how I found out."

"My God!" Rafe could scarcely imagine it.

Nate shifted, looking as if he was shaking off a memory. "Anyway, to make a long story short, I got over the fact that she gave the boy up a lot faster than I got over the fact that she lied to me all those years. I could understand why she didn't keep the baby, but I sure as hell couldn't understand why she lied. I made an ass of myself over that, I'll tell you. Had half the county wondering if I'd lost my marbles."

"I can imagine."

Nate's eyes met Rafe's, sharp and intent. "What I'm saying here, son, is that I can understand why you thought of finding someone to take the baby. And you didn't just hand him to a stranger, you wanted to give him to someone you could trust. Nothing wrong with that, not under the circumstances. But I would mightily appreciate it if you'd never lie to me again about important things. Not even by omission."

"I wasn't lying," Rafe said. "By the time I got here, I pretty much knew I couldn't give the kid up, not even to you."

Nate nodded. "Okay, then. I don't see that you did anything wrong at all. Now, if you want Marge and me to take the baby for a few weeks or months while you figure out how to settle things, that's fine. And if you still wanted us to take him for good, we would. We're family, son. We don't leave family hanging in the breeze. It just ain't done that way."

Rafe's throat was suddenly so tight he couldn't speak. He managed a nod and looked down at the baby, wondering crazily if he would ever grow up to be a man like Nate Tate.

The worst part about not being related, Rafe discovered, was that the doctor wouldn't tell him or Nate anything about Angela's medical condition. The most they got was, "She's going to be all right. You should be able to take her home in an hour or so."

"Which I guess is as good as we can ask for," Nate said. He turned to Rafe. "If you want to take the baby home, I'll drive her when they let her go."

But Rafe couldn't bring himself to do that. "We'll be all right. I'll take her home."

Nate nodded. "Okay, then. I'll head on back to work."

"Wait a moment. There was something else I needed to tell you. I spoke with an attorney this morning."

Nate nodded. "And?"

"She says if I say I'm asking you to care for the child for a while, until I get my life sorted out, we can fight the custody case here. And that she thinks there isn't a single judge or jury in this town who'd give custody to Manny when you're an option and I'm your brother."

A smile spread across Nate's face. "That's a good idea. Did you see Connie Crandall? I thought she was smart as a whip. Well, that suits me fine, and I'm sure it'll suit Marge fine, too."

"It might not work, of course," Rafe said, giving voice to his fear. "I mean, I have no *proof* that this is the child's residence, and the judge might just throw it out, in which case Manny can take the case up in Miami."

"It's worth a try." Nate hesitated. "It might also be worth considering whether you want to go back to Miami at all."

Rafe thought about that after Nate left. Considering the way

Manny had hounded him all the way to Wyoming, maybe he really *didn't* want to go back to Miami, where he would be a much easier target. He didn't think he wanted to spend the rest of his life wondering if every time he answered the door he was going to find Manny standing there, demanding to see the child.

And he was beginning to think that Manny's behavior wasn't born of real interest in the child, anyway. He was beginning to think that this was payback for what he had done to Eduardo. Manny probably figured there was no worse way to hurt Rafe than to take the child.

And he was right.

A long time later, Angela appeared, looking rumpled and embarrassed but a whole lot better than the last time he'd seen her. On the back of her hand was a bandage, probably from an IV.

"I'm sorry," she said as soon as she saw him. Now she looked miserably embarrassed.

"What happened?"

"My blood sugar got too low and I didn't pay enough attention to it." She tried to shrug it off. "Stupid, huh?"

Still holding the baby, he reached out and took her unbandaged hand. "It's not stupid at all. We had a lot going on. But I'll tell you what *is* stupid. I didn't think to bring a jacket for you, and it's colder than hell out there."

"I'll be okay."

"Let me give you my jacket."

She shook her head. "I'm more used to the cold than you are. If you just want to warm the car up a little and pick me up at the door, I'll be fine."

"Okay. You want to hold the baby while I do that?"

She seemed surprised that he asked, and that struck him as odd.

"Are you sure you want to trust me?" she asked finally.

"Trust you? Of course I trust you."

"After the way I passed out…"

He shook his head, pointed her to a chair, made her sit and

put the baby in her arms. "I have a feeling your blood sugar is just fine right now, so don't argue with me and make it fall again."

Then he left her, glancing back just long enough to see the bemused expression on her face as she looked down at the child in her arms.

Before darkfall, an early snowstorm hit Conard County. Unexpected piles of the cold white stuff began to drift across the streets and along the buildings. After dinner, Rafe and Gage went out to the store to get some supplies in case the roads wound up being closed. Alone with the sleeping baby, Angela and Emma made cups of herbal tea and settled in the living room to listen to the wind howl.

"This was only supposed to be a flurry," Emma remarked, looking toward the window as snow rattled against it.

"Somebody fooled the weatherman."

Emma laughed and sipped her tea. "I like it when it gets like this. At least early in the winter. Along about March I'm sick of it, but right now it feels cozy, and it's making me think about Christmas. You *will* stay for Christmas, won't you?"

Angela was astonished. "Emma, I can't impose like that! You must already be sick of having houseguests, and to keep me around until Christmas..." She started to shake her head.

"There is only one reason I'll let you leave any sooner," Emma replied. "If you really feel you have to get back to your own life, I'll understand. But if you're not in any hurry, I'd love for you to stay."

"Gage couldn't possibly—"

"Gage likes having you here as much as I do. And you're no trouble at all, Angela. We're enjoying your company. Sometimes this big old house can seem so empty, even when the two of us are here...." Her voice trailed off, and she looked away. "I'm going to miss having the baby around, too."

"So will I."

Their eyes met in perfect understanding. Both of them knew what the loss of that dream meant.

"Anyway," Emma continued briskly, "having you here is like having family, so if you're not in any rush to get home, stay with us."

"I'll think about it. Thanks, Emma." But she knew she couldn't stay. Her savings would only stretch so far, and the longer she was out of work, the harder it would be to find a new job. She could conceivably look for something here, but she doubted she would find the kind of job that would further her career in any meaningful way. There just weren't that many jobs available in a town this small.

But Emma, in an attempt to get Angela to stay, had brought up the very subject that Angela had been avoiding thinking about: her future. Like it or not, the best thing she could do for herself would be to go home in the next few days and start job hunting. Go home and get away from Rafe and the baby before she got any more attached to either of them.

She *was* getting attached to Rafe. It wasn't just the baby. He was a frustrating man, alternately cold and hot, and utterly inscrutable. He was exactly the kind of man who could bring her nothing but heartache.

Their lovemaking had been wonderful, but she knew better than to base hopes for a relationship on that. It had been a mistake. They had given in to a momentary need, a momentary lust, and now neither of them wanted to recall those minutes.

And just supposing that for some reason they *did* get together, she could imagine only one future: a stormy one. She couldn't imagine any two people more ill-suited. The only thing they seemed to have in common was love for Peanut. And that just wasn't enough.

Why was she even thinking about this? Disturbed, she looked at Emma and saw knowledge in her friend's eyes. She could have ignored it, but she had always shared everything with Emma in the past, and she found herself doing so instinctively now.

"What do you think of Rafe?"

A twinkle appeared in Emma's green eyes. "He'll never be boring."

Angela felt her cheeks flush. "That isn't what I meant."

Emma smiled. "Of course not. What do I think of him? I think he's been more wounded than even he realizes."

Angela nodded slowly. "I made up my mind a long time ago that if I ever got involved with anybody, I wanted him to check his issues at the door. I had enough issues with He Whose Name Will Never Pass My Lips Again."

Emma laughed outright. "Good old Lance. You don't know how often I wanted to wipe the floor with his face."

"You never even met him!"

"But I read your letters, and I talked to you on the phone, and he was the most self-centered, selfish son of a gun."

Angela nodded slowly. "I was the last to realize it, of course."

"Of course. Love blinds—but only for a little while."

"I'm not going to be blind again."

"Of course not."

Angela felt herself smiling. "Don't agree so easily."

"Why not? It's true. Once burned, twice shy. That's you. But sometimes you still have to use the stove if you want to cook dinner."

"Meaning?"

Emma sipped her tea and looked thoughtful. "I'm not sure," she said finally. "I just get this feeling…well, Ange, think about it. You don't really want a man who checks his issues at the door."

"I don't?"

"Of course not. That would be boring. That's no foundation for a relationship. What you want is a man who can open up and share, one who will also listen to you. Issues become a lot easier to handle when two people share them. Of course, that's not to say there aren't certain kinds of issues you'd be better off avoiding. I just mean…well, we're all wounded in some way by life. And some of those wounds can be soothed or even healed by sharing them."

"Okay…" Angela shook her head. "So which issues are all right to have?"

"That depends on you. Basically, you need to look at the problems and ask yourself if you can deal with them. Because everybody has issues."

"No kidding." Angela wrapped her hands around her teacup, warming them. "I've gotten kind of selfish, too, since Lance."

"Hardly surprising, considering how he hurt you. But a little selfishness isn't bad for anyone."

"Not too much, though. No relationship should be a one-way street." She put her cup down and rose, walking slowly around the living room, thinking about Rafe. She really shouldn't be wasting any thought on him, she told herself, but she kept right on thinking about him, anyway.

She loved the way he loved the baby. And considering what Emma had just said about his wounds, she suspected that he loved the child because Peanut was the one person in this world who couldn't hurt him. The one person who needed him so completely that Rafe had nothing to fear.

She doubted he could give the same love to someone who wasn't dependent. That would be too big a risk for him.

And why was she thinking about *his* risks when hers were the ones she ought to be worrying about? She couldn't take the risk, either. This was getting entirely too dangerous.

She turned to Emma suddenly and said, "I'll have to leave by the end of the week, Em. I really need to get back and start job hunting."

"You could job hunt from here."

"There are other things I need to do."

Emma nodded, her expression enigmatic, but said only, "Whatever's best for you."

Angela didn't know what was best for her anymore. She only knew what she needed to do. And getting away from Rafe was rapidly becoming her top priority.

Chapter 10

They didn't get snowed in. The storm blew over before midnight, and the plows cleared the streets by dawn. Emma and Gage went to work, and Rafe stood in the kitchen, blinking in the incredibly bright sunlight that bounced off the snow outside and in through the windows. He had never seen light so unremittingly white and bright. Even in the subtropics at high noon, the light didn't have this kind of hard edge to it.

Peanut was sitting in his little seat on the table, cooing happily and waving his arms as if he were trying to catch handfuls of the light. Too bad he wasn't older, Rafe thought. They could have gone out and built a snowman.

Instead, they stayed inside, Rafe squinting against the brightness and thinking about what he needed to do.

Something had shifted inside him yesterday at the hospital when he and Nate had talked. It was as if some things had gotten very clear for him. And he suddenly knew why he had been flailing around the way he had. Now he just had to nerve himself up to do what he needed to do.

Angela came in the back door, stomping the snow off her

running shoes. He turned and looked at her, taking in her reddened cheeks and the sparkle in her eyes.

"It's *beautiful* out there," she said breathlessly.

"You look cold."

"To the bone."

"Want me to make you something hot to drink?"

"Coffee would be great. I've gotta go shower."

He watched her leave, hoping she wouldn't have a repeat of yesterday. But Angela was a capable woman, and he figured she'd probably adjusted her insulin somehow this morning. Either that or she had eaten more.

And he thought *he* had problems? Comparing his difficulties to her diabetes made his own problems seem inconsequential. But he still couldn't bring himself to pick up the phone.

When Angela returned twenty minutes later, she looked a lot warmer. She'd changed into a navy-blue sweater and wool pants, and her blond hair had the feathery look of being freshly washed and blow-dried.

"Food," she said, flashing him a smile as she headed for the cupboard and the crackers.

"Juice?" His heart skipped nervously.

"No, I adjusted my insulin this morning. I'm doing pretty good, actually. Crackers will take care of it."

"Good." He said that more emphatically than he had intended, but she seemed not to notice. He did, though, and somewhere deep inside he admitted that he never again wanted to see her look the way she had yesterday when she passed out.

She brought her crackers and coffee to the table and sat with him and Peanut. The baby recognized her and cooed happily. She reached out to let him curl his fingers around one of hers while she nibbled and sipped coffee.

The look she sent Rafe was humorous. "You really need to take yourself outside and get really cold and wet in the snow. Next thing you know, you'll be back in Miami baking and wishing you could be cold."

"We don't bake in Miami, we steam."

She laughed.

"But I'm not going back all that soon."

It seemed to him that she grew still for a moment, a stillness that came to her face more than her body. Her smile vanished, and he wondered why.

"How come?" she asked.

"This custody case is probably going to take a while. I need to stay here and see it out. If I take the baby and go, Manny will just file back home."

She nodded slowly. "I see."

He was surprised that he felt better for actually having voiced the decision he'd reached during the night. It was as if it hadn't been fully made until he spoke it. But now it was final, and he felt a measure of peace.

"I'm going to need an apartment or something," he continued, talking of details rather than the emotional consequences of what he had just said. "The baby and I can't keep living here with Emma and Gage. Not for as long as this is going to take."

"And your job?"

He shrugged. "I don't know. Maybe I can get compassionate leave. If not, I'll find another job."

"But…I thought your job was very important to you."

"'Was' is the key word. My perspective seems to have changed."

She nodded again, and ate a cracker as if she was using it as an excuse to say nothing. He couldn't blame her. He probably sounded as if he'd lost his mind.

But he was pretty sure he hadn't. He had a much stronger feeling that he was just becoming sane.

"Well, I'm glad you've got it all figured out, then," she said presently. "There's only one hitch in your plan."

"What's that?"

"Your make-believe fiancée is going home at the end of the week."

He didn't answer, feeling suddenly wary.

She continued, a faint edge in her voice. "You'll need to

think of something to tell Manny. But then, you're good at lies, you told me.''

He didn't think he'd done anything to earn that last shot from her, but instead of getting angry, he found himself perplexed, searching over all the things they'd said in the past few minutes, wondering what had made her want to try to hurt him. He couldn't figure it out.

Finally, all he said was, "Yeah, I'm real good at lies."

"Good. Well, I wish you all the best. I'm sure it'll all work out. After all, I can't imagine why anyone would think Manny would do a better job with this baby than you."

Then she gave him a thin smile. "I just remembered something." She got up and walked out of the room, leaving him to wonder what the hell was going on.

And the silence reminded him that you couldn't trust people, because sooner or later they all tried to hurt you.

Life was hell, Angela decided. Much as she wanted to hibernate in her room until Emma came home, she couldn't avoid the fact that she needed to go down and make herself some lunch at the usual time. Making lunch began to loom before her like a dread deadline, and all because she didn't want to see Rafe again.

She wasn't even sure what had set her off down in the kitchen. She'd made up her mind that he wasn't for her—not that there had ever been any possibility of that—so what was the big deal? Why was she suddenly feeling raw and hurt, as if he had done something wrong? Why had she struck out at him like that?

Because he hadn't expressed regret that she was leaving so soon, when he was staying? Could it be as simple and stupid as that? Had she really been silly enough to expect that much from him?

She must be going nuts. Or maybe her blood sugar was lower than she thought. Taking out her kit, she checked it again and was dismayed to find it right on the money. So the problem was emotional. She couldn't worm out of it by blaming it on something else.

Okay. She was disappointed. After their lovemaking Saturday, somewhere deep inside her she had expected something to deepen between them. She had expected something more than a continuation of their casual acquaintance.

How dumb could she be? The man said he was a good liar, but as far as she could tell, he'd never lied to *her*. He'd never promised her anything. He'd never offered any sweet talk or hinted at anything more. It was her own fault for harboring romantic delusions about a casual affair. Affair? It didn't even qualify as that. It had been a one-night stand, nothing more.

And she had nobody but herself to blame for the aftermath. At her age, she ought to know better.

She sat there grimly considering her own folly and the price she was going to pay for it. She had let herself do what she had sworn never to do again: she had become involved with a man who had nothing to offer her.

She hoped she'd learned her lesson this time. From now on, she wasn't going to let herself even consider such possibilities until a man knew everything about her and was offering her a ring. Maybe then she would consider falling in love. Or maybe not. She'd had a ring from Lance, after all. A ring and a baby.

Not that she had fallen in love with Rafe. Oh, no. The man wouldn't let her close enough to feel any such thing. This aching in her heart, this empty abandoned feeling, wasn't love. It was infatuation, nothing more.

Finally, though, she couldn't hide any longer. It was time for her insulin, and then she was going to have to go downstairs to eat, and act as if she hadn't just spent hours up here brooding about imaginary hurt.

All she had to do was get through the next three days. Then she could go home, far, far away from Rafe and his child.

She felt a serious pang every time she thought of Peanut, but that was neither here nor there. Neither the baby nor the baby's father was hers to lose. She had no business feeling this way.

She gave herself her injection, waited a few minutes, then went down to make lunch. Rafe, thank goodness, was nowhere to be seen. She was able to make a sandwich and a cup of soup for herself, and eat in utter peace.

And utter loneliness.

Thursday morning the sun dawned bright and warm, and the blizzard was nothing but a remnant, melting drifts along the roadside and in the shadows of houses and trees. It was an unexpected burst of Indian summer, and Angela had to restrain herself from running farther and longer than usual.

When she got back to the house, she headed straight for the shower, avoiding Rafe as she had been doing since Tuesday, which he didn't seem to mind. It was as if whatever closeness they'd had evaporated entirely after her outburst. Which was a good thing, she told herself for the hundredth time.

Knowing it was good didn't make it any more comfortable, however. Even when he was out of sight, she felt his presence, like a subliminal warning of storms to come.

It would be a lot better when she got home. Her other problems would wipe this one out of her mind.

So she wasn't exactly thrilled when she came back downstairs for her snack to find Rafe and the baby waiting for her at the foot of the stairs.

"After you have your snack," he said almost diffidently, "could you do me a favor?"

She supposed he wanted her to watch the baby. She knew she should say no, but there was no way she could refuse to take Peanut. For the past couple of days, she'd been missing that child as if he were part of her.

"Sure," she said, then wanted to kick herself.

"Great. We're going house hunting, and I'd like you to come along."

She could hardly believe her eyes. "Why? It's going to be *your* home."

"Yeah, but...well, I've never looked for a *home*. I always just get some efficiency apartment where I can hang the clothes I'm not wearing and sleep when I'm not sleeping somewhere else."

"And?"

"Well..." He actually looked uncomfortable and a little bit embarrassed. "I don't know exactly how to get a place with a baby in mind. I mean...I might be here long enough for Peanut to start crawling and walking. So I'd like a backup opinion."

"But I don't know anything more than you do."

"Two heads have got to be better than one. Who else can I ask?"

"Gage would probably have a better idea. He's had children."

"But Gage is working. I'm sorry. I'm imposing. I shouldn't have asked."

She hated it when he got polite. She could deal better with his coldness and bluntness. Worse, when he got polite, she didn't know how to say no. "Okay," she said finally. "But I don't promise to be much help." And she didn't really have anything better to do to pass the afternoon. Or so she told herself. The truth was, the idea of spending an afternoon with Rafe appealed to her.

And for once she didn't argue with herself about it. She would be gone tomorrow, so how much more trouble could she get into?

"I'll buy you lunch," Rafe said, "so just bring your travel kit with you."

In spite of herself, she was touched that he had considered her needs without prompting. He had the potential to be a really wonderful guy, she thought. But he had too many problems, and she just plain didn't want to deal with them. Quite frankly, she didn't think he would ever let anyone inside his barriers for long before he found a way to evict them.

Before lunch they looked at two apartments, both of which

they agreed might not be wise, since they were on the second floor.

"Of course," Angela said as they headed for Maude's and lunch, "we're probably being overly cautious. You probably don't need to worry much about that until Peanut starts walking."

"For all I know, I'll be battling this case here for the next five years."

"What about the job? What happened with that?"

Rafe shrugged a shoulder. "I've got a leave of absence for the next three months. After that—well, I'll deal with that when I get to it."

"You've really made up your mind, haven't you?"

"About the kid? You bet. I'll do whatever I have to."

She liked him more in that minute than she ever had. Maybe she'd been judging him too harshly, she found herself thinking. Maybe he wasn't as difficult as she thought.

Whoa, there, girl, she told herself. Thinking like that was only going to get her in more trouble.

Maude's service was the usual abrupt, slightly unfriendly approach to taking care of her customers. She even scowled at Rafe and said, "I don't like your friend."

"My friend?" He lifted an eyebrow.

"That guy who followed you from Miami."

"What did he do?"

"Telling me how to run my restaurant, like I haven't been doing it just fine these forty years! What makes him think he can tell me what to do?"

Rafe started to smile. "That's Manny, all right. He runs a restaurant in Miami."

"This ain't Miami."

"I know that. Apparently he doesn't."

"Well, you tell him for me that if he don't like my service and my food, he can damn well eat somewhere else."

"Tell him yourself, Maude. He's not my friend."

She humphed. "I told him, all right, but he just keeps coming back. Man's going to drive me to murder." She stomped away with their orders.

Rafe grinned at Angela. "I wish Maude were going to be the judge on this case."

She laughed. "It'd be settled in the time it took her to bang the gavel."

She excused herself to go to the ladies' room for her injection. When she got back to the table, she found that Rafe had apparently taken the baby to change him. She settled back into their booth, but not before she was spotted by Manny Molina, who was just entering the diner.

She groaned when he started to walk toward her and busied herself looking at the table.

He didn't take the hint. "Well, well, well," he said with false joviality. "Rafe's fiancée."

She almost winced at the word but managed to keep her face composed as she looked up at him. "Mr. Molina. You shouldn't be talking to me."

"Why not? You're not part of the case." He squeezed into the booth, facing her. "So where's the big man and the kid? Did they abandon you?"

She didn't answer directly. She figured she had to be very careful, so that she didn't say or do something that might cause Rafe trouble with his case. "Just what exactly is your problem, Mr. Molina?"

"My problem? It isn't my problem, lady. It's *his* problem. He took the kid away from the family."

"He *is* the baby's family."

Manny shook his head. "He's nothing but a stud who knocked my sister up and then vanished. He can talk about my brother Eduardo all he wants, but I'll tell you something. He's been living on the streets like a bum and a crook for years. He hangs out with people I wouldn't let within ten miles of my kids."

"It's his job."

"It doesn't matter, lady. The only difference between these D.E.A. agents and the people they're after is that the agents got government permission to do it. They get all high and mighty about it, when they're no different than the people they're after—except maybe they lie more. Rafael Ortiz isn't any better than my brother. And I'm going to prove it in court.''

Rafe was suddenly there, holding the baby, looking livid. "You bothering my fiancée, Manny?"

"Fiancée, shmiancée. Just keep lying, Ortiz. Those lies are gonna hang you in court."

Maude suddenly joined them. "Do I need to call the cops?" She was looking straight at Manny. "I told you to get out of here and stay out of here, and I meant it. You're bothering my other guests. You got thirty seconds to get your butt outta here!"

Manny left, muttering. Angela's heart was still pounding, and she sat for a few moments, staring at her clasped hands. Finally she spoke. "He's getting…nasty."

"What did he say?"

"That you're no better than the people you arrest."

Rafe shrugged and settled Peanut into his seat. "He might be right. Except I don't get people addicted to drugs, and I don't supply drugs to addicts. Oh, and I don't break the law."

"Ever?"

His eyes suddenly fixed on her. "No," he said flatly. "Never. Which is not to say I never get tempted to, to speed up the process. I'm sure some agents cross the line. But I never have and never will. Sooner or later, the crooks make the mistakes I need to catch them. I can be patient when I need to." He sighed and shook his head. "Maybe Manny's started to worry that he's not going to win this custody battle."

"I don't see how he possibly can."

"I wish I were as confident."

After lunch they stopped at the real estate office, where the busy agent handed them keys to a couple of houses and told them to check them out.

"I'm beginning to love small towns," Rafe remarked as

they drove to the first house. "Where else would a real estate agent trust you with the keys?"

"Nowhere that I know of."

He flashed her a smile, and she felt a little catch in her breathing, accompanied by a feeling of warmth. It wasn't fair that a simple smile could affect her so strongly. She looked away quickly, staring out at the sun-drenched world with its patches of melting snow, and wondered how she could be so close to tears so quickly.

The first house they looked at had one bedroom and floors that sloped drastically.

"I don't think so," Rafe said.

"Me neither," Angela agreed.

The second house smelled like cat urine, and they were out the door before they'd hardly stepped in.

Rafe gave her a wry look. "Something tells me this is going to be harder than I expected."

"It might be."

"It's not that I need perfection. But I do need to be comfortable and feel the kid will be safe."

She nodded.

"You're not saying much."

"It's not exactly my decision."

He sighed. "I asked for your input. Tell me what you like. Please. Or I'm going to wind up in another efficiency that I'll be cursing for months."

"Come on! You're not that helpless!"

He laughed, his dark eyes suddenly twinkling. "I'm a guy. It gives me an inferiority complex when it comes to things like this."

"And because I'm a woman, I'm supposed to know more?"

He laughed again. "Sure. Aren't you the ones with the nesting instincts?"

She was torn between an urge to laugh and an urge to needle him. Unable to think of a good retort, though, she fell back on laughter and again felt that strange warmth when his eyes smiled at her.

The next house was more to their liking. It had been freshly painted inside and out, there were two bedrooms, and the kitchen and bathroom had been modernized within the past five years. Whoever had last lived in it had taken good care of it.

Angela found herself talking about the possibilities she saw, speaking of curtains and plants and where a couch would fit. When she realized Rafe was listening to her with a bemused smile, her voice trailed off. "I'm sorry."

He shook his head. "I was enjoying it. Really. You have some nice ideas."

She felt her cheeks warm. "Thanks."

He stepped toward her, the baby in his arm, and came to a halt no more than twelve inches away. "You want a real home, don't you?"

"I *have* a home."

"Not the kind I'm talking about."

It was true, she thought, mesmerized by his gaze. She didn't really think of her apartment as a *home*. The kind of place that made her feel safe and warm, not just the place where she happened to live. But she'd never seen her apartment as a permanent thing. It had always been a way station.

"I want a home," he said. "I've never really had one, either. This house won't be it, of course. It'll just be me and Peanut marking time. But I really want a *home*."

"You could make it a home."

He shook his head. "My life isn't here, Angel. Just like yours isn't. Sometimes I think I'm still looking for my life."

She caught her breath as the truth of what he had just said sank home. She knew exactly what he meant. She was still looking for her life, too, like some kind of Sleeping Beauty waiting for the prince's kiss. Only for her there would be no prince. A wave of ineffable sadness washed over her.

"Don't look like that," he said almost gruffly.

"Like what?"

"Like you want to cry..."

He leaned closer, bringing his face to within inches of hers, until she could feel the whisper of his breath against her cheek and lips. "You'll find your home, Angel. You will."

"No…" She pulled away from him. "No, I won't. No man is ever going to want me. Just stop it, Rafe! Stop it and take me home. This house is fine. You can live in it for a few months, and I need to pack.…"

"Angel—"

"Don't call me that! I'm not your angel. I'm not anybody's angel. Now, will you take me home, or do I have to walk?"

He drove her home and dropped her off, then roared away, leaving her standing on the sidewalk, wondering if she ought to just get in her car and leave right now before he managed to twist her emotions any more.

Turning, she hurried into the house and up to her bedroom, where she started packing in a fury, throwing her things into her suitcases without regard, which led to her being unable to close the suitcases. It was the last straw. She lay on her bed and gave in to her tears.

Life, she thought miserably, could be so damn unfair. She should never have come to visit Emma. All her two weeks here had done was show her all the things she was missing in life. Watching the way Emma and Gage looked at one another was enough to give her heartache, and being near Rafe…

Well, being near Rafe was like being on the other side of a plate-glass window from food when you were starving.

There was a quiet, insistent knocking at her door, but she ignored it, determined to indulge her stupid mood, then get up, close those damn suitcases and leave.

But someone else had a very different idea. The door opened, and she rolled over quickly to find Rafe standing there.

"Just leave me alone," she said.

He sighed. "I get the feeling I've been doing something very wrong where you're concerned, and I want to know what it is."

"Just go away. I'm in no mood to be rational."

He stepped in and slammed the door behind him. "Neither am I!"

She realized she had never seen him angry before, and what she was seeing right now was intimidating. But she wasn't easily frightened. "Don't act like a gorilla! Slamming doors won't frighten me."

"I didn't slam it to frighten you, damn it! I'm just so frustrated I could...I could..."

"What? Hit me?"

He swore. "I've never in my life hit a woman, and I'm not about to start!" He ran his fingers through his hair and glared at her. "Look, Angel—"

"I told you not to call me that!"

"All right. *Angela.* Now look..."

"I don't want to look. I just want to be left alone."

"Just tell me what the hell I did wrong!" He roared the words, and they were followed by a silence so profound that Angela could hear the beating of her own heart.

"I'm sorry," he said abruptly. "I shouldn't have shouted. I apologize. But please, tell me what I keep doing that's making you so mad."

"Nothing."

"Nothing?" The frustrated note crept back into his voice. "You're getting mad about nothing?"

"Yes."

"I don't believe you."

"Well, that brings us to a pretty pass, doesn't it?" She sat up, scowling at him. "Now if you'll just go, I'll finish packing."

But he dropped into the chair facing her, crossed his legs loosely and regarded her over the steeple of his fingers. "Let's try it this way. I know I'm a screwed up son of a gun. I already figured that out. But I don't know how I'm going to get un-screwed-up if people won't tell me what I'm doing wrong."

In spite of her anger and contrariness, she felt herself aching for him. That couldn't be a pleasant way to feel. "You're not screwed up."

"No? Funny, every time I look at the mess my life is, I get a very strong feeling that I'm missing something basic."

"So? What's new? Everyone's life is a mess. Everyone's missing something they need."

He never took those dark eyes from her, and she was beginning to feel uncomfortable, as if he could look right past all her defenses and see to her soul.

"You know," he said finally, "I thought I had some pretty good defenses, but yours beat all."

She caught her breath, feeling as if she had just been punched. "I don't know what you're talking about."

"No? Then how about we get back to the discussion we were having earlier? I was willing to admit I want to find a home. What's your problem with that?"

She shrugged, words deserting her.

"See? You can't even discuss it. The difference between us is that I'm willing to admit what I want, and willing to hope I might find it. You aren't even willing to hope."

"That's not true!"

"Sure it is. I drive you crazy, don't I?"

"I never said that!"

"You never would. But the bottom line is that I can read it in your face. One of my talents learned from a life of foster homes and risking my neck on the streets. I drive you nuts with the way I get close and then pull back. It's obvious. And I don't blame you for feeling that way."

She didn't answer, pressing her lips closed.

"But you...you're different. You don't just get close then pull away because you get afraid of what you might feel. No, you shut the doors and pull up the drawbridge *before* anybody can get close."

"That's not true."

"It sure as hell is. And it's getting more and more obvious, so I must be getting too close."

She hated him right then. If a smoldering look could have turned him to a cinder, she would have done so.

"Go ahead and glare at me. I suppose I deserve it. But keep

one thing in mind, Angel. I may pull back when I get scared, but I keep coming back. You…you're going to leave town. That makes it kind of hard for anybody to have a chance.''

"What chance? I'm just another Raquel to you.''

His lips tightened into a thin, white line. "Low blow, baby.''

"I'm not your baby!''

"And you're never going to be anybody's baby if you don't take a chance.''

She continued to glare at him, some part of her recognizing that she was being deliberately contrary, but unable to stop. She absolutely had to get out of this place as quickly as she could. It was the only way she could be safe.

"You've been avoiding me ever since we made love!'' The words burst out of her unbidden, and she was horrified. She had never, ever, wanted to say that, never wanted to admit that much.

"I have,'' he agreed. "I was scared. So what's your excuse? You haven't exactly been trying to get closer yourself. Are you scared, too, Angela?''

"Look, this whole discussion is academic. I'm going home, and you're going to do whatever it is you want to do with the rest of your life, and we're never going to meet again. So who the hell cares if you're scared or I'm scared, or who's the biggest idiot between us?''

"I do. It's real important to me to know that I haven't been the idiot this time.''

She gaped at him, wondering what in the world he meant, but then he was kneeling in front of her, catching her face between his hands and giving her a kiss that shook her to her very soul.

"You be the idiot if you have to,'' he said quietly, while she was still gasping for breath. "But I'm damned if I'm going to make the same mistake twice.''

Before she could even begin to divine what he meant by that, he snatched her breath away with another kiss, one that seemed to reach deep within her and pluck at feelings she had been desperately trying to bury. Feelings that responded to his touch as if it were an earthquake.

She wanted him. Whatever part of her had been denying it was lost in the onslaught of the needs he awoke within her. Every sensible thought fled before the attack of his mouth. Her arms lifted and wrapped around his shoulders as if they belonged there, and when he bent her back so that she was lying on the bed with him kneeling between her legs, she was just glad that she didn't have any more decisions to make, that she didn't have to muster another argument. What was about to happen was as inevitable as sunrise, and every bit as potent.

His weight between her legs felt good, so good that she lifted her legs and wrapped them around his hips, bringing him even closer. It might have been a signal for him, because he shoved her blouse up and unhooked her bra in one fevered movement.

She felt the air on her bare skin, felt its coolness pucker her. Or maybe it was the way he was looking at her, as if her breasts filled him with longing and wonder. Then, before she could do more than recognize his look, she felt his mouth on her, hot and wet and hungry.

She was lost, and she didn't care. If there was a way back from this madness, she didn't want to find it. Not now. She would deal with the aftermath later, because she knew even in the throes of what she was feeling that there was going to be pain.

But she couldn't make herself care enough to deny herself what he was offering. She needed the sensations and the closeness. She needed this gift he was offering her, however brief it would be.

His mouth warmed her breast, tugging gently until it was swollen and aching. Then he moved to the other one, giving it the same wondrous treatment. She clutched at his shoulders, holding him close, wishing this closeness could be hers forever.

Then, as if from a distance, she heard her own voice say, "This doesn't solve anything, Rafe."

He lifted his head, leaving her feeling bereft, and said, "No, but it sure makes the issues a hell of a lot clearer."

"We shouldn't..." Oh, God, that couldn't be her saying that, not when every cell in her body was screaming for his touch.

"We *should,*" he said flatly, and caught her face between his hands. "I can't get close to you any other way. If this is all I can have, I'm going to take it."

So this was all he wanted, she thought hazily as his mouth found her breast again. Just this. Nothing else. And much as she wanted that to matter, it couldn't, not right now, when she wanted him every bit as much as he seemed to want her.

She felt him pop the button on her slacks and knew that this was it, that she wasn't going to stop him.

Knew, in her deepest heart, that she was going to soar on these moments with him and cherish every one of them.

Tomorrow was soon enough to crash and burn.

Chapter 11

At some level, Angela almost seemed to rise above herself. Everything except his touches seemed unreal, distant, utterly unimportant. Reality was his kiss, his caress, his warm weight pressing her down.

Her slacks slid away, then her panties, and she lifted herself so he could pull her shirt and bra off. Then he covered her, cradling himself between her thighs, and she felt the most erotic sensation she had ever known, the press of a fully clothed man's body against her unprotected nakedness.

She caught her breath, awash in textures, her senses heightened by her own delightful vulnerability. She could feel denim and Oxford cloth, could feel the hardness of him behind the hardness of his zipper. And she was suddenly in no hurry to have him undress. There was a wicked pleasure in what she was feeling now, and she wanted to savor it.

As if he knew it, he caught her hands with his own, holding them prisoner. He scattered kisses all over her, from her mouth down the column of her throat, across her breasts.

Then lower. Trailing down across her waist, her belly. Traveling lower, until she was holding her breath in anticipation, in expectation of something she had never experienced before.

She felt him nuzzle her curls, and she gasped, arching instinctively. He obliged, teasing her curls until she was throbbing and gasping his name, making silent promises until she feared that he would not keep them.

But he did. When she felt the first touch of his tongue on her sensitive nub, the sensation was so powerful that she almost cried out in pain. What escaped her was a long, low moan. Then his tongue stroked her again, and the pain became pleasure. Her entire world became the tiny knot of nerves that he had found in her moist folds.

She gasped again as he slipped a finger within her, then cried out as his tongue lashed her again. She had never dreamed that her body could know such intense sensations, had never dreamed the pleasures to be found in utter vulnerability.

She could feel the heat of his breath on her in a place she had never expected to feel anyone's breath, could feel the moist heat of his tongue, the faint scratch of beard stubble, and all of it added to the fire that was building in her.

Higher she rose, straining toward that exquisite moment of completion, yet reluctant to arrive there too soon. She wanted this to go on forever, and ever and ever....

But it didn't. All too soon, it seemed, she exploded in a cataclysm so intense that she was blinded by it. All too soon she was on the other side, sinking slowly back to earth, with his face pressed hard to her womanhood.

Then he stood. She opened her eyes just enough to watch as he stripped away his clothes. She couldn't move. Couldn't make a sound. Even though she yearned to touch him, she felt too weak to lift a hand.

Oh, he was beautiful, she thought, watching him through her lashes. Just perfect. Compactly muscled, lean, bronzed. She wished she could have a picture of him to carry with her always.

Before anticipated sorrow could wedge its way into her consciousness, however, he turned her on the bed and stretched out beside her, kissing her, letting her know he wasn't done with her.

For a little while there was nothing but kisses, as if he sensed she needed time to recover from what she had just discovered.

And as she recovered, as the strength seeped back into her limbs, she discovered she wanted him every bit as much as she ever had. She would never, ever, feel that she had had enough of Rafe.

But this would be her last chance to have him at all.

Suddenly full of energy, she lifted herself on her elbow, so that she looked down at him. His dark eyes were slumberous, and he lay back, as if inviting her to take her fill of him. Bending, she kissed him again, tasting herself on him.

He smiled when she began to run her hands over him.

"What do you like?" she asked, her voice catching. She had never asked that question before; it had never seemed important enough. But then, no one had ever made love to her the way Rafe just had, as if all that mattered was giving her pleasure.

"Whatever you like. Everything you like."

The huskiness of his voice thrilled her, and she felt a dawning sense of power. Her hands grew bolder, sweeping over his chest and belly, down his thighs. His smile deepened, and his eyelids grew even heavier.

She discovered that his small nipples hardened when she brushed over them. Curious and excited by her discovery, she brushed them again and heard a sigh escape him. He was just like her, she realized. She had never guessed that before.

And now she had a road map. Whatever pleased her would probably please him, as well. Bending, she teased one brown nipple with her tongue and heard a soft groan escape him.

Pleased, she devoted herself to teasing him as he had teased her, licking, sucking, and at one point nipping gently. The sensation caused him to arch, and he groaned more loudly.

The sound renewed the aching between her own legs, and she unconsciously moved closer to him.

Wanting so much more, she began to kiss him everywhere he had kissed her, enjoying his obvious pleasure in her touches.

And finally she kissed his shaft, learning from his reactions how he responded to her touches, watching his hands grip the coverlet, listening to him moan. Her power was complete, she realized. He was now as helpless as she had been.

But before she could pursue that any further, he half sat up, grabbing her shoulders and pulling her over him. "Lift up," he said hoarsely, and guided himself into honeyed depths.

She straddled him, not moving, paralyzed by the exquisite sensation of having him fill her. Her eyes were closed, her head thrown back, her body nothing but a vessel for him and for the magic they made together.

Then he reached up and touched her breasts, gently squeezing her swollen nipples. She groaned and began to move against him, finding herself once more on the climb to ecstasy.

The next minutes were a total blur as sensation blinded her. She never remembered them clearly, but she would never ever forget the moment when they reached the apex together and tumbled over.

She shattered then into a thousand flaming pieces. And deep inside she knew she would never again be the same.

They cuddled under the blankets. Angela was past trying to put any distance between them. After what they had just shared, she needed these minutes of closeness, needed to hold him and be held by him. Needed to pretend this could go on forever.

He seemed to feel the same. He dozed for a minute or two, but other than that, his dark eyes stayed open, stayed fixed on her, as if he were afraid to lose sight of her.

Or afraid of what she might do next. She couldn't blame him for that. His analysis of her psyche might be all wet, but she couldn't deny that she had been difficult and contrary.

None of that belonged right here, right now, and she didn't even want to think about it. Tomorrow would be here soon enough, and when she was on the road she could tell herself what a fool she had been.

"Do you need to eat something?" he asked lazily.

"I'm fine." Much as she hated the illness that made that question necessary, she was touched that he cared enough to remember.

"You're sure?"

"Positive."

"Well, *you* might be 'fine,' but *I'm* super."

She had to smile at that. "Yes, you are."

"No. I mean, you made me feel super."

"Thank you."

He smiled and placed a kiss on her shoulder. In response, she snuggled closer.

The afternoon was waning, she realized. Light was no longer pouring in through the windows, and the room had become dim. Much as she wanted to stay like this forever, she knew that reality was about to intrude again. The baby would wake. She would need to take her insulin. It would be time go down to dinner with Emma and Gage. Then would follow a long evening while everyone tried to be cheerful and no one wanted to say goodbye.

"You look sad," Rafe remarked.

"I guess I am, a little." It was hard to make the admission, but she forced herself.

"Me, too." He sighed and hugged her tighter for a moment. "Do you really have to leave?"

"It's time to get on with my life."

"Yeah. I guess. I'm kind of stuck in limbo here for a while."

"It'll pass."

"Sure. But are you sure you can't stay another week? It's not like you have to get back to your job."

Her heart skipped a beat; then she asked herself why he wanted her to stay. Because she was a convenient lay? Even as she asked the bitter question, she knew it was unjustified. Rafe had never treated her that way.

"What good could it possibly do for me to stay another week?" she asked finally.

"Well, you'd have more time to relax. Get your sugar sorted out. I'm still worried about what happened on Monday."

"That was just a blip."

"What if you have another blip on the road?"

"I'll be more careful. What happened Monday was sheer carelessness on my part."

"Okay." He was silent for a while. Then he looked straight at her and said, "I wish you wouldn't go."

Her heart seemed to stop. She searched his face, trying to divine his meaning, but he offered her nothing more than that. *I wish you wouldn't go.* That could mean so much—or so little.

She closed her eyes, wrestling with internal doubts, wondering if she dared take this risk for nothing more than an *I wish you wouldn't go.* Inevitably her thoughts returned to Lance and how he had hurt her.

But today she saw the whole relationship in a different light. Lance had fallen for her quickly. He had been surprisingly ready to announce his love for her, and they'd become engaged before he'd ever really seen what diabetes could do. Oh, he'd known about it intellectually, but she'd been so careful not to make a to-do about her shots and her need to eat that the disease had been virtually invisible to him.

Until they started living together. Little by little he'd begun to resent the way her disease hemmed them in, and now she wondered if the engagement wouldn't have ended a lot sooner if she hadn't become pregnant.

"Angel?"

She opened her eyes and found Rafe's dark gaze on her, steady and unblinking.

"Stay," he said again. "Just another week."

All he wanted was another week. Some part of her resented that, but some part of her wanted it every bit as much as he did. And after the loneliness of her life since Lance, she was no longer certain she would ever again have an opportunity to hear a man say, "Stay."

It was a week. Just a week. It couldn't get much worse than it already was, she reasoned. And wasn't she entitled to steal just one week out of her life? Wasn't she entitled to pretend that she was a normal woman, having a normal love affair, for just one week?

"Okay," she heard herself say.

He smiled and squeezed her tight, sprinkling kisses over her face until she laughed and forgot her impending sorrow.

"Great," he said, with a huge smile. "Now, unless I'm mistaken, it's time for you to take your insulin."

"It's that late?" She twisted her head and looked at the clock. "It is!"

"Yup. And I can hear Emma and Gage downstairs making dinner."

She felt a blush creep up her throat into her face. "They're home?"

"They sure are. But if they suspect anything, I don't think either one of them is going to embarrass you by mentioning it. But we need to get down there and help them."

She nodded, embarrassed, and started to sit up.

"Wait," he said.

She paused and looked at him.

"Let me watch you take your insulin. Tell me all about it."

She started to shake her head.

"No," he said, stilling her with a finger over her lips. "It's part of you. You don't need to hide it from me."

"But there's no need...."

"Yes, there is," he said. "Until you trust me with this, you don't trust me."

Trust! As if they needed trust to have a week-long fling. But part of her understood what he was saying, and when she thought about it, she decided to do it. After all, if he was going to get disgusted, she might as well find out right now, before she unpacked her bags.

But it was a terrible intimacy. Lance had wanted no part of it, and she couldn't see any reason why another person should want to see such a thing.

Except...except she had the feeling that he was trying to tell her that he didn't think her needing insulin was any worse than brushing her teeth or combing her hair.

That didn't make it any easier to do it while he watched, though. She was suddenly painfully conscious of her nakedness, of the dimples on her thighs from so many injections. She fumbled as she pricked her finger for the blood test.

"Four times a day?" he said. "Your fingers must be sore a lot."

"A little." She didn't really think about it anymore. Sometimes she noticed it, but mostly she was so accustomed to it that it was unnoticeable to her.

She filled the syringe, swabbed her thigh with alcohol, pinched it and inserted the needle. When she finished, she swabbed her thigh again and tossed the used syringe in the wastebasket with its brothers.

Then Rafe astonished her by bending to kiss her leg where she had just given herself the injection.

"I'm sorry you have to do that," he said, "but I'm damn glad you can. Now I'm going to check on the baby."

He rose, pulled on his briefs and jeans, grabbed his shoes and shirt from the floor, gave her a quick kiss on the lips and left her room.

What had gotten into him? she wondered. If she didn't know better, she might start to think he was sensitive.

"Of course we want you to stay another week," Emma said eagerly when Angela brought up the subject at dinner. "Didn't I tell you we'd like it if you'd stay until Christmas?"

"That's right," Gage agreed. "We're enjoying your company, Angela. Stay as long as you want."

"Just another week," Angela hastened to say. "I really *do* have to get back to job hunting. But I hate to leave." For now. She hated to leave for now.

Her eyes met Rafe's across the table, and he gave her a smile that caused her heart to flutter. When she glanced at Emma, she saw knowledge in her friend's eyes. But Emma didn't say anything, just looked gently understanding.

There was nothing to understand, Angela reminded herself. Rafe wanted a week, not a lifetime. And she had decided to take that week rather than miss it. No big deal.

After dinner, Rafe suggested a walk. Emma excused herself, because she needed to bathe and get things ready to go to work in the morning. Gage excused himself to stay with Emma.

Which left Rafe, Peanut and Angela to take a lazy walk down the darkened street. Peanut slept comfortably in his father's arm, oblivious to the star-studded sky and the lights pouring through the windows along the street.

Rafe reached out and took Angela's hand, and she felt a tingle of pure delight as their warm palms met.

"I'm convinced," Rafe said, "that there are more stars here than there are in Miami."

It took a second, but Angela started laughing. "It's the same sky!"

"It couldn't possibly be. We don't have half this many stars." He paused as they rounded a corner onto a dark street. "See? There's the Milky Way. We don't have that in Miami."

She was still laughing. "It might be the city lights, you know."

He flashed her a grin. "Nah. We just don't have the same sky."

"You're silly."

"Occasionally." They walked on to the end of the block, then turned again, circling back toward the house. "It's too bad they don't need any D.E.A. agents here. I could get used to this."

"Maybe you ought to look into it. I mean, they might not need you here—the town is too small—but there are other places in Wyoming."

"I'd probably be working out of Denver. But maybe that wouldn't be so bad."

"I take it you're getting used to the cold?"

"Ask me that again when it gets really cold."

As if she would be around then. Much as she tried to prevent it, her heart skipped a hopeful beat. Maybe she'd made a serious mistake by agreeing to spend another week here. It *could* get worse, she realized. It could get much, much worse.

She felt as if she were standing on a bridge between hope and disappointment, between eager anticipation and dread. She felt as if she kept bouncing between one and the other, feeling joy and despair all at once.

Rafe did that to her. It might have been wiser to leave in the morning, as she had planned, but it was too late now. She had signed on for the ride, wherever it led.

When they got back to the house, Rafe went to feed the baby and put him to bed. Alone at last, Angela went to her room and gave herself her insulin injection for the night. Then she went to take a shower.

Standing under the hot spray, she told herself that she might as well not try to sort out all of this now, because she had agreed to stay the week. Next week, after she left, would be soon enough to evaluate everything that was going on.

For now she ought to just give herself over to the pleasures that were being offered to her.

She felt a cold draft and turned around to find Rafe climbing into the shower with her. He gave her a lazy smile and took the bar of soap from her hand. He took a washcloth from the rack, soaped it, then began to wash her all over in gentle, stroking movements.

The sensation was so erotic that her knees turned instantly weak. Instinctively, she reached out and grabbed his shoulders for support.

"That good, huh?" he asked softly, and gave her another lazy smile. She felt herself smiling back, even as her eyelids insisted they were heavy, felt herself giving herself up to the marvelous feelings he was evoking in her, both physically and emotionally. She felt so *cared* for. So...sexy.

The hot soapy washcloth, rough and smooth all at once, stroked her back, rubbed her bottom, then slid around to caress her breasts and belly. When he bent to wash her legs, she bit her lip and hung on for dear life. He went down the outsides of her legs first, long, soothing strokes, then came back up the insides to touch the most secret part of her and rub gently.

She was burning, a slow, lazy burn that felt so good she never wanted it to end. But then she felt him press the soap and washcloth into her hands, and she knew it was her turn.

And it was every bit as wonderful. It gave her an unimpeded opportunity to admire the rippling muscles of his back and shoulders, his tight, flat butt, his long, strong legs. His chest, broad and firm, his belly flat and hard. His manhood, hard for her. Just for her. She stroked him sensuously, enjoying the low sound he made, as if he were purring.

Then she found the scars in his side and paused there, looking up at him.

"Knife wounds," he said with a shrug.

The thought froze her. She didn't know why she hadn't noticed the scars before, but she noticed them now, and they filled her with pain.

"Angel, it was a long time ago. Don't worry about it."

But her mood was destroyed, and so was the hazy, devil-may-care determination with which she had embarked on this week out of time. In an instant it all became too entirely real.

He was a cop. People tried to kill him. She was leaving in a week. What was wrong with her? She must be out of her mind!

She turned from him abruptly, rinsing as quickly as she could.

"Angel?"

"It's okay," she heard herself say. "It's okay. I just need...I need to be alone for a little while, okay?"

She hardly dared look at him, but finally she stole a glance and found his face as frozen as an Arctic tundra, as hard as ice.

"Okay," he said flatly.

She climbed out of the tub, grabbed a towel and wrapped it around herself. Then, picking up her nightgown and slippers, she ran for her bedroom, locking the door behind her.

She couldn't go on with this, she realized. She couldn't ignore reality, even for one week. When it came to Rafe Ortiz, life promised absolutely nothing but pain. Nothing.

Well, screw her, then, Rafe thought as he rinsed himself off. Little tease. He was really getting sick to death of the way she would suddenly run from him, closing him out. And for no good reason that he could figure out.

His scars? Well, what about them? They'd been there so long he'd nearly forgotten them, and he had told her about the time the guy stabbed him. He was sure he had. So what was it with this running away?

He turned off the water and stepped out onto the bathmat. Using a towel, he wiped off the mirror on the back of the door and took a long look at those scars. Hell, there wasn't much to see, certainly not when compared with the way they'd looked for months afterward. Now they were little more than wide silvery lines in his darker skin. A little puckered, but when all was said and done, the doc had done a fine job of sewing him back together. They sure weren't any worse than the scars from knee surgery.

So what the hell was going on with her? Was she that repulsed by a few scars? Somehow he didn't think so. Then what?

He was about ready to throw in the towel on this one. He'd begun to feel something with her that he hadn't felt since Raquel, a passion commingled with a warmth unlike anything he'd ever known before.

It killed him to admit that. He didn't want to admit that he'd tumbled into bed with Raquel for any reason other than lust. But in retrospect, in moments of brutal honesty, he admitted that there had been something more. Something that had drawn him to her. Something that had touched him in ways he'd never been touched before.

But she had turned her back on him the same way Angela kept doing. With Raquel, he'd never gone back. And it was remembering that fact every time he looked at his son that made him reluctant to walk away from Angela.

He'd made a mistake with Raquel, and he didn't want to make the same mistake twice. But how many times was he supposed to keep going back before he admitted it was a lost cause?

Frustrated, he toweled himself dry, yanked on his slacks and headed for his own room. He would probably wake up in the morning and discover that Angela had gone home, after all.

And that was probably for the best. How many times and in how many ways did a woman have to tell him to get lost before he believed she meant it? The fact that he might have made a mistake with Raquel by listening the first time didn't mean he had to spend the rest of his life taking this kind of crap from some woman.

Nope, he was going overboard here. Angela kept telling him, and it was high time he started listening.

She didn't want him. Period. End of story.

But accepting that didn't make going to sleep any easier.

By Monday morning, Angela was wondering why she had ever agreed to stay the week. Rafe was scarcely talking to her—although, to be fair, she couldn't blame him.

What stung, she admitted, what *really* stung, was that for the first time in her life she was being rejected by a man not because of her diabetes, but because of the way she had acted.

Throughout her morning run she wondered if she should apologize to him. But how could she explain her own actions? It was as if every time he got a little too close to something that mattered, she bolted like an unbroken horse.

God, she almost hated herself when she thought about it. If she were him, she would avoid her, too.

Entering the house, she found Rafe and Peanut in the kitchen, making a late breakfast.

"Good morning," she said.

"Morning." He looked grumpy and rumpled.

"Did the baby keep you up last night?" she asked.

"Nope. Not the baby."

She almost asked what had disturbed his sleep, then decided against it. She might not like the answer. "Look, I wanted to tell you I'm sorry about how I've been behaving."

He didn't look particularly receptive. He scraped scrambled eggs onto a plate, beside four pieces of toast, then sat facing Peanut, who was sitting in his recliner seat.

"It doesn't matter," he said finally.

"Yes, it does. I don't know what's gotten into me, but I'm sorry."

He shrugged with supreme indifference. "Whatever. Forget it."

She wanted to scream with frustration, but instead she went to get her snack. Then, pointedly, she sat at the table to eat. "I don't mean to act like that," she said. "I never have before."

He said nothing. She gave up and concentrated on her crackers and milk.

The phone rang. Without getting up, Rafe twisted and grabbed the receiver. "Dalton residence. Oh, hi, Connie. How's it going?"

Connie? Angela felt an uncharacteristic surge of jealousy. Who was Connie? Must be someone he worked with, she told herself. Maybe it was even his boss. She tried not to listen, and listening wouldn't have told her much, anyway. He asked a few short questions that revealed nothing, then hung up and went back to his meal.

"Well," she said eventually, "I guess there's no reason to hang around the rest of the week," she said. "I'll pack and leave tomorrow."

The reaction she got wasn't at all what she expected.

"You might want to wait until Wednesday," he said.

Even as her heart was plummeting because he didn't want her to stay longer, her irritation began to rise. Who was *he* to tell her when she could go? "Why?"

He looked at her. "That was my lawyer, about the custody case. The judge wants to talk to both of us. I told her not to wait too long, because I figured you'd be going back to Iowa soon. She said she's going to set it up for tomorrow if she can. So you might want to hang around until Wednesday."

"Why? I have nothing to say about any of this. Unless the judge thinks we're engaged?" Her annoyance began to rise. "That's probably it. That stupid Manny probably shot his mouth off about that, and now the judge wants to know what kind of person I am. Man! I can't believe this."

He didn't say anything, just resumed eating.

"Well, I'll leave this afternoon, then," she said. "Then you can go in there and tell whatever lies you want about your fiancée."

"I don't lie," he said levelly.

"Except when it suits you."

"Except when it's necessary, and never under oath."

"Pretty narrow definition of telling the truth, don't you think?"

He looked at her. "At least I don't lie to *myself.*"

Her hackles rose. "And just what does that mean?"

"I suppose it'll mean whatever you want it to, the way everything else I've said does." He rose from the table and carried his plate to the sink. "I'll tell you one thing, Angel. You could be a really wonderful person if you could come out of that shell long enough to care just a little bit about somebody besides yourself."

Then he picked up the baby and was gone.

Oh, God, she thought, she'd done it again. What in the world was the matter with her?

She and Rafe went to the courthouse the next morning to see the judge. For all she'd squawked about it, Angela hadn't had the heart to pack. If there was something she could do to help Rafe keep his child, she would do it. But riding in the car with him was like riding to an execution. Neither of them said a word, and the emotional temperature was below zero.

They were met at the courthouse by Rafe's attorney, Constance Crandall. "This shouldn't be difficult," Connie said. "The judge is already strongly leaning our way."

Judge Williams was a pleasant-looking woman in her forties, dressed in a navy-blue business suit. She invited them into her chambers and offered them comfortable upholstered chairs facing her desk. She waited while Rafe removed Peanut's bunting, then asked the court reporter, who was sitting in the corner, to administer the oath to both Rafe and Angela.

"I've been reviewing this custody case, Mr. Ortiz. I don't see any reason to drag this process out unnecessarily, so I thought I'd ask you a few questions to clarify some of the issues. I hope this will be sufficient to come to a conclusion in this matter. Now, I understand from your lawyer that you have absolute proof you're the child's natural father?"

"Yes, Your Honor. I had a DNA test done."

The judge nodded. "And we can get a copy of those results?"

"I don't see why not. I had it done through my regular doctor. He should have a copy of it."

"Good. Can you give me his name and phone number? Maybe my clerk can get him to fax those results up today."

Rafe pulled out his wallet and offered a business card.

"Thank you." The judge passed it to the reporter, who typed all the information in. Then the card was given back to Rafe.

"Now," the judge continued, "the complaint from Mr. Molina alleges that you absconded with the child in order to prevent Mr. Molina and his family from having access to the child. How do you answer that?"

Rafe looked down at the baby in his arms. Angela found herself holding her breath, wondering what he was going to say, and afraid of the impact it might have on his case.

"That's partly true, Your Honor," Rafe said finally. "When

Raquel—that's the baby's mother, Raquel Molina—was dying, she left word with her doctor that she wanted me to raise the child far away from her family. I agreed with her."

"And why was that?"

"Because the Molina family is deeply involved in drug trafficking, including the importation of cocaine from South America."

"And how do you know that?"

"I'm an agent for the Drug Enforcement Agency."

"Ah." The judge sat back in her seat. "How many family members are involved?"

"Well, I arrested Mr. Molina's brother last year for trafficking. We have evidence that Mr. Molina's mother—the baby's grandmother—is also involved, and for a time the baby's mother was involved as a mule—a person who carried the drugs across international boundaries."

"And Mr. Manuel Molina?"

Rafe hesitated, and Angela found herself holding her breath. "As of this time, we have no evidence that he's directly involved."

Judge Williams nodded and looked down at the papers before her. "He says he's a restauranteur."

"He appears to be."

The judge made a note. "What were your other reasons for bringing the child here?"

"Well, there were a couple," Rafe said slowly. "I probably wouldn't have left Miami quite so precipitously, except that Manny Molina showed up at my apartment one night. He had me followed."

"And this was bad?"

"I am—*was*—an undercover street operative. He blew my cover and found my residence, and he associates with persons known to be involved in drug trafficking. Worse, I had arrested his brother. I wasn't about to hang around and find out how much worse it could get. I was worried about the child being taken. Or being used against me somehow."

Again a noncommittal nod from the judge. "So you came here. Was there any other reason for your departure?"

Angela suspected this could be an important point, and she found herself on the edge of her seat, wondering how Rafe was going to answer it.

"Well," Rafe said, drawing the word out, "I have a brother here. Half-brother. Nathan Tate. I thought perhaps he could take care of my son while I got my affairs in order."

"What affairs?"

"Well, it was obvious to me that with a small child I couldn't continue working on the streets. That meant reassessing my job, and what I want to do from here on out."

"Did you leave the child with your brother?"

Rafe shook his head. "I found out I couldn't bear to."

Angela felt her heart turn over, aching for him.

"Are you planning to take the child back to Miami?"

Rafe shook his head. "No way. I may need to go back briefly to settle a few things, but there's no way I'm going to raise my son there."

"So where do you consider the child's residence to be?"

Angela, suspecting a problem, spoke out of turn. "He's looking for a place to rent here."

The judge frowned at her, but looked at Rafe. "Is that true, Mr. Ortiz?"

Rafe nodded. "Yes, it is."

"So for now, at least, you consider this to be the child's place of residence?"

"Yes, I do."

"Well, then, I think jurisdiction is clear. Mr. Molina accepted this court's jurisdiction by filing his complaint here, and you say this is the child's residence at this time. Under law, the court of jurisdiction is decided by the child's place of residence, and apparently you and Mr. Molina are agreed on this much." She sat forward, resting her elbows on her desk. "Mr. Ortiz, if you leave the child here while you go back to Miami, who will you leave it with?"

"Nathan Tate."

Angela thought the judge almost smiled. "Sheriff Tate's character is well known to this court. Now, Mr. Molina said something else I need to ask you about. He said you've been leaving the child in the care of a total stranger whom you claim is your fiancée."

Angela's heart skipped a beat, and she felt her mouth go dry.

"Is Ms. Jaynes a stranger to you?"

Rafe looked at Angela, and she at him. On his face she read a variety of emotions, and she couldn't blame him. Right now he probably hated her. But then he said something that astonished her.

"Ms. Jaynes is not a stranger, Your Honor. I consider her a friend."

"Ms. Jaynes?"

She found herself smiling almost stupidly. "We're not strangers, Your Honor. I know Mr. Ortiz very well, and I have great admiration and respect for him."

"Are you engaged to him?"

There it was. Angela could almost see the question lying on the floor like a thrown gauntlet. She hesitated a moment, then looked at the judge. "No, Your Honor, we're not engaged. Mr. Ortiz said that to shut Mr. Molina up when he showed up at the house and was being so obnoxious. We're just friends."

"Are you living in sin?"

Angela caught her breath. Then she looked the judge right in the eye and said, "No, we are not. We are both staying at the house of friends, but we're not living together. Which is not to say that I don't wish we were."

Rafe jerked as if startled and stared at her.

"It's quite simple, Judge," Angela said. "Mr. Ortiz puts the baby's welfare before everything else in his life. I've seen it. And he would never, ever, do anything that would be bad for his son. No child could ask for a better father."

Again Angela thought the judge was hiding a smile. But she turned to Rafe. "Basically, Mr. Ortiz, I'm trying to judge the claim that you are prepared to abandon your child to a stranger.''

Rafe looked Judge Williams right in the eye and said firmly, ''It may have crossed my mind once or twice at the beginning, Your Honor. I was a little shocked to find myself a father with full responsibility for an infant when I hadn't realized that my…that the child's mother was pregnant. She never saw fit to inform me of the fact, probably because I had arrested her brother Eduardo for trafficking. So I was utterly shocked when I was called to the hospital and informed I had a son.''

The judge nodded encouragingly.

''It was utterly unexpected,'' Rafe continued. ''It was overwhelming. Frankly, I *did* consider having the child adopted, because I didn't feel adequate. I didn't know how I could take proper care of him while still working undercover.''

He sighed. ''Anyway, I took this trip up here hoping Nate could care for the child while I sorted things out, because every time I thought of giving the baby up for adoption, I discovered I simply *could not* do it. As it turns out, coming up here was the smartest thing I could have done, because I've had the opportunity to care full-time for my son, and I've discovered that *nothing* on earth could make me give him up to anyone, for any reason. I'll quit my job and do whatever else is necessary to ensure that I'm a good father. And that, Judge, is the beginning and end of it.''

The judge's face betrayed nothing. ''Thank you, Mr. Ortiz,'' she said. ''That concludes my questions. You'll have my decision within a few days.''

Outside, at the foot of the courthouse steps, they all stopped. Rafe looked at his lawyer. ''I blew it, didn't I? I never should have told her I thought about giving Peanut up for adoption.''

Connie looked doubtful. ''I don't know. But if you'd told me about that before, I would have warned you not to mention it.''

Rafe nodded. ''I blew it.''

''I don't think so,'' Angela said. ''Rafe, that was a beautiful,

heartfelt speech. You couldn't have done a better job of telling
the judge how much you care for Peanut."

He grimaced. "I blew it. But thanks for being so supportive,
Angel. I really appreciate it."

"What are you going to do now?"

"Wait for the decision."

"Don't despair, Rafe," Connie said. "You're the baby's
legal father. And that carries more weight in a court than an
uncle's claim any day."

"Small comfort," Rafe said as he watched Connie walk to
her car. "Manny probably painted a beautiful picture of a big
loving family, grandmothers, uncles and cousins. It's bound to
sound a lot better than a single dad with only one living relative in the world."

"Ah, but your relative is Nate Tate," Angela said bracingly.
"He's worth a dozen grandmas."

Rafe tried to laugh, but he didn't quite succeed. "We'd
better get you home," he said. "It's almost time for your
insulin." Then he added, "Thanks for what you said in there
about wishing you could live with me."

She had the worst urge to reach out to him, to hug him to
try to offer him some comfort, but he was already moving
away. Besides, she'd given up her right to do that by acting
like such an idiot so many times.

She'd been so eager to protect herself that she'd made it
impossible for anyone to get close to her, and by preventing
anyone from getting close to her, she'd shut herself off from
being able to offer comfort.

She didn't like herself very much anymore. And she had
the feeling that she'd sacrificed something very, very special.

Chapter 12

It started snowing again that afternoon. While the peanut took his afternoon nap, Rafe stood at the living room wall and watched the snowflakes fall gently. At first they melted when they kissed the ground, but after a while they began to stay, and little by little the brown grass disappeared beneath their icy blanket.

He felt like that grass, he thought. Brown and dead, and being suffocated beneath a blanket of ice. Angela was probably upstairs packing right this minute. And in a few days the judge would probably order him to turn the baby over to Manny. Manny was right about one thing: he hadn't lived his life much better than the dealers he'd been trying to catch. He'd never invested anything of himself in anyone until that little child came into his life.

And now he was so heavily invested he was having wild thoughts about what he would do if he couldn't keep the baby.

"What will you do?"

Angela's voice startled him out of his thoughts. He turned and found her standing just inside the living room doorway.

"Do?" he asked.

"If they don't let you keep Peanut."

"I'll pack him up and hit the road. I'm not giving my kid up. Not to anyone for any reason."

She nodded. "I figured that's what you'd say."

"What else *can* I say? I'm not going to let anyone else raise my son, and certainly not the Molinas. God!"

He turned back to the window, half wishing she would just go away and leave him to wallow in his moroseness. But the other half of him wished she would come to him and put her arms around him and remind him that there were good things in life. Good things like Angela.

"The worst of it is," he said, trying to speak through a suddenly tight throat, "is that I'm convinced Manny is doing this just to spite me. Just because the family hates me."

"Why do you think that?"

"Because I know how a person feels about a baby he doesn't even know. There's no real caring. This is about this kid being a Molina, about him being Rocky's son, about me not having him. It's not about who can take the best care of the baby, or who loves him most."

"You might be right."

"I know I'm right. Problem is, after three months, I *love* the kid. I may be the only person in the world who really does. And I'm not giving him up."

"You won't have to."

"I wish I could be sure of that. The judge is probably sitting there right now wondering about a father who wanted to give his kid up for adoption."

"She's probably sitting there right now thinking about what an honest man you are. And how much courage it took for you to be that honest when it might cost you everything."

He gave a short laugh. "Aren't I the guy who said he'd lie to protect someone who was important to him? I should have lied."

"You said you never lie under oath. And I don't think you said anything wrong."

He turned to face her. "What do you think of me, knowing that there was a time when I actually thought about giving the baby up for adoption?"

"I think that was probably a pretty normal reaction under the circumstances. You didn't see how you could take care of him. Lots of people give up their babies when they don't believe they can take care of them. That's not necessarily such a bad thing."

"Maybe not. But in my case, I just didn't *want* to take care of him."

"Maybe not at first. Not until you started to care for him." She shrugged. "I think you're right. Nobody can really love someone they don't know. You had to get to know Peanut. And the whole thing came as such a shock to you. It's not like you had eight or nine months to get used to the idea of being a father before the child was born."

"Well, I'm still appalled at myself."

"Only because you love Peanut so much now."

"Maybe." He started to turn toward the window again, then hesitated. "Thanks, Angel. Thanks for all your help."

"No problem."

"Did you really mean what you said about wishing we were living together?"

The question startled her. He could see it in the way her eyes widened, in the way she seemed to stop breathing. He expected her to turn tail the way she usually did when he started to get close to her real yearnings. He almost took the question back, to spare her the discomfort, then decided not to. She'd been the one who said it, after all.

He could feel the seconds slipping by while she just stared at him. Just as he was about to give up hope that she would ever answer, she spoke.

"Yes."

The single word fell into the silence, and it seemed to him that he could feel the shockwaves radiating from it, buffeting his heart and mind. Things inside him began to shift, and a deep fear erupted in him.

"Just yes?" he asked finally. "No qualifications? No caveats?"

"Just yes," she said, her voice going husky. "Just yes."

Finally he turned toward the window again, putting his back to her. "Good, I hope that damn judge lets me keep my baby."

He could feel her unspoken question, but he didn't answer it, and finally she went away. Just as well. As long as there was any possibility that he might have to hit the road with Peanut, he couldn't make any other plans. It wouldn't be fair.

Angela considered leaving. She was still half packed and ready to run, but she couldn't bring herself to do it. Something deep inside her held her back, insisting she wait for the custody decision.

Through the next two days, she and Rafe spent a lot of time together, playing cards. There was a quiet desperation in the air, as if Rafe was wild to distract himself. They didn't discuss anything personal, as if everything in their lives was in abeyance until the decision came down.

They did talk a lot, though, casually, about their childhoods and their friends and their jobs, and about what they might do now that they were both facing career changes.

"I could probably get a job with a police department," Rafe said.

"On the streets?"

"No, I can't do that now. Peanut's only got one parent. But there are other useful things I could do. Or maybe I'll take a desk job with the agency. What about you?"

"I'm thinking about going back to school to take a few courses. I majored in English. I think I'd like to teach."

He nodded. "You're good with kids."

She laughed at that. "I'm good with *one* kid."

Peanut, who was lying on a blanket on the floor nearby, gurgled agreement.

"How does an English major become a loan officer?"

"She takes the first decent job she's offered."

"Ah. I always knew what I wanted to do."

"So leaving your job will be really difficult."

He smiled faintly at that. "Not as much as I would have thought."

By Friday morning, Rafe took to pacing the entire downstairs of the house, and Angela skipped her morning run, not wanting to leave him alone. It was like being stuck in a pressure cooker, she thought. There was no escape from the tension.

At around eleven o'clock the phone rang. He grabbed it, answered it, listened, then hung up.

When he turned to face Angela, his face was almost gaunt, his eyes hollow. "The decision's ready. Connie's going over to the courthouse to pick it up so we don't have to wait on the mail."

"What is it?"

"She doesn't know."

Now the minutes ticked by even more slowly, until Angela began to feel that they weren't moving at all. She began to have a wild urge to reach out and move the clock hands, just to speed things up.

Twenty minutes. Twenty-five. Then a knock at the front door.

They both hurried to answer it, but Rafe reached it first. He threw it open to see Connie standing there, a huge smile on her face.

"Here," she said, handing him a sheaf of stapled papers. "I wanted to hand it to you myself. Dismissed with prejudice."

Rafe looked at the papers, then at her. "What does that mean?"

"The judge threw Molina's case out. And she dismissed it with prejudice, which means he can never file it again. You're safe, Rafe. The baby is yours."

Rafe's hand started to shake, rattling the papers, and Angela felt her heart squeeze as she saw his eyes begin to glisten with tears.

Then he threw back his head and let out a "Wahoo!" that just about rattled the windows. Angela started laughing, then squealed when he suddenly picked her up and whirled her in a circle. Connie was laughing, too, and hugged them both.

When he had calmed a little, he asked Connie, "Did the judge say why?"

Connie shook her head. "No need. That's the point of dismissing it with prejudice. Basically Judge Williams is saying that Molina doesn't have a case. Period. And she leaves him no wiggling room for appeal. It's over and done."

It certainly was, Angela thought a few minutes later, after Connie left. She looked at Rafe, sitting on the living room floor with his son, quite seriously telling the boy that now he never had to worry about losing his father.

She stood watching them for a few minutes, feeling her chest ache with so many emotions, then she turned and went upstairs to pack.

He didn't need her anymore. It was time to go.

"Where do you think you're going?"

Angela turned from her suitcase to face Rafe, who stood in her doorway looking like a thunderstorm.

"Home," she said, glad that her voice remained level. "You don't need me anymore."

"Who said that? Did I say that?"

She shook her head, feeling her heartbeat grow heavy. "You don't have to say it, Rafe. You asked me to stay until the judge had questioned me. I stayed longer because I thought you needed company to get you through the last few days. But now it's settled, and I need to get on with my life."

"Mmm. So…you're running away again?"

"I'm not running away!"

"Really? Funny, that's how it looks to me."

She shook her head and turned back to her suitcase. "No, it's just that…well, you need to get on with your life, too."

"But you're not running."

"Of course not!"

"So…if I tell you I want you to hang around, you won't bolt like a frightened horse?"

She turned to glare at him.

"Good," he said. "We're getting better at this. So now it's safe for me to tell you I want a home with you?"

Her heart stopped. Her ears strained with disbelief. Finally, dragging in a gasp of air, she asked, "What do you mean?"

"I mean, I want you and me to get together. I mean, I want you to put your life on hold just a little while longer while I go back to Miami, get my stuff together and sort out my future."

"Why? Do you mean you want me to watch Peanut?"

"I mean, I want you to *help* me watch Peanut. I want you to come with me. I'll get a new job out of the agency, I'll get transferred to some place where you can go to school, and we'll make a home for ourselves. You, me and Peanut."

Her chest was so tight now that she could barely breathe. Her throat was aching, and she was afraid, so afraid, to believe what she was hearing.

"But we fight all the time," she said, her voice a breathless croak.

"Not all the time. Just a lot of the time. I don't know about you, but I don't mind that at all. We'll probably squabble a lot until we get used to each other. Until you start trusting me."

Her legs were beginning to feel weak, and she sat on the edge of the bed, looking at him through eyes that wanted to fill with hopeful tears. Oh, she didn't dare believe him! But what he had said about trusting him… She took a leap.

"I trust you," she said quietly.

"Maybe a little. But not completely. However," he said with an almost embarrassed smile, "I believe that eventually you will trust me completely. What's not to trust, anyway?"

A shaky laugh escaped her.

He came to kneel in front of her, taking both her hands in his. "I understand why you don't trust me, Angel. But you've got to give me a chance to prove that I'm not like that other guy. That's all I'm asking for. A chance."

"But *why*, Rafe. Why?"

"Because," he said simply, "I love you."

Her heart slammed, and she had to close her eyes for a moment against an overwhelming wave of feelings, of joy, love, hope and fear. "Really…?" she heard herself whisper.

"Yes, really," he said firmly. "Trust me, this is one feeling you can't misidentify. I love you. And I'd do anything for you, just the way I would for Peanut. I need you. And I need you to need *me*."

"But…I'm sick.…" She had to say it. She had to hear him address it before she would dare to believe.

"So?" he said. "Someday I'll be sick. Where's the guarantee that in ten years I won't have cancer and you'll be nursing me through it? What guarantee does anyone have? As near as I can tell, you just need to be a little more cautious about your schedule than most people, and you need to take shots. God, if that's an illness, I'd rather have that one than a lot of others I can think of."

"I could…I could die at any moment, Rafe." She looked at him then, needing to see his face.

"So could I. So could anyone. When you come right down to it, that's all any of us has to look forward to. But most of us refuse to let it control our lives."

"I can't have kids."

"I already have one of those. I don't feel any particular need for another one. But if *you* do, we can sure as hell consider adoption. I hear there are all kinds of kids who can't find homes, if you're not too particular about health issues. I'd be willing to bet we could adopt a kid with diabetes, if you want."

Something was blossoming inside her, something beautiful and wonderful, and it was bringing more tears to her eyes.

"The thing is, Angel, we can do just about anything we put our minds to. That includes you. You just have to stop saying you can't and start saying you can."

She nodded slowly, feeling hot tears run down her cheeks.

"So," he said, looking at her from dark eyes that were alive with warmth, "the question is, are you crying from horror or happiness?"

"Happiness," she said huskily. Then, unable to help herself, she threw her arms around his neck and hugged him as tightly as she could, and when she felt his arms close around her, she knew she had come home.

"I love you, Rafe."

He stiffened, then pulled back until he could see her face. "Say that again, Angel. Please."

"I love you, Rafe."

"Oh, God, I've been waiting my entire life to hear that. Say it again, and again...."

So she said it over and over, each time with more joy, and he echoed her.

"I love you...."

It was right, and it was good, and it was all that mattered.

Epilogue

"Angel? Are you ready?" Rafe called from the kitchen of their house in Virginia. Morning sun poured through the windows as he stuffed the last cereal bowl in the dishwasher and turned it on. Then he yanked his tie off the back of a chair and donned it.

After five years, he still wasn't comfortable in a suit, but what the hell. His street days were long over. Besides, he was enjoying his job as an instructor at Quantico. And looking forward to spending Christmas in Conard County with his brother's family. He had a lot to be thankful for these days, so he wasn't about to complain about a tie.

"We're ready," Angela said from the doorway. He turned and smiled as he saw his wife and three children. Peanut, who these days preferred to be called Rafie, was looking spit and polished in slacks and a sport shirt, ready for his first day in first grade. Beside Rafie stood his twelve-year-old sister, Melinda, the child Rafe and Angel had adopted three years ago.

Melinda had diabetes, and had been orphaned by the death of her birth parents. She was smiling and pretty in a corduroy jumper, her brown hair gleaming as it fell to her waist. On the verge of tumbling into womanhood, but still tomboyish and coltish. Melinda, he thought, was a lot healthier than she had been when they'd adopted her, and that had a lot to do with Angel's knowledge of her disease.

And finally there was Squirrel, whose real name was Jason, but who insisted everyone call him Squirrel. They'd adopted him as a toddler because his single mother couldn't care for him. He was mildly autistic, but doing very well in the school for special children where Angela taught. And this morning he was actually holding Angela's hand, a remarkable achievement.

"Are we ready?" Rafe asked.

"Ready!" they all responded, even Squirrel.

"Then pile in the car, troops. We're off."

On the way out the door, Angela paused to give Rafe a kiss. "I love you," she whispered.

"I love you, too," he whispered back. He loved them all. And in loving them, he'd found the home he'd never had.

Grinning from ear to ear, he locked the door and climbed into the family van.

It just didn't get any better than this.

* * * * *

If you enjoyed what you just read,
then we've got an offer you can't resist!

Take 2 bestselling
love stories FREE!
Plus get a FREE surprise gift!

Clip this page and mail it to Silhouette Reader Service™

IN U.S.A.
3010 Walden Ave.
P.O. Box 1867
Buffalo, N.Y. 14240-1867

IN CANADA
P.O. Box 609
Fort Erie, Ontario
L2A 5X3

YES! Please send me 2 free Silhouette Intimate Moments® novels and my free surprise gift. Then send me 6 brand-new novels every month, which I will receive months before they're available in stores. In the U.S.A., bill me at the bargain price of $3.57 plus 25¢ delivery per book and applicable sales tax, if any*. In Canada, bill me at the bargain price of $3.96 plus 25¢ delivery per book and applicable taxes**. That's the complete price and a savings of over 10% off the cover prices—what a great deal! I understand that accepting the 2 free books and gift places me under no obligation ever to buy any books. I can always return a shipment and cancel at any time. Even if I never buy another book from Silhouette, the 2 free books and gift are mine to keep forever. So why not take us up on our invitation. You'll be glad you did!

245 SEN CNFF
345 SEN CNFG

Name _____ (PLEASE PRINT)

Address _____ Apt.#

City _____ State/Prov. _____ Zip/Postal Code

* Terms and prices subject to change without notice. Sales tax applicable in N.Y.
** Canadian residents will be charged applicable provincial taxes and GST.
    All orders subject to approval. Offer limited to one per household.
    ® are registered trademarks of Harlequin Enterprises Limited.

INMOM99   ©1998 Harlequin Enterprises Limited

Don't miss Silhouette's newest cross-line promotion,

Four royal sisters find their own Prince Charmings as they embark on separate journeys to find their missing brother, the Crown Prince!

The search begins in October 1999 and continues through February 2000:

On sale October 1999: **A ROYAL BABY ON THE WAY** by award-winning author **Susan Mallery** (Special Edition)

On sale November 1999: **UNDERCOVER PRINCESS** by bestselling author **Suzanne Brockmann** (Intimate Moments)

On sale December 1999: **THE PRINCESS'S WHITE KNIGHT** by popular author **Carla Cassidy** (Romance)

On sale January 2000: **THE PREGNANT PRINCESS** by rising star **Anne Marie Winston** (Desire)

On sale February 2000: **MAN...MERCENARY...MONARCH** by top-notch talent **Joan Elliott Pickart** (Special Edition)

ROYALLY WED
Only in—
SILHOUETTE BOOKS

Available at your favorite retail outlet.

Silhouette®

Visit us at www.romance.net

SSERW

INTIMATE MOMENTS®

Silhouette®

COMING NEXT MONTH